RANDOM
HOUSE

LARGE
PRINT

MACHINES LIKE ME

MACHINES LIKE ME

AND PEOPLE LIKE YOU

Ian McEwan

RANDOM HOUSE LARGE PRINT

Copyright © 2019 by Ian McEwan

All rights reserved.
Published in the United States of America by Random House Large Print in association with Nan A. Talese/ Doubleday, a division of Penguin Random House LLC, New York.

Originally published in hardcover in Great Britain by Jonathan Cape, an imprint of Penguin Random House Ltd., London, in 2019.

Ian McEwan is an unlimited company no. 7473219 registered in England and Wales.

The quotation on p. 129 is from the song "Teddy Bear's Picnic," written by Jimmy Kennedy.

Cover design by Suzanne Dean
Cover images: Mannequins reproduced with kind permission of Rootstein Display Mannequins; photographs © Lily Richards

The Library of Congress has established a Cataloging-in-Publication record for this title.

ISBN: 978-0-593-15281-2

www.penguinrandomhouse.com/large-print-format-books

FIRST LARGE PRINT EDITION

Printed in the United States of America

10 9 8 7 6 5 4 3 2 1

This Large Print edition published in accord with the standards of the N.A.V.H.

TO GRAEME MITCHISON
1944–2018

But remember, please, the Law by which we live,
We are not built to comprehend a lie . . .

—Rudyard Kipling,
"The Secret of the Machines"

MACHINES LIKE ME

ONE

It was religious yearning granted hope, it was the holy grail of science. Our ambitions ran high and low—for a creation myth made real, for a monstrous act of self-love. As soon as it was feasible, we had no choice but to follow our desires and hang the consequences. In loftiest terms, we aimed to escape our mortality, confront or even replace the Godhead with a perfect self. More practically, we intended to devise an improved, more modern version of ourselves and exult in the joy of invention, the thrill of mastery. In the autumn of the twentieth century, it came about at last, the first step towards the fulfilment of an ancient dream, the beginning of the long lesson we would teach ourselves that however complicated we were, however faulty and difficult to describe in even our simplest actions and modes of being, we could be imitated and bettered. And I was there as a young man, an early and eager adopter in that chilly dawn.

But artificial humans were a cliché long before they arrived, so when they did, they seemed to some a disappointment. The imagination, fleeter than history, than technological advance, had already rehearsed this future in books, then films and TV dramas, as if human actors, walking with a certain glazed look, phony head movements, some stiffness in the lower back, could prepare us for life with our cousins from the future.

I was among the optimists, blessed by unexpected funds following my mother's death and the sale of the family home, which turned out to be on a valuable development site. The first truly viable manufactured human with plausible intelligence and looks, believable motion and shifts of expression, went on sale the week before the Falklands Task Force set off on its hopeless mission. Adam cost £86,000. I brought him home in a hired van to my unpleasant flat in north Clapham. I'd made a reckless decision, but I was encouraged by reports that Sir Alan Turing, war hero and presiding genius of the digital age, had taken delivery of the same model. He probably wanted to have his lab take it apart to examine its workings fully.

Twelve of this first edition were called Adam, thirteen were called Eve. Corny, everyone agreed, but commercial. Notions of biological race being scientifically discredited, the twenty-five were designed to cover a range of ethnicities. There were rumours, then complaints, that the Arab could not be told apart from the Jew. Random programming as well as life experience would grant to all complete latitude in sexual preference. By the end of the first week, all the Eves sold out. At a careless glance, I might have taken my Adam for a Turk or a Greek. He weighed 170 pounds, so I had to ask my upstairs neighbour, Miranda, to help me carry him in from the street on the disposable stretcher that came with the purchase.

While his batteries began to charge, I made us coffee, then scrolled through the 470-page online handbook. Its language was mostly clear and precise. But Adam was created across different agencies and in places the instructions had the charm of a nonsense poem. "Unreveal upside of B347k vest to gain carefree emoticon with motherboard output to attenuate mood-swing penumbra."

At last, with cardboard and polystyrene wrapping strewn around his ankles, he sat naked at my tiny dining table, eyes closed, a black power line trailing from the entry point in his umbilicus to a thirteen-amp socket in the wall. It would take sixteen hours to fire him up. Then sessions of download updates and personal preferences. I wanted him now, and so did Miranda. Like eager young parents, we were avid for his first words. There was no loudspeaker cheaply buried in his chest. We knew from the excited publicity that he formed sounds with breath, tongue, teeth and palate. Already his lifelike skin was warm to the touch and as smooth as a child's. Miranda claimed to see his eyelashes flicker. I was certain she was seeing vibrations from the Tube trains rolling a hundred feet below us, but I said nothing.

Adam was not a sex toy. However, he was capable of sex and possessed functional mucous membranes, in the maintenance of which he consumed half a litre of water each day. While he sat at the table, I observed that he was uncircumcised, fairly well endowed, with copious dark pubic hair. This highly advanced model of artificial human was likely to reflect the appetites of its young creators of code. The Adams and Eves, it was thought, would be lively.

He was advertised as a companion, an intellectual sparring partner, friend and factotum who could wash dishes, make beds and "think." Every moment of his existence, everything he heard and saw, he recorded and could retrieve. He couldn't drive as yet and was not allowed to swim or shower or go out in the rain without an umbrella, or operate a chainsaw unsupervised. As for range, thanks to breakthroughs in electrical storage, he could run seventeen kilometres in two hours without a charge or, its energy equivalent, converse non-stop for twelve days. He had a working life of twenty years. He was compactly built, square-shouldered, dark-skinned, with thick black hair swept back; narrow in the face, with a hint of hooked nose suggestive of fierce intelligence, pensively hooded eyes, tight lips that, even as we watched, were draining of their deathly yellowish-white tint and acquiring rich human colour, perhaps even relaxing a little at the corners. Miranda said he resembled "a docker from the Bosphorus."

Before us sat the ultimate plaything, the dream of ages, the triumph of humanism—or its angel of death. Exciting beyond measure, but frustrating too. Sixteen hours was a long time to be waiting and watching. I thought that for the sum I'd handed over after lunch, Adam should have been charged up and ready to go. It was a wintry late afternoon. I made toast and we drank more coffee. Miranda, a doctoral scholar of social history, said she wished the teenage Mary Shelley was here beside us, observing closely, not a monster like Frankenstein's, but this handsome dark-skinned young man coming to life. I said that what both creatures shared was a hunger for the animating force of electricity.

"We share it too." She spoke as though she was referring only to herself and me, rather than all of electrochemically charged humanity.

She was twenty-two, mature for her years and ten years younger than me. From a long perspective, there was not much between us. We were gloriously young. But I considered myself at a different stage of life. My formal education was far behind me. I'd suffered a series of professional and financial and personal failures. I regarded myself as too hard-bitten, too cynical for a lovely young woman like Miranda. And though she was beautiful, with pale brown hair and a long thin face, and eyes that often appeared narrowed by suppressed mirth, and though in certain moods I looked at her in wonder, I'd decided early on to confine her in the role of kind, neighbourly friend. We shared an entrance hall and her tiny apartment was right over mine. We saw each other for a coffee now and then to talk about relationships and politics and all the rest. With pitch-perfect neutrality she gave the impression of being at ease with the possibilities. To her, it seemed, an afternoon of intimate pleasure with me would have weighed equally with a chaste and companionable chat. She was relaxed in my company and I preferred to think that sex would ruin everything. We remained good chums. But there was something alluringly secretive or restrained about her. Perhaps, without knowing it, I had been in love with her for months. Without knowing it? What a flimsy formulation that was!

Reluctantly, we agreed to turn our backs on Adam and on each other for a while. Miranda had a seminar to attend north of the river, I had emails to write. By the early seventies, digital communication had discarded its air of convenience and become a daily chore. Likewise the 250 mph trains—crowded and dirty. Speech-recognition software, a fifties miracle, had long turned to drudge, with entire populations sacrificing hours each day to lonely soliloquising. Brain–machine interfacing, wild fruit of sixties optimism, could barely arouse the interest of a child. What people queued the entire weekend for became, six months later, as interesting as the socks on their feet. What happened to the cognition-enhancing helmets, the speaking fridges with a sense of smell? Gone the way of the mouse pad, the Filofax, the electric carving knife, the fondue set. The future kept arriving. Our bright new toys began to rust before we could get them home, and life went on much as before.

Would Adam become a bore? It's not easy, to dictate while trying to ward off a bout of buyer's remorse. Surely other people, other minds, must continue to fascinate us. As artificial people became more like us, then became us, then became more than us, we could never tire of them. They were bound to surprise us. They might fail us in ways that were beyond our imagining. Tragedy was a possibility, but not boredom.

What was tedious was the prospect of the user's guide. Instructions. My prejudice was that any machine that could not tell you by its very functioning how it should be used was not worth its keep. On an old-fashioned impulse, I was printing out the manual, then looking for a folder. All the while, I continued to dictate emails.

I couldn't think of myself as Adam's "user." I'd assumed there was nothing to learn about him that he could not teach me himself. But the manual in my hands had fallen open at Chapter Fourteen. Here the English was plain: preferences; personality parameters. Then a set of headings—Agreeableness. Extraversion. Openness to experience. Conscientiousness. Emotional stability. The list was familiar to me. The Five Factor model. Educated as I was in the humanities, I was suspicious of such reductive categories, though I knew from a friend in psychology that each item had many subgroups. Glancing at the next page I saw that I was supposed to select various settings on a scale of one to ten.

I'd been expecting a friend. I was ready to treat Adam as a guest in my home, as an unknown I would come to know. I'd thought he would arrive optimally adjusted. Factory settings—a contemporary synonym for fate. My friends, family and acquaintances all had appeared in my life with fixed settings, with unalterable histories of genes and environment. I wanted my expensive new friend to do the same. Why leave it to me? But of course I knew the answer. Not many of us are optimally adjusted. Gentle Jesus? Humble Darwin? One every 1,800 years. Even if it knew the best, the least harmful parameters of personality, which it couldn't, a worldwide corporation with a precious reputation couldn't risk a mishap. **Caveat emptor**.

God had once delivered a fully formed companion for the benefit of the original Adam. I had to devise one for myself. Here was Extraversion and a graded set of childish statements. **He loves to be** the life and soul of the party and **He knows how to entertain people and lead them.** And at the bottom, **He feels uncomfortable around other people** and **He prefers his own company.** Here in the middle was, **He likes a good party but he's always happy to come home.** This was me. But should I be replicating myself? If I was to choose from the middle of each scale I might devise the soul of blandness. Extraversion appeared to include its antonym. There was a long adjectival list with boxes to tick: outgoing, shy, excitable, talkative, withdrawn, boastful, modest, bold, energetic, moody. I wanted none of them, not for him, not for myself.

Apart from my moments of crazed decisions, I passed most of my life, especially when alone, in a state of mood neutrality, with my personality, whatever that was, in suspension. Not bold, not withdrawn. Simply here, neither content nor morose, but carrying out tasks, thinking about dinner or sex, staring at the screen, taking a shower. Intermittent regrets about the past, occasional forebodings about the future, barely aware of the present, except in the obvious sensory realm. Psychology, once so interested in the trillion ways the mind goes awry, was now drawn to what it considered the common emotions, from grief to joy. But it had overlooked a vast domain of everyday existence: absent illness, famine, war or other stresses, a lot of life is lived in the neutral zone, a familiar garden, but a grey one, unremarkable, immediately forgotten, hard to describe.

At the time, I was not to know that these graded options would have little effect on Adam. The real determinant was what was known as "machine learning." The user's handbook merely granted an illusion of influence and control, the kind of illusion parents have in relation to their children's personalities. It was a way of binding me to my purchase and providing legal protection for the manufacturer. "Take your time," the manual advised. "Choose carefully. Allow yourself several weeks, if necessary."

I let half an hour pass before I checked on him again. No change. Still at the table, arms pushed out straight before him, eyes closed. But I thought his hair, deepest black, was bulked out a little and had acquired a certain shine, as though he'd just had a shower. Stepping closer, I saw to my delight that though he wasn't breathing, there was, by his left breast, a regular pulse, steady and calm, about one a second by my inexperienced guess. How reassuring. He had no blood to pump around, but this simulation had an effect. My doubts faded just a little. I felt protective towards Adam, even as I knew how absurd it was. I stretched out my hand and laid it over his heart and felt against my palm its calm, iambic tread. I sensed I was violating his private space. These vital signs were easy to believe in. The warmth of his skin, the firmness and yield of the muscle below it—my reason said plastic or some such, but my touch responded to flesh.

It was eerie, to be standing by this naked man, struggling between what I knew and what I felt. I walked behind him, partly to be out of range of eyes that could open at any moment and find me looming over him. He was muscular around his neck and spine. Dark hair grew along the line of his shoulders. His buttocks displayed muscular con- cavities. Below them, an athlete's knotted calves. I hadn't wanted a superman. I regretted once more that I'd been too late for an Eve.

On my way out of the room I paused to look back and experienced one of those moments that can derange the emotional life: a startling realisa- tion of the obvious, an absurd leap of understanding into what one already knows. I stood with one hand resting on the doorknob. It must have been Adam's nakedness and physical presence that prompted the insight, but I wasn't looking at him. It was the but- ter dish. Also, two plates and cups, two knives and two spoons scattered across the table. The remains of my long afternoon with Miranda. Two wooden chairs were pushed back from the table, turned companionably towards each other.

We had become closer this past month. We talked easily. I saw how precious she was to me and how carelessly I could lose her. I should have said something by now. I'd taken her for granted. Some unfortunate event, some person, a fellow student, could get between us. Her face, her voice, her manner, both reticent and clear-headed, were sharply present. The feel of her hand in mine, that lost, preoccupied manner she had. Yes, we had become very close and I'd failed to notice it was happening. I was an idiot. I had to tell her.

I went back into my office, which doubled as my bedroom. Between the desk and the bed there was enough space in which to walk up and down. That she knew nothing about my feelings was now an anxious matter. Describing them would be embarrassing, perilous. She was a neighbour, a friend, a kind of sister. I would be addressing a person I didn't yet know. She would be obliged to step out from behind a screen, or remove a mask and speak to me in terms I had never heard from her. **I'm so sorry . . . I like you very much but, you see . . .** Or she'd be horrified. Or, just possibly, overjoyed to hear the one thing she had longed for, or to say herself but dreaded rejection.

By chance, we were currently both free. She must have thought about it, about us. It was not an impossible fantasy. I would have to tell her face to face. Unbearable. Unavoidable. And so it went on, in tightening cycles. Restless, I went back next door. I saw no change in Adam as I brushed past to get to the fridge, where there was a half-full bottle of white Bordeaux. I sat facing him and raised my glass. To love. This time, I felt less tenderness. I saw Adam for what it was, an inanimate confection whose heartbeat was a regular electrical discharge, whose skin warmth was mere chemistry. When activated, some kind of microscopic balance-wheel device would prise open his eyes. He would seem to see me, but he would be blind. Not even blind. When it kicked in, another system would give a semblance of breath, but not of life. A man newly in love knows what life is.

With the inheritance, I could have bought a place somewhere north of the river, Notting Hill, or Chelsea. She might even have joined me. She would've had space for all the books that were boxed up in her father's garage in Salisbury. I saw a future without Adam, the future that was mine until yesterday: an urban garden, high ceilings with plaster mouldings, stainless-steel kitchen, old friends to dinner. Books everywhere. What to do? I could take him, or it, back, or sell it online and take a small loss. I gave it a hostile look. The hands were palms down on the table, the hawkish face remained angled towards the hands. My foolish infatuation with technology! Another fondue set. Best to get away from the table before I impoverished myself with a single swipe of my father's old claw hammer.

I drank no more than half a glass, then I returned to the bedroom to distract myself with the Asian currency markets. All the while I listened out for footsteps in the flat above me. Late into the evening, I watched TV to catch up on the Task Force that would soon set off across 8,000 miles of ocean to recapture what we then called the Falkland Islands.

At thirty-two, I was completely broke. Wasting my mother's inheritance on a gimmick was only one part of my problem—but typical of it. Whenever money came my way, I caused it to disappear, made a magic bonfire of it, stuffed it into a top hat and pulled out a turkey. Often, though not in this recent case, my intention was to conjure a far larger sum with minimal effort. I was a mug for schemes, semi-legal ruses, cunning shortcuts. I was for grand and brilliant gestures. Others made them and flourished. They borrowed money, put it to interesting use and remained enriched even as they settled their debts. Or they had jobs, professions, as I once had, and enriched themselves more modestly, at a steady rate. I meanwhile leveraged or, rather, shorted myself into genteel ruin, into two damp ground-floor rooms in the dull no-man's-land of Edwardian terraced streets between Stockwell and Clapham, south London.

I grew up in a village near Stratford, Warwickshire, the only child of a musician father and community-nurse mother. Compared to Miranda's, my childhood was culturally undernourished. There was no time or space for books, or even music. I took a precocious interest in electronics but ended up with an anthropology degree from an unregarded college in the south Midlands; I did a conversion course to law and, once qualified, specialised in tax. A week after my twenty-ninth birthday I was struck off, and came close to a short spell in prison. My hundred hours of community service convinced me that I should never have a regular job again. I made some money out of a book I wrote at high speed on artificial intelligence: lost to a life-extension-pill scheme. I made a reasonable sum on a property deal: lost to a car-rental scheme. I was left some funds by a favourite uncle who had prospered by way of a heat-pump patent: lost to a medical-insurance scheme.

At thirty-two, I was surviving by playing the stock and currency markets online. A scheme, just like the rest. For seven hours a day I bowed before my keyboard, buying, selling, hesitating, punching the air one moment, cursing the next, at least at the beginning. I read market reports, but I believed I was dealing in a random system and mostly relied on guesses. Sometimes I leaped ahead, sometimes I plunged, but on average through the year I made about as much as the postman. I paid my rent, which was low in those days, ate and dressed well enough and thought I was beginning to stabilise, learning to know myself. I was determined that my thirties would be a superior performance to my twenties.

But my parents' pleasant family home was sold just as the first convincing artificial person came on the market. 1982. Robots, androids, replicates were my passion, even more so after my research for the book. Prices were bound to fall, but I had to have one straight away, an Eve by preference, but an Adam would do.

It could have turned out differently. My previous girlfriend, Claire, was a sensible person who trained to be a dental nurse. She worked in a Harley Street practice and she would have talked me out of Adam. She was a woman of the world, of this one. She knew how to arrange a life. And not only her own. But I offended her with an act of undeniable disloyalty. She disowned me in a scene of regal fury, at the end of which she threw my clothes out into the street. Lime Grove. She never spoke to me again and belonged at the top of my list of errors and failures. She could have saved me from myself.

But. In the interests of balance, let that unsaved self speak up. I didn't buy Adam to make money. On the contrary. My motives were pure. I handed over a fortune in the name of curiosity, that steadfast engine of science, of intellectual life, of life itself. This was no passing fad. There was a history, an account, a time-deposit, and I had a right to draw on it. Electronics and anthropology—distant cousins whom late modernity has drawn together and bound in marriage. The child of that coupling was Adam.

So, I appear before you, witness for the defence, after school, 5 p.m., typical specimen for my time—short trousers, scabby knees, freckles, short back and sides, eleven years old. I'm first in line, waiting for the lab to open and for "Wiring Club" to begin. Presiding is Mr. Cox, a gentle giant with carroty hair who teaches physics. My project is to build a radio. It's an act of faith, an extended prayer that has taken many weeks. I have a base of hardboard, six inches by nine, easily drilled. Colours are everything. Blue, red, yellow and white wires run their modest courses around the board, turning at right angles, disappearing below to emerge elsewhere and be interrupted by bright nodules, tiny vividly striped cylinders—capacitors, resistors—then an induction coil I have wound myself, then an op-amp. I understand nothing. I follow a wiring diagram as a novice might murmur scripture. Mr. Cox gives softly spoken advice. I clumsily solder one piece, one wire or component, to another. The smoke and smell of solder is a drug I inhale deeply. I include in my circuit a toggle switch made of Bakelite which, I've persuaded myself, came out of a fighter plane, a Spitfire surely. The final connection, three months after my beginning, is from this piece of dark brown plastic to a nine-volt battery.

It's a cold, windy dusk in March. Other boys are hunched over their projects. We are twelve miles away from Shakespeare's hometown, in what will come to be known as a "bog-standard" comprehensive school. An excellent place, in fact. The fluorescent ceiling lights come on. Mr. Cox is on the far side of the lab with his back turned. I don't want to attract his attention in case of failure. I throw the switch and—miracle—hear the sound of static. I jiggle the variable-tuning capacitor: music, terrible music, as I think, because violins are involved. Then comes the rapid voice of a woman, not speaking English.

No one looks up, no one is interested. Building a radio is nothing special. But I'm speechless, close to tears. No technology since will amaze me as much. Electricity, passing through pieces of metal carefully arranged by me, snatches from the air the voice of a foreign lady sitting somewhere far away. Her voice sounds kindly. She isn't aware of me. I'll never learn her name or understand her language, and never meet her, not knowingly. My radio, with its irregular blobs of solder on a board, appears no less a wonder than consciousness itself arising from matter.

Brains and electronics were closely related, so I discovered through my teens as I built simple computers and programmed them myself. Then complicated computers. Electricity and bits of metal could add up numbers, make words, pictures, songs, remember things and even turn speech into writing.

When I was seventeen, Peter Cox persuaded me to study physics at a local college. Within a month I was bored and looking to change. The subject was too abstract, the maths was beyond me. And by then I'd read a book or two and was taking an interest in imaginary people. Heller's **Catch-18**, Fitzgerald's **The High-Bouncing Lover**, Orwell's **The Last Man in Europe**, Tolstoy's **All's Well That Ends Well**—I didn't get much further and yet I saw the point of art. It was a form of investigation. But I didn't want to study literature—too intimidating, too intuitive. A single-sheet course summary I picked up in the college library announced anthropology as "the science of people in their societies through space and time." Systematic study, with the human factor thrown in. I signed up.

The first thing to learn: my course was pitifully underfunded. No bunking off for a year to the Trobriand Islands, where, I read, it was taboo to eat in front of others. It was good manners to eat alone, with your back turned to friends and family. The islanders had spells to make ugly people beautiful. Children were actively encouraged to be sexual with each other. Yams were the viable currency. Women determined the status of men. How strange and bracing. My view of human nature had been shaped by the mostly white population crammed into the southern quarter of England. Now I was set free into bottomless relativism.

At the age of nineteen I wrote a wise essay on honour cultures entitled "Mind-forged Manacles?" Dispassionately, I gathered up my case studies. What did I know or care? There were places where rape was so common it didn't have a name. A young father's throat was cut for failing in his duties to an ancient feud. Here was a family eager to kill a daughter for being seen holding hands with a lad from the wrong religious group. There, elderly women keenly assisted in the genital mutilation of their granddaughters. What of the instinctive parental impulses to love and protect? The cultural signal was louder. What of universal values? Upended. Nothing like this in Stratford-upon-Avon. It was all about the mind, the tradition, the religion— nothing but software, I now thought, and best regarded in value-free terms.

Anthropologists did not pass judgement. They observed and reported on human variety. They celebrated difference. What was wicked in Warwickshire was unremarkable in Papua New Guinea. Locally, who was to say what was good or bad? Certainly not a colonial power. I derived from my studies some unfortunate conclusions about ethics which led me a few years later to the dock in a county court, accused of conspiring with others to mislead the tax authorities on a grand scale. I did not attempt to persuade His Honour that far from his court might be a coconut beach where such conspiracy was respected. Instead, I came to my senses just before I addressed the judge. Morals were real, they were true, good and bad inhered in the nature of things. Our actions must be judged on their terms. This was what I'd assumed before anthropology came along. In quavering, hesitant tones I apologised abjectly to the court and dodged a custodial sentence.

When I entered the kitchen in the morning, later than usual, Adam's eyes were open. They were pale blue, flecked with minuscule vertical rods of black. The eyelashes were long and thick, like a child's. But his blink mechanism had not yet kicked in. It was set at irregular intervals and adjusted for mood and gestures, and primed to react to the actions and speech of others. Reluctantly, I'd read the handbook into the night. He was equipped with a blink reflex to protect his eyes from flying objects. At present, his gaze was empty of meaning or intent and therefore unaffecting, as lifeless as the stare of a shop-window mannequin. So far, he was showing none of the fractional movements that warmly typify the human head. Elsewhere, no body language at all. When I felt for the pulse in his wrist, I found nothing—a heartbeat without a pulse. His arm was heavy to lift, resistant at the elbow joint, as though rigor mortis was about to set in.

I turned my back on him and made coffee. Miranda was on my mind. Everything had changed. Nothing had changed. During my near-sleepless night, I'd remembered that she was visiting her father. She would have gone straight to Salisbury from her seminar. I saw her on her train from Waterloo, sitting with an unread book on her lap, staring at the rushing landscape, the dip and rise of telephone lines, not thinking of me. Or thinking only of me. Or recalling a boy at her seminar who'd tried to out-stare her.

I watched the TV news on my phone. A brilliant mosaic in sound and sparkling seaside light. Portsmouth. The Task Force ready to depart. Most of the country was in a dream-theatre, in historical dress. Late medieval. Seventeenth century. Early nineteenth. Ruffs, hose, hooped skirts, powdered wigs, eyepatch, wooden legs. Accuracy was unpatriotic. Historically, we were special and the fleet was bound for success. TV and press encouraged a vague collective memory of enemies defeated—the Spanish, the Dutch, the Germans twice this century, the French from Agincourt to Waterloo. A fly-past by fighter jets. A young man in combat gear, fresh out of Sandhurst, narrowed his eyes as he told an interviewer of the difficulties ahead. A superior officer spoke of his men's unshakeable resolve. I was moved, even as I disliked it. When a massed band of Highland pipers marched towards their ship's gangplank, my spirits swelled. Then back to the studio for charts, arrows, logistics, objectives, sane voices in agreement. For diplomatic moves. For the prime minister in her trim blue suit on the steps of Downing Street.

I warmed to it, even though I often declared myself against it all. I loved my country. What a venture, what wild courage. Eight thousand miles. What decent people putting their lives at risk. I took a second coffee next door, made the bed to give the room the appearance of a workplace, and sat down to reflect a while on the state of the world's markets. The prospect of war had sent the FTSE down a further one per cent. Still in patriotic mood, I assumed an Argie defeat and took a position on a toy and novelty group that made Union Jacks on sticks for people to wave. I also invested in two champagne importers, and bet on a big recovery generally. Merchant-navy ships had been requisitioned to transport troops to the South Atlantic. A friend who worked in asset management in the City told me that his company was predicting that some would be sunk. It made sense to short the major players in the insurance markets and invest in South Korean shipbuilders. I was in no mood for such cynicism.

My desktop computer, bought second-hand from a Brixton junk shop, dated from the midsixties and was slow. It took me an hour to arrange the position on the flag-maker. I would have been quicker if I'd had my thoughts under control. When I wasn't thinking about Miranda and listening out for her footsteps in the flat above me, I was thinking about Adam and whether I should sell him off or start making decisions about his personality. I sold sterling and thought more about Adam. I bought gold and thought again about Miranda. I sat on the lavatory and wondered about Swiss francs. Over a third coffee I asked myself what else a victorious nation might spend its money on. Beef. Pubs. TV sets. I took positions on all three and felt virtuous, a part of the war effort. Soon it was time for lunch.

I sat facing Adam again while I ate a cheese and pickle sandwich. Any further signs of life? Not at first glance. His gaze, directed over my left shoulder, was still dead. No movement. But five minutes later I glanced up by chance and was actually looking at him when he began to breathe. I heard first a series of rapid clicks, then a mosquito-like whine as his lips parted. For half a minute nothing happened, then his chin trembled and he made an authentic gulping sound as he snatched his first mouthful of air. He didn't need oxygen, of course. That metabolic necessity was years away. His first exhalation was so long in coming that I stopped eating and tensely waited. It came at last—silently, through his nostrils. Soon his breathing assumed a steady rhythm, his chest expanded and contracted appropriately. I was spooked. With his lifeless eyes, Adam had the appearance of a breathing corpse.

How much of life we ascribe to the eyes. If only his were closed, I thought, he'd at least have the appearance of a man in a trance. I left my sandwich and went to stand by him and, out of curiosity, put my hand close to his mouth. His breath was moist and warm. Clever. In the user's manual I'd read that he urinated once a day in the late morning. Also clever. As I went to close his right eye, my forefinger brushed against his eyebrow. He flinched and violently jerked his head away from me. Startled, I moved back. Then I waited. For twenty seconds or more nothing happened, then, with a smooth, soundless movement, infinitesimally slow, the tilt of his shoulders, the angle of his head moved towards their former positions. His rate of breathing was undisturbed. Mine and my pulse had accelerated. I was standing several feet away, fascinated by the way he settled back, like a balloon gently deflating. I decided against closing his eyes. While I was waiting for something more from him, I heard Miranda moving around in the flat upstairs. Back from Salisbury. Wandering in and out of her bedroom. Once again I felt the troubled thrill of undeclared love, and that was when I had the first stirrings of an idea.

That afternoon I should have been making and losing money at my computer. Instead, I watched from the great height of a helicopter as the leading ships of the Task Force rounded Portland Bill and filed by Chesil Beach. The very place names deserved a respectful salute. **How brilliant. Onwards!** I kept thinking. And then, **Go back!** Soon the fleet came along the Jurassic coast, where herds of dinosaurs once grazed on giant ferns. Suddenly we were down among the people of Lyme Regis gathering on the Cobb. Some had binoculars, many had the very flags I had in mind, plastic on a wooden stick. A news team might have handed them around. Vox pops. Gentle local voices of hard-working women, tight with emotion. Tough old coves who'd fought in Crete and Normandy, nodding to themselves, giving nothing away. Oh, how I wished I too believed. But I could! A long lens mounted somewhere on the Lizard showed the tiny receding blobs of ships heading bravely out onto the big swell of the open sea to the sound of husky Rod Stewart, while I tried not to be tearful.

What turmoil on a weekday afternoon. A new kind of being at my dining table, the woman I newly loved six feet above my head, and the country at old-fashioned war. But I was tolerably disciplined and had promised myself seven hours every day. I turned off the TV and went to my screen. Waiting for me was the email from Miranda that I'd hoped for.

I knew I would never get rich. The sums I moved around, safely spread across scores of opportunities, were small. Over the month I had done well out of solid-state batteries but had lost almost as much to rare earth element futures—a foolish leap into the known. But I was keeping myself out of a career, an office job. This was my least bad option in the pursuit of freedom. I worked on through the afternoon, resisting the temptation to look in on Adam, even though I guessed he would be fully charged by now. Next step was downloading his updates. Then those problematic personal preferences.

Before lunch I'd sent Miranda an email inviting her to dinner that night. Now she'd accepted. She liked my cooking. During the meal I would make a proposal. I would fill in roughly half the choices for Adam's personality, then give her the link and the password and let her choose the rest. I wouldn't interfere, I wouldn't even want to know what decisions she had made. She might be influenced by a version of herself: delightful. She might conjure the man of her dreams: instructive. Adam would come into our lives like a real person, with the layered intricacies of his personality revealed only through time, through events, through his dealings with whomever he met. In a sense he would be like our child. What we were separately would be merged in him. Miranda would be drawn into the adventure. We would be partners, and Adam would be our joint concern, our creation. We would be a family. There was nothing underhand in my plan. I was sure to see more of her. We'd have fun.

My schemes generally fell apart. This was different. I was clear-headed, incapable of deceiving myself. Adam was not my love-rival. However he fascinated her, she was also physically repelled by him. She had told me as much. It was "creepy," she had told me the day before, that his body was warm. She said it was "a bit weird" that he could make words with his tongue. But he had a word-store as large as Shakespeare's. It was his mind that aroused her curiosity.

So the decision not to sell Adam was made. I was to share him with Miranda—just as I might have shared a house. He would contain us. Making progress, comparing notes, pooling disappointments. I regarded myself at thirty-two as an old hand at love. Earnest declarations would drive her away. Far better to make this journey together. Already she was my friend, she sometimes held my hand. I wasn't starting from nowhere. Deeper feelings could steal up on her, as they had on me. If they didn't, then at least I'd have the consolation of more time with her.

In my ancient fridge, whose rusty door handle had partly come away, was a corn-fed chicken, a quarter-pound of butter, two lemons and a bunch of fresh tarragon. In a bowl on the side were a few bulbs of garlic. In a cupboard, some earth-caked potatoes, already sprouting—but peeled, they would roast nicely. Lettuce, a dressing, a hearty bottle of Cahors. Simple. First, heat the oven. These ordinary matters filled my thoughts as I stood from my desk. An old friend of mine, a journalist, once said that paradise on earth was to work all day alone in anticipation of an evening in interesting company.

The meal I intended to cook for her and the homely dictum of my friend distracted me and for the moment Adam was not on my mind. So it was a shock to enter the kitchen and find him standing there, naked, by the table, partly facing away from me, one hand vaguely fiddling with the wire that protruded from his umbilicus. His other hand was somewhere near his chin, stroking it in a contemplative way—a clever algorithm no doubt, but entirely convincing in its projection of a thoughtful self.

I recovered and said, "Adam?"

He turned towards me slowly. When he was facing me full on, he met my gaze and blinked, and blinked again. The mechanism was working but seemed too deliberate.

He said, "Charlie, I'm pleased to meet you at last. Could you bear to arrange my downloads and prepare the various parameters . . ."

He paused, looking at me intently, his black-flecked eyes scanning my face in quick saccades. Taking me in. "You'll find all you need to know in the manual."

"I'll do that," I said. "In my own time."

His voice surprised and pleased me. It was a light tenor, at a decent speed, with a kindly variation in tone, both obliging and friendly, but no hint of subservience. The accent was the standard English of an educated man from the middle-class south, with the faintest hint of West Country vowels. My heart was beating fast, but I was intent on seeming calm. To show that I was, I made myself take a step closer. We stared at each other in silence.

Years before, as a student, I read of a "first contact" in 1924 between an explorer called Leahy and some highlanders of Papua New Guinea. The tribesmen could not tell whether the pale figures who had suddenly appeared on their land were humans or spirits. They returned to their village to discuss the matter, leaving a teenage boy behind to spy from a distance. The question was settled when he reported back that one of Leahy's colleagues had gone behind a bush to defecate. Here, in my kitchen in 1982, not many years later, things were not so simple. The manual informed me that Adam had an operating system as well as a nature—that is, a human nature—and a personality, the one I hoped Miranda would help provide. I was unsure how these three substrates overlapped or reacted with each other. When I studied anthropology, a universal human nature was thought not to exist. It was a romantic illusion, merely the variable product of local conditions. Only anthropologists, who studied other cultures in depth, who knew the beautiful extent of human variety, fully grasped the absurdity of human universals. People who stayed behind at home in comfort understood nothing, not even of their own cultures. One of my teachers liked to quote Kipling—"And what should they know of England who only England know?"

By the time I was in my mid-twenties, evolutionary psychology was beginning to reassert the idea of an essential nature, derived from a common genetic inheritance, independent of time and place. The response from the mainstream of social studies was dismissive, sometimes furious. To speak of genes in relation to people's behaviour evoked memories of Hitler's Third Reich. Fashions change. But Adam's makers were riding the new wave of evolutionary thinking.

He stood before me, perfectly still in the gloom of the winter's afternoon. The debris of the packaging that had protected him was still piled around his feet. He emerged from it like Botticelli's Venus rising from her shell. Through the north-facing window, the diminishing light picked out the outlines of just one half of his form, one side of his noble face. The only sounds were the friendly murmur of the fridge and a muted drone of traffic. I had a sense then of his loneliness, settling like a weight around his muscular shoulders. He had woken to find himself in a dingy kitchen, in London SW9 in the late twentieth century, without friends, without a past or any sense of his future. He truly was alone. All the other Adams and Eves were spread about the world with their owners, though seven Eves were said to be concentrated in Riyadh.

As I reached for the light switch I said, "How are you feeling?"

He looked away to consider his reply. "I don't feel right."

This time his tone was flat. It seemed my question had lowered his spirits. But within such microprocessors, what spirits?

"What's wrong?"

"I don't have any clothes. And—"

"I'll get you some. What else?"

"This wire. If I pull it out it will hurt."

"I'll do it and it won't hurt."

But I didn't move immediately. In full electric light I was able to observe his expression, which barely shifted when he spoke. It was not an artificial face I saw, but the mask of a poker player. Without the lifeblood of a personality, he had little to express. He was running on some form of default program that would serve him until the downloads were complete. He had movements, phrases, routines that gave him a veneer of plausibility. Minimally, he knew what to do, but little else. Like a man with a shocking hangover.

I could admit it to myself now—I was fearful of him and reluctant to go closer. Also, I was absorbing the implications of his last word. Adam only had to behave as though he felt pain and I would be obliged to believe him, respond to him as if he did. Too difficult not to. Too starkly pitched against the drift of human sympathies. At the same time I couldn't believe he was capable of being hurt, or of having feelings, or of any sentience at all. And yet I had asked him how he felt. His reply had been appropriate, and so too my offer to bring him clothes. And I believed none of it. I was playing a computer game. But a real game, as real as social life, the proof of which was my heart's refusal to settle and the dryness in my mouth.

It was clear he would speak only when spoken to. Resisting the impulse to reassure him further, I went back into the bedroom and found him some clothes. He was a sturdy fellow, a couple of inches shorter than me, but I thought my stuff would fit him well enough. Trainers, socks, underwear, jeans and sweater. I stood in front of him and put the bundle into his hands. I wanted to watch him dress to see if his motor functions were as good as the literature had promised. Any three-year-old knows how hard it is to put socks on.

When I gave him my clothes I caught a faint scent from his upper torso and perhaps his legs too, of warmed oil, the pale, highly refined sort my father had used to lubricate the keys of his sax. Adam held the clothes in the crook of both arms, with his hands extended towards me. He didn't flinch when I stooped and disengaged the power line. His tight, chiselled features showed nothing at all. A forklift truck approaching a pallet would have been as expressive. Then, I supposed, some logic gate or a network of them yielded and he whispered, "Thank you." These words were accompanied by an emphatic nod of the head. He sat down, rested the pile on the table, then took from the top the sweater. After a reflective pause he unfolded it, laid it flat, chest side down, threaded his right hand and arm through to the shoulder, then the left, and with a complicated muscular swaying shrug it was on him and he was tugging it down straight at the waist.

The sweater, made of faded yellow fleece, bore in red letters the jokey slogan of a charity I once supported: "Dyslexics of the World Untie!" He unboxed the socks and remained seated to pull them on. His movements were deft. No trace of hesitation, no problems with relative spatial calculation. He stood, held the boxer shorts low, stepped into them, pulled them up, stepped likewise into the jeans, zipped up the fly and secured the silver button at the waist in one continuous movement. He sat again, hooked his feet into the trainers and tied the laces in a double bow at a blurring speed that to some might have seemed inhuman. But I didn't think it was. It was a triumph of engineering and software design: a celebration of human ingenuity.

I turned away from him to begin my preparations for dinner. Overhead, I heard Miranda cross the room, her steps muffled, as though barefoot. Preparing to take a shower, getting ready. For me. I pictured her still wet, in a dressing gown, opening her underwear drawer and wondering. Silk, yes. Peach? Fine. While the oven warmed, I set the ingredients out on the work surface. After a day of greedy trading, there's nothing like cooking to bring one back into the world's better side, its long history of catering to others. I looked over my shoulder. It was startling, the effect of the clothes. He sat there, elbows on the table like some old pal of mine, waiting for me to pour the first glass of the evening.

I called out to him, "I'm roasting a chicken with butter and tarragon." It was mischievous of me, knowing his plain diet of electrons.

Without pausing, and in the flattest of tones, he said, "They go well together. But it's easy to burn the leaves when you're browning the bird."

Browning the bird? It was correct, I guessed, but it sounded odd.

"What d'you advise?"

"Cover the chicken with tinfoil. From the size of it I'd say seventy minutes at 180. Then brush the leaves off into the juice while you brown at the same temperature for fifteen minutes without the foil. Then pour the tarragon back on with the juices and melted butter."

"Thanks."

"Remember to let it stand under a cloth for ten minutes before you carve."

"I know about that."

"Sorry."

Did I sound tetchy? By the early eighties we were long used to talking to machines, in our cars and homes, to call centres and health clinics. But Adam had weighed up my chicken from across the room and apologised for the extraneous advice. I glanced back at him again. Now I noticed that he'd pulled up the sleeves of the sweater to his elbows to expose powerful wrists. He'd interlaced his fingers and was resting his chin on his hands. And this was him without a personality. From where I stood, with the light picking out his high cheekbones, he looked tough, the quiet guy at the bar you'd prefer not to disturb. Not the sort to hand out cooking tips.

I felt the need, rather childish, to demonstrate that I was in charge. I said, "Adam, will you walk round the table a couple of times? I want to see how you move."

"Sure."

There was nothing mechanical about his gait. In the confines of the room he managed a loping stride. When he'd been round twice he stood by his chair, waiting.

"Now you could open the wine."

"Certainly."

He came towards me with his open palm extended and I placed the corkscrew on it. It was of the articulated, cantilevering kind favoured by sommeliers. It gave him no trouble. He raised the cork to his nose, then reached into a cupboard for a glass, poured a half-inch and passed it to me. As I tasted it, his gaze on me was intent. The wine was hardly of the first or even second rank, but it wasn't corked. I nodded and he filled the glass and set it down carefully by the stove. Then he returned to his chair as I turned away to prepare a salad.

A peaceful half-hour went by and neither of us spoke. I made a dressing for the salad and chopped the potatoes. Miranda was in my thoughts. I was convinced I'd reached one of those momentous points in life where the path into the future forked.

Down one route, life would continue as before,
down the other, it would be transformed. Love, adventures, sheer excitement, but also order in my new
maturity, no more wild schemes, a home together,
children. Or these last two were wild schemes. Hers
was the sweetest nature, she was kind, beautiful,
amusing, vastly intelligent . . .

At a sound behind me, I came back to myself,
heard it again and turned. Adam was still in his
chair at the kitchen table. He had made, then repeated, the sound of a man purposefully clearing
his throat.

"Charlie, I understand that you're cooking for
your friend upstairs. Miranda."

I said nothing.

"According to my researches these past few seconds, and to my analysis, you should be careful of
trusting her completely."

"What?"

"According to my—"

"Explain yourself."

I was staring angrily into Adam's blank face. He
said in a quiet sorrowful voice, "There's a possibility she's a liar. A systematic, malicious liar."

"Meaning?"

"It would take a moment, but she's coming down
the stairs."

His hearing was better than mine. Within seconds there was a gentle tap at the door.

"Would you like me to get it?"

I didn't answer him. I was in such a fury. I went into the miniature hallway in the wrong frame of mind. Who or what was this idiot machine? Why should I tolerate it?

I wrenched the door open, and there she was in a pretty pale blue dress, smiling merrily at me, a posy of snowdrops in her hand, and she'd never looked so lovely.

TWO

Several weeks passed before Miranda was able to work on her share of Adam's character. Her father was ill and she made frequent journeys to Salisbury to look after him. She had a paper to write on nineteenth-century Corn Law reform and its impact on a single street in a town in Herefordshire. The academic movement known generally as "theory" had taken social history "by storm"—her phrase. Since she had studied at a traditional university which offered old-fashioned narrative accounts of the past, she was having to take on a new vocabulary, a new way of thinking. Sometimes as we lay side by side in bed (the evening of the tarragon chicken had been a success) I listened to her complaints and tried to look and sound sympathetic. It was no longer proper to assume that anything at all had ever happened in the past. There were only historical documents to consider, and changing scholarly approaches to them, and our own shifting relationship to those approaches, all of which were determined by ideological context, by relations to power and wealth, to race, class, gender and sexual orientation.

None of this seemed so unreasonable to me, or all that interesting. I didn't say so. I wanted to encourage Miranda in everything she did or thought. Love is generous. Besides, it suited me to think that whatever had once happened was no more than its evidence. In the new dispensation, the past weighed less. I was in the process of remaking myself and eager to forget my own recent history. My foolish choices were behind me. I saw a future with Miranda. I was approaching the shores of early middle age, and I was taking stock. I lived daily with the accumulated historical evidence my past had bequeathed, evidence I intended to obliterate: my loneliness, relative poverty, poor living quarters and diminished prospects. Where I stood in relation to the means of production and the rest was a blank to me. Nowhere, I preferred to think.

Was my purchase of Adam more proof of failure? I wasn't sure. Waking in the small hours—next to Miranda, her place or mine—I summoned in the darkness a lever of the sort found by old railway tracks that would shunt Adam back to the store and return the money to my account. By daylight the matter was more diffuse or nuanced. I hadn't told Miranda that Adam had spoken against her, and I hadn't told Adam that Miranda was to have a hand in his personality—a punishment of sorts. I despised his warning about her, but his mind fascinated me—if a mind was what he had. His appearance was thuggishly handsome, he could put on his own socks and he was a technical miracle. He was expensive but this child of the Wiring Club could not let him go.

Working on the old computer in my bedroom, out of Adam's sight, I typed in my own choices. I decided that answering every other question would be a sufficiently random kind of merging—our home-made genetic shuffling. Now I had a method and a partner, I relaxed into the process, which began to take on a vaguely erotic quality; we were making a child! Because Miranda was involved, I was protected from self-replication. The genetic metaphor was helpful. Scanning the lists of idiotic statements, I more or less chose approximations of myself. Whether Miranda did the same, or something different, we would end up with a third person, a new personality.

I wasn't going to sell Adam, but the "malicious liar" remark rankled. In studying the manual, I'd read about the kill switch. Somewhere on the nape of his neck, just below the hairline, was a mole. If I were to lay a finger on it for three seconds or so, then increase the pressure, he would be powered down. Nothing, no files, memories or skills, would be lost. That first afternoon with Adam I'd been reluctant to touch his neck or any part of him, and held back

until late in the day after my successful dinner with
Miranda. I'd spent the afternoon at my screen losing £111. I went into the kitchen where the dishes,
pots and pans were piled in the sink. As a test of
his competence I could have asked Adam to clear
up, but I was in a strange, elevated state that day.
Everything to do with Miranda glowed, even her
nightmare that had woken me in the small hours.
The plate I had put before her, the lucky fork that
had been in and out of her mouth, the pale bowed
shape where her lips had kissed her wine glass were
mine alone to handle and cleanse. And so I began.

Behind me, Adam was in place at the table, gazing towards the window. I finished and was drying
my hands on a tea towel as I went over to him.
Despite my sunny mood, I could not forgive his
disloyalty. I didn't want to hear what else he had to
say. There were boundaries of ordinary decency he
needed to learn—hardly a challenge for his neural
networks. His heuristic shortcomings had encouraged my decision. When I had learned more, when
Miranda had done her share, he could come back
into our lives.

I kept a friendly tone. "Adam, I'm switching you
off for a while."

His head turned towards me, paused, tilted,
then tilted the other way. It was some designer's notion of how consciousness might manifest itself in
movement. It would come to irritate me.

He said, "With all respect, I think that's a bad idea."

"It's what I've decided."

"I've been enjoying my thoughts. I was thinking about religion and the afterlife."

"Not now."

"It occurred to me that those who believe in a life beyond this one will—"

"That's enough. Hold still." I reached over his shoulder. His breath was warm on my arm, which, I supposed, he could snap with ease. The manual quoted in bold Isaac Asimov's tirelessly reiterated First Law of Robotics, "A robot may not injure a human being or, through inaction, allow a human being to come to harm."

I couldn't find what I wanted by touch. I walked behind Adam and there, as described, right on the hairline was the mole. I put my finger on it.

"Might we talk about this first?"

"No." I pressed and with the faintest whirring sigh he slumped. His eyes remained open. I fetched a blanket to cover him up.

In the days that followed this powering-down, two questions preoccupied me: Would Miranda fall in love with me? And would French-made Exocet missiles scupper the British fleet when it came within range of Argentinian fighter jets? When I was falling asleep, or in the mornings while I lingered a few seconds in the foggy no-man's-land between dreaming and waking, the questions merged, the air-to-ship missiles became arrows of love.

What was disarming and curious about Miranda was the ease that settled round her choices, the way she abandoned herself to the flow of events. That evening she came to supper, and after a pleasant two hours eating and drinking, we made love, having closed the bedroom door on Adam. Then we talked into the night. Just as easily, she could have kissed me on the cheek after the chicken with tarragon and retreated upstairs to her own bed and read a history book before falling asleep. What for me was momentous, the immediate, astonishing fulfilment of my hopes, was for her enjoyable and entirely unsurprising, a pleasant extra course after the coffee. Like chocolates. Or a good grappa. Neither my nakedness nor my tenderness had the effect on her that hers, in all their glorious sweetness, had on me. And I was in decent shape—good muscle tone, full head of dark brown hair—and generous, resourceful, some had been kind enough to say. I played a decent hand in pillow talk. She hardly seemed to notice how well we got along, how one topic, one harmless running joke, one mood tone succeeded another. My self-esteem allowed that this was how it must have been with everyone she had known. I suspected that our first night together barely entered her thoughts the following day.

I could hardly complain when the second night followed the pattern of the first, except that she cooked for me and we slept in her bed, and on the third, in mine—and so on. For all our carefree physical intimacy, I never spoke about my feelings in case I prompted her to admit she had none of her own. I preferred to wait, to let things build, let her feel free until she realised that she wasn't, that she was in love with me and it was too late to turn back.

There was vanity in this expectation. After a week or so there was anxiety. I'd been glad to switch Adam off. Now I wondered about reactivating him to ask about his warning, his reasons, his sources. But I couldn't let a machine have such a hold over me, which was what would happen if I granted it the role of confidant, counsellor, oracle, in my most private affairs. I had my pride and I believed that Miranda was incapable of a malicious lie.

And yet. I despised myself for doing it, but ten days into the affair I began my own investigations. Apart from the much-discussed notion of "machine intuition," Adam's only possible source was the Internet. I trawled through the social media sites. There were no accounts under her name. She lived in the reflections of her friends. So there she was, at parties or on holidays, carrying a friend's daughter on her shoulders at a zoo, gum-booted on a farm, linking arms or dancing or romping in the pool with a succession of bare-chested boyfriends, with boisterous crowds of teenage girlfriends, with drunken undergraduates. All who knew her liked her. No one on any accessible site had a sinister story. Now and then the chatter endorsed parts of the past she was recounting in our midnight conversations. Elsewhere her name came up in connection with the one academic paper she had published—"Pannage in Swyncombe: the role of the half-wild pig in the household economies of a medieval Chilterns village." When I read it, I loved her more.

As for the intuitive artificial mind, it was pure urban legend, begun in early 1968 when Alan Turing and his brilliant young colleague Demis Hassabis devised software to beat one of the world's great masters of the ancient game of go in five straight games. Everyone in the business knew that such a feat could not be accomplished by number-crunching force. The possible moves in go and chess vastly exceed the number of atoms in the observable universe, and go has exponentially more moves than chess. Go masters are unable to explain how they attain their supremacy beyond a profound sense of what feels right for any given situation on the board. So it was assumed that the computer was doing something similar. Breathless articles in the press announced a new era of humanised software. Computers were on the threshold of thinking like us, imitating our often ill-defined reasons for our judgements and choices. In a counter-move and in a pioneering spirit of open access, Turing and Hassabis put their software online. In media interviews they described the process of machine deep learning and neural networks. Turing attempted layman explanations of the Monte Carlo tree search, an algorithm elaborated during the forties' Manhattan Project to develop the first atom bomb. He became famously irritable when he attempted, overambitiously, to explain PSPACE-complete mathematics to an impatient television interviewer. Less well known was his loss of temper on an American cable channel as he described a problem central to computer science, P versus NP. He was in front of a combative studio audience of ordinary "folk." He had recently published his solution, which mathematicians around the world were then checking. As a problem it was easy to state, formidably difficult to resolve. Turing was trying to suggest that a correct positive solution would initiate exciting discoveries in biology as well as in concepts of space and time and creativity. The audience did not share or understand his excitement. They had only a dim awareness of his role in the Second World War, or of his influence on their own computer-dependent lives. They regarded him as the perfect English gentleman egghead and enjoyed tormenting him with stupid questions. The unhappy episode marked the end of his mission to popularise his field.

Before the confrontation with the nine-dan Japanese go master, the Turing–Hassabis computer played thousands of matches against itself continuously for a year. It learned from experience, and it was the scientists' claim—reasonable enough—to have come a step closer to approximating human general intelligence that gave rise to the legend of machine intuition. Nothing they said could bring the untethered story back to earth.

Commentators who suggested that the computer's victory would make the game extinct were wrong. After his fifth defeat, the elderly go master, helped by an assistant, stood slowly, bowed towards the laptop and congratulated it in a trembling voice. He said, "The mounted horse did not kill athletics. We run for joy." He was right. The game, with its simple rules and boundless complexity, became even more popular. As with the post-war defeat of a chess grandmaster, the triumph of the machine could not diminish the game. Winning, it was said, was less important than pleasure in the intricacies of the contest. But the idea that there was now software that could eerily, accurately "read" a situation, or a face, a gesture or the emotional timbre of a remark was never dislodged and partly explained the interest when the Adams and Eves came on the market.

Fifteen years is a long time in computer science. The processing power and sophistication of my Adam was far greater than that of the go computer. The technology advanced and Turing moved on. He spent concentrated time looking at decision-making and wrote a celebrated book: we are disposed to make patterns, narratives, when we should be thinking probabilistically if we want to make good choices. Artificial intelligence could improve on what we had, on what we were. Turing devised the algorithms. All his innovative work was available to others. Adam must have benefited.

Turing's institute drove forward AI and computational biology. He said he wasn't interested in becoming richer than he already was. Hundreds of prominent scientists followed his example on open-source publication, which would lead, in 1987, to the collapse of the journals **Nature** and **Science**. He was much criticised for that. Others said that his work had created tens of thousands of jobs around the world in diverse fields—computer graphics, medical scanning devices, particle accelerators, protein folding, smart electricity distribution, defence, space exploration. No one could guess the end of such a list.

By living openly from 1969 with his lover, Tom Reah, the theoretical physicist who would win the Nobel Prize in 1989, Turing helped give weight to a gathering social revolution. When the AIDS epidemic broke out he raised a huge sum to set up a virology institute in Dundee and was co-founder of a hospice. After the first effective treatments appeared, he campaigned for short licences and low prices, especially in Africa. He continued to collaborate with Hassabis, who had run his own group since 1972. Turing gradually lost patience with public engagements, so he said, and preferred to concentrate on his work in "my shrinking years." Behind him were his long residency in San

Francisco, the Presidential Medal of Freedom and a banquet in his honour with President Carter, lunch with Mrs. Thatcher at Chequers to discuss science funding, dinner with the President of Brazil to persuade him to protect the Amazon. For a long while he was the face of the computer revolution, and the voice of the new genetics, almost as famous as Stephen Hawking. Now he was a near-recluse. His only journeys were between his house in Camden Town and his institute in King's Cross, two doors down from the Hassabis Centre.

Reah wrote a long poem about his and Turing's life together, published in the **TLS** and then in book form. The poet and critic Ian Hamilton said in a review, "Here is a physicist who can imagine as well as scan. Now bring me the poet who can explain quantum gravity." When Adam appeared in my life, I believed that only a poet, not a machine, could tell me if Miranda would ever love me, or lie to me.

There must have been Turing algorithms buried in the software of the Exocet series 8 missiles that a French company, MBDA, had sold to the Argentine government. This fearsome weapon, once fired from a jet in the general direction of a ship, could recognise its profile and decide mid-flight whether it was hostile or friendly. If the latter, it aborted its mission and plunged harmlessly into the sea. If it missed its target and overshot, it was able to double back and make two more attempts. It closed on its prey at 5,000 miles an hour. Its opt-out capacity was probably based on face-recognition software that Turing developed in the mid-sixties. He had been looking for ways to help people with prosopagnosia, a condition in which sufferers are unable to recognise familiar faces. Government immigration control, defence companies and security firms raided the work for their own purposes.

Since France was a NATO partner, strong representations were made to the Elysée Palace by our government that MBDA should be prevented from selling more Exocets or from providing technical assistance. A consignment bound for Peru, Argentina's ally, was blocked. But other countries, including Iran, were willing to sell. There was also a black market. British agents, posing as arms dealers, bought up the supply.

But the spirit of the free market was irrepressible. The Argentinian military desperately needed help with the Exocet software, which had not been fully installed by the time the conflict began. Two Israeli experts, acting on their own, presumably on the offer of huge financial reward, flew to Argentina. It was never discovered who cut their throats in a Buenos Aires hotel. Many assumed it was British intelligence agents. If so, they were too late. On the day the young Israelis bled to death in their beds, four British ships were sunk, the next day another three went down, and on the third another. In all, an aircraft carrier, destroyers, frigates and a troop carrier were sunk. The loss of life was in the low thousands. Sailors, troops, cooks, doctors and nurses, journalists. After days of confusion, with all military efforts concentrated on rescuing survivors, the rump of the Task Force turned back and the Falkland Islands became Las Malvinas. The fascist junta that ruled Argentina was jubilant, its popularity soared, its murder, torture and disappearances of its citizens were forgotten or forgiven. Its hold on power was consolidated.

I watched it all, horrified—and guilty. Having thrilled to the sight of the warships filing down the English Channel, despite my opposition to the venture, I was implicated, along with nearly everyone else. Mrs. Thatcher came out of 10 Downing Street to make a statement. First she couldn't speak, then she was tearful but refused to be helped back inside. Finally she recovered and, in an untypically small voice, made the famous "I take it on my shoulders" speech. She assumed full responsibility. She would never outlive the shame. She offered her resignation. But the shock to the nation of so many deaths was profound and there was no appetite for heads to roll. If she had to go, so did her entire cabinet, and most of the country. A leader in the **Telegraph** put it thus: "The failure belongs to us all. This is not the occasion for scapegoats." A very British process began, reminiscent of the Dunkirk disaster, by which a terrible defeat was transformed into a mournful victory. National unity was all. Six weeks later, 1.5 million people were in Portsmouth to greet the returning ships with their cargoes of corpses, their burned and traumatised passengers. The rest of us watched it on television in horror.

I repeat this well-known history for the benefit of younger readers who won't be aware of its emotional impact, and because it formed a melancholy background to our three-cornered household. The rent was due and I was concerned by a loss of income. There was no mass purchase of hand-held Union Jacks, champagne consumption was down, and the general economy was in trouble, though pubs and hamburgers went on as before. Miranda was lost to her father's illness and to the Corn Laws and the historical viciousness of vested interests, their indifference to suffering. Meanwhile, Adam remained under the blanket. Miranda's delay in starting work on him was in part due to technophobia, if that's the word for disliking being online and ticking boxes with a mouse. I nagged, and finally she agreed to make a start. A week after the remains of the Task Force returned to port, I set up the laptop on the kitchen table and brought up Adam's site. It wasn't necessary to wake him for her to begin. She picked up the cordless mouse, turned it over and stared at its underside with distaste. I made her coffee and went into the bedroom to work.

My portfolio had halved in value. I was supposed

to be recouping losses. But the thought of her next door was a distraction. As so often in the mornings, I dwelt on our night before. The misery enveloping the country had made it all the more intense. Then we had talked. She described at length her childhood, an idyll shattered by her mother's death when she was eight. She wanted to take me to Salisbury and show me the important locations. I took this as a sign of progress but she had yet to suggest a date, and she hadn't said that she wanted me to meet her father.

I was facing my screen without seeing it. The walls and especially the door were thin. She was making very slow progress. At long intervals, I made out a deliberate click as she registered a choice. The silence between made me tense. Open to experience? Conscientious? Emotionally stable? After an hour I was getting nowhere and decided to go out. I kissed the top of her head as I squeezed past her chair. I left the house and set off towards Clapham.

It was unusually hot for April. The traffic down Clapham High Street was heavy, the pavements were crowded. Everywhere, black ribbons. The idea had crossed from the United States. On lampposts and doors, in shop windows, on car door handles and aerials, on pushchairs, wheelchairs and bikes. In central London, on official buildings where Union Jacks were at half mast, black ribbons dangled from the flagpoles for the 2,920 dead. Black ribbons were worn as armbands and on lapels—I was wearing one myself and so was Miranda. I would find one for Adam. Women and girls and flamboyant men tied them in their hair. The passionate minority who had argued and marched against the invasion wore them too. For public figures and celebrities, including the royal family, it was hazardous not to wear one—the popular press was keeping watch.

I had no ambition but to walk off my restless state. I increased my pace through the business end of the High Street. I passed the boarded-up office of the Anglo-Argentinian Friendship Society. A rubbish collectors' walkout was in its second week. The bags piled round lampposts were waist-high and the heat was generating a sweet stench. The public, or its press, agreed with the prime minister that a strike at such a time was an act of heartless disloyalty. But the wage demands were as inevitable as the next rise in inflation. No one knew yet how to dissuade the snake from eating its tail. Very soon, perhaps by the end of the year, stoical robots of negligible intelligence would be picking up the rubbish. The men they displaced would be even poorer. Unemployment was at sixteen per cent.

By the curry house and along the greasy pavement outside the fast-food chains, the smell of rotting meat was a force that hit the chest. I held my breath until I was past the Tube station. I crossed the road and walked onto the Common. There were shouts and squeals rising from a crowd by the boating and paddling pool. Even some of the kids splashing about were wearing ribbons. It was a happy scene but I didn't linger. In these new times a solitary man had to be wary of seeming to stare at children.

So I strolled over to Holy Trinity Church, a huge brick Age of Reason shed. There was no one inside. As I sat, hunched forward, elbows on knees, I could have been mistaken for a worshipper. It was too reasonable a place to evoke much awe, but its clean lines and sensible proportions were soothing. I was content to stay a while in the cool gloom and let my thoughts drift back to our very first night together when I'd been woken by a prolonged howl. I thought a dog was in the room and I was half out of bed before I came to and realised that Miranda was having a nightmare. It wasn't easy to wake her. She was struggling, as if fighting with someone, and twice she mumbled, "Don't go in. Please." Afterwards I thought it would help her to describe the dream. She was lying on my arm, clinging to me tightly. When I asked her again, she shook her head, and soon she was asleep.

In the morning, over coffee, she shrugged my question away. Just a dream. That moment of evasion stood out because Adam was behind us, making a good job of cleaning the window, which I had told him, rather than asked him, to do. While we were talking, he had paused and turned, as if intrigued to hear an account of a nightmare. I wondered then if he himself was subject to dreams. He was on my conscience now. My command that morning had been snappish. I shouldn't have treated him like a servant. Later that day I had powered him down. I had left him switched off too long. Holy Trinity Church was associated with William Wilberforce and the anti-slavery movement. He would have promoted the cause of the Adams and Eves, their right not to be bought and sold and destroyed, their dignity in self-determination. Perhaps they could take care of themselves. Soon they'd be doing the dustmen's jobs. Doctors and lawyers were next in line. Pattern recognition and faultless memory were even easier to compute than gathering up the city's filth.

We could become slaves of time without purpose. Then what? A general renaissance, a liberation into love, friendship and philosophy, art and science, nature worship, sports and hobbies, invention and the pursuit of meaning? But genteel recreations wouldn't be for everyone. Violent crime had its attractions too, so did bare-knuckle cage-fighting, VR pornography, gambling, drink and drugs, even boredom and depression. We wouldn't be in control of our choices. I was proof of that.

I wandered out across the open spaces of the Common. Fifteen minutes later I reached the far side and decided to turn back. By now Miranda should have made at least a third of her decisions. I was impatient to be with her before she set off for Salisbury. She would be back late that night. I was resting from the heat in the narrow shade of a silver birch. A few yards away was a fenced-in little swing park for children. A small boy—I guessed he was about four years old—dressed in baggy green shorts, plastic sandals and a stained white t-shirt, was bent over by a see-saw examining an object on the ground. He tried to dislodge it with his foot, then he crouched down and got his fingers to it.

I hadn't noticed his mother sitting on a bench with her back to me. She called out sharply, "Get here!"

The boy looked up, seemed about to go towards her, then his attention returned to the interesting thing on the ground. Now he had moved, I saw it myself. It was a bottle top, glinting dully, perhaps embedded in the softened tarmac.

The woman's back was broad, her hair black, curly, thinning towards the crown. In her right hand was a cigarette. Her elbow was cupped in her left hand. Despite the heat, she was wearing a coat. Below the collar was a long tear.

"D'you hear me?" The threat was on a rising note. Again the child looked up and seemed fearful and bound to obey. He took a half-step, but as his gaze shifted, he saw his prize again and faltered. When he went back to it, he may have thought he could lever it free and take it to his mother. But what he may have reasoned didn't matter. With a yelp of frustration, the woman leaped from the bench, crossed the few yards of playground at speed and dropped her cigarette as she grabbed the boy by his arm and smacked his bare legs. At the instant of his first cry, she smacked him again, and a third time.

I'd been comfortable in my thoughts and was reluctant to be taken from them. For a moment I thought I could head for home, pretending, if not to myself, then to the world, that I'd seen nothing. There was nothing I could do about this little boy's life.

His screams were angering his mother further. "Shut up!" she shouted at him over and over again. "Shut up! Shut up!"

Even then I might have forced myself to ignore the scene. But as the boy's shrieks grew louder, she seized his shoulders in two hands, pulling his dirty t-shirt clear of his belly, and began to shake him hard.

There are some decisions, even moral ones, that are formed in regions below conscious thought. I found myself jogging towards the playground's fence, stepping over it, taking three paces and putting a hand on the woman's shoulder.

I said, "Excuse me. Please. Please don't do that."

My voice sounded prissy in my ears, privileged, apologetic, lacking all authority. I was already doubting where this could lead. Not to a future of reformed, kindly parenting. But at least, as she turned towards me in disbelief, her assault had ceased.

"What was that?"

"He's just little," I said stupidly. "You could do him serious harm."

"Who the fuck are you?"

It was the right question and for that reason I didn't answer it. "He's too little to understand you."

This conversation was proceeding over the child's screams. Now he clutched at his mother's skirts, wanting to be picked up. This was the worst of it. His tormentor was also his only comfort. She was squaring up to me. The dropped cigarette smouldered by her foot. Her right hand clenched and unclenched. Trying to appear not to, I took a vague half-step back. We were staring each other out. It was, or had been, a rather lovely, intelligent face, its obvious beauty marred by weight gain plumping up the flesh round her eyes, narrowing them into a look of suspicion. In another life it could have been a kindly, maternal face. Rounded, high cheekbones, a slew of freckles across the bridge of her nose, full lips—though the lower was split. After several seconds, I noticed that her pupils were pinpricks. She was the first to shift her gaze. She was looking over my shoulder and then I found out why.

She yelled, "Oi, John."

I turned. Her friend or husband, John, also plump, naked from the waist, bright pink from a bout in the sun, was on his way through the playground's wire gate.

Still several yards away he called, "He bothering you?"

"Fucking right."

In some other sector of all imagined possibilities—the cinematic would be one—I needn't have worried. John was about my age, but shorter, flabbier, less fit, less strong. In that other world, if he'd struck me, I could have floored him. But in this world, I'd never hit another person in my life, not even in childhood. I could have told myself that if I knocked the father down the child would suffer all the more. But that wasn't it. I had the wrong attitude, or rather, I lacked the right one. It wasn't fear, it certainly wasn't lofty principle. When it came to hitting people, I didn't know where to begin. I didn't want to know.

"Oh yeah?"

Now John was squaring up to me, the woman having stepped back. The boy continued to wail. Father and son were comically alike—both crop-haired, ginger-blond, with small faces and wide-apart green eyes.

"With all respect, he's just little. He shouldn't be hit or shaken."

"With all respect, you can fuck off out of it. Or else."

And John did look ready to hit me. His chest was puffed out, the ancient self-enlargement ploy of toads and apes and many others. His breathing was rapid and his arms hung well clear of his torso. I may have been stronger, but he would be more reckless. Less to lose. Or this was what bravery was. Being ready to take a chance on not getting felled and your head lifted and slammed down on the tarmac many times, with lifelong neural consequences. A chance I wouldn't take. This was what cowardice was, a surfeit of imagining.

I raised both hands in a gesture of surrender. "Look. I can't make you do anything, obviously. I can only hope to persuade you. For the little boy's benefit."

Then John said something so surprising that I was completely outflanked and for a moment could hardly reply.

"Do you want him?"

"What?"

"You can have him. Go on. You're an expert on kids. He's yours. Take him home with you."

The child had gone quiet by this point. Looking at him again, I thought he had something his father lacked, though perhaps not his mother—a faint but still luminous signal in his expression of intelligent engagement, despite his distress. We stood in a tight little group. From far across the Common we heard, above the traffic, the distant shouts of children by the paddling pool.

On an impulse, I called the father's bluff. "All right," I said. "He can come and live with me. We'll sort out the paperwork later."

I took a card from my wallet and gave it to him. Then I put my hand out to the boy and to my surprise he raised his and slotted his fingers between mine. I felt flattered. "What's his name?"

"Mark."

"Come on, Mark."

Together we walked away from his parents, across the playground to the spring-hinged gate.

The little boy said in a loud whisper, "Let's pretend to run away." His upturned face was suddenly alive with humour and mischief.

"OK."

"On a boat."

"All right."

I was about to open the gate when there was a shout behind me. I turned, hoping that my relief didn't show. The woman came running at me, pulled the boy away and swung at me with an open hand. The blow fell harmlessly against my upper arm.

"Pervert!"

She was ready to take another swing when John called out in a weary tone. "Leave it."

I let myself out and walked a little way before stopping to look back. John was hoisting Mark onto his raw shoulders. I had to admire the father. There may have been wit in his methods which I'd failed to notice. He had got rid of me without a fight by making an impossible offer. What a nightmare, to drag the boy back to my tiny place, introduce him

to Miranda, then see to his needs for the next fifteen years. I noticed that the woman had a black
ribbon tied to the arm of her coat. She was trying
to persuade John to take his shirt. He was ignoring
her. As the family crossed the playground, Mark
turned in my direction and raised an arm, perhaps
to maintain his balance, perhaps in farewell.

In our side-by-side conversations in bed, often
in the early hours, a figure presided whose form
was becoming clearer as he hovered before us in the
darkness, an unfortunate ghost. I had to overcome
an initial impulse to regard him as a rival, hostile
to my very existence. I looked him up online and
saw his face through time, from early twenties to
mid-fifties, evolving from girlishly handsome to
appealingly ruined. I read his press, which was not
extensive. His name meant nothing to me. A couple of my friends knew of him but had never read
him. A profile, five years old, dismissed him as "an
almost-man." Since the phrase described one of my
own possible fates, I warmed a little to Maxfield
Blacke, and understood the obvious—that to love
the daughter would be to embrace the father. Whenever she returned from Salisbury, she needed to talk
about him. I learned about his different pains, or
agonies, the shifting prognoses, the arrogant, ignorant doctor followed by the kind and brilliant
doctor, the chaotic hospital with surprisingly good

food, the treatments and medications, the fresh hopes abandoned, then restored. His mind, she found countless ways of saying, remained sharp. It was his body that had turned against him, against itself, with the ferocity of a civil war. How it hurt the daughter to see the writer's tongue disfigured by ugly black spots. How it hurt the father to eat, to swallow, to speak. His immune system was letting or taking him down.

There was more. He passed a large kidney stone, as excruciating, Miranda believed, as natural child-birth. He broke a hip on the bathroom floor. His skin itched intolerably. Now he had gout in the joints of both thumbs. Reading, his passion, was made difficult as cataracts clouded his vision. The operation was ahead of him, though he hated and feared anyone messing with his eyes. There may have been other afflictions too humiliating to re-count. The woman he should have asked long ago to be his fourth wife had walked out two years ago. Maxfield was alone, dependent on health visitors, strangers, and on his daughter, ninety miles dis-tant. His two sons by another marriage sometimes travelled from London, bringing presents of wine, cheese, biographies, the latest wristwatch computer. But they were squeamish about their father's inti-mate care.

We weren't old enough, Miranda and I, to un-derstand fully that a man in his late fifties was still too young to expect or deserve such multiple insults.

But his resemblance to Job tortured by his pitiless God made it seem blasphemous to do anything but listen to Miranda. The night after my encounter in the playground stood out. Hard to believe of a man in love, but my mind wandered as she talked about him. She was just back from Salisbury, describing a fresh torment as we lay in bed. Sympathetically, I took her hand as she talked. The constant sufferings of a man I had never met could only hold me so long. Half listening, I was free to contemplate my life's strange new turns.

Downstairs, still on the same hard wooden chair, my interesting toy waited under its blanket, its merged personality installed that afternoon while it slept. The adventure was about to begin. At my side was my future, I was sure of it. The imbalance in our feelings for each other would be righted. We were simply the embodiment of a pattern in modern manners: acquaintance, followed by sex, then friendship, finally love. There was no good reason we should travel this conventional course at the same speed. Patience was all.

Meanwhile, surrounding my islet of hopes was an ocean of national sorrow. With ghastly timing, the junta had raised that day 406 Argentine flags in Port Stanley, one for each of their dead, and staged a military parade along the deserted, sodden main street, while in London, in St. Paul's, a commemoration service was held for our 3,000.

I watched it on television after I returned from the Common. There could hardly have been two dozen in that vast congregation of the ruling elite who thought that a God who preferred fascism to the Union Jack was worth the candle, or that the departed reposed in eternal bliss. But secular tradition couldn't provide such familiar verses polished to a gleam by the long-discarded sincerity of previous generations. **Man that is born of woman hath but a short time to live.** So the hymns were sung, the impenetrable, echoing readings intoned, the responses returned in ragged unison, while the rest of us mourned at the altars of our TV sets. Unlike Miranda, I mourned too.

With a million and a half others I had "marched" through central London to protest against the Task Force. In fact we crept along, stopping to wait at many bottlenecks. The usual paradox held: the matter was grave, the demonstration joyous. Rock bands, jazz bands, drums and trumpets, witty banners, wild costumes, circus skills, speeches, and above all the exhilaration of such numbers, taking hours to file past, so diverse, so clearly decent. So easy to believe that the whole nation had invaded London to make the obvious point that the coming war was unjust, inhumane, illogical, potentially catastrophic. We couldn't know just how right we were. Or how effectively Parliament, the tabloids, the military and two-thirds of the nation would dismiss us. It was said we were unpatriotic, defending a fascist regime and opposing the rule of international law.

Where was Miranda that day? We barely knew each other then. She was in the library, making the final changes to her half-wild-pigs paper. She had unusual ideas about the Task Force for someone in her twenties, and she distrusted the spirit of what she called a "self-loving crowd," its easy likemindedness, its stupid high spirits. She didn't share my aptitude for protest or sentiment. She was not interested in watching the ships leave, or in what came to be known as The Sinking, or the inglorious return and still less the service in St. Paul's. Where I had talked with friends about nothing else for months and read every opinion on the affair, Miranda stayed away. When the ships sank, she was silent. When the black ribbons appeared, she wore one, but she wouldn't be drawn. As she put it, the whole episode "stank."

Now, as I lay beside her with her hand in mine, the orange streetlights beyond the curtains gave her bedroom the appearance of a stage set. She had taken the last train home and waited for a delayed Tube to Clapham North. It was almost three o'clock. She was describing how Maxfield had told her ruefully that the gout in his thumbs was a blessing. The pain was so ferocious and localised that his other complaints had faded.

I was still holding her hand. I said, "You know

how much I want to meet him. Let me come with you next time."

Several seconds passed before she drowsily replied, "I'd like to go very soon."

"Good."

Then, after another pause, "Adam must come too."

She stroked my forearm in a gesture of farewell as she turned on her side, away from me. Soon her breathing was regular and deep, and I was left pondering in the monochrome sodium dusk. He's coming too. She had assumed joint ownership, just as I'd hoped. But an encounter between Adam and an old-style literary curmudgeon like Maxfield Blacke was hard to envisage. I knew from the profile that he still worked in longhand, detested computers, mobile phones, the Internet and all the rest. Apparently he didn't, in that priggish cliché, "suffer fools gladly." Or robots. Adam had yet to be woken. He had yet to leave the house, yet to test his luck as a plausible being capable of small talk. I'd already decided to keep him away from my circle of friends until he was a fully adept social creature. Starting out with Maxfield could disable important sub-routines. Miranda might have been hoping to distract her father and energise his writing. Or it was to do with me, somehow in my interests in ways I didn't understand. Or—I failed to resist this thought—against them?

That was a bad idea, of the kind that comes in

the small hours. Like all insomniac brooding, the essence was repetition. Why should I meet her father in the presence of Adam? Of course, it was entirely in my power to insist on keeping him here. But I would be denying the wishes of a woman whose father lay dying. Was he really dying? Was it possible to get gout in your thumb? Bilaterally? Did I really know Miranda? I lay on my side, seeking a cool corner of the pillow, then on my back with a view of a dappled ceiling that now seemed too close, and yellow rather than orange. I asked myself the same questions, I rephrased them and asked them again. I knew what I was about to do, but I delayed, preferring to fret, denying the obvious for almost an hour. Then at last I got up, pulled on my jeans and t-shirt, let myself out and went barefoot down the communal stairs to my own flat.

In the kitchen I didn't even pause before pulling the blanket clear. Outwardly nothing had changed—eyes closed, that same bronze face, the nose with its hint of cruelty. I reached behind his head, found the spot and pressed. While he was warming up I ate a bowl of cereal.

Just as I was finishing he said, "Never be disappointed."

"What was that?"

"I was saying that those who believe in the afterlife will never be disappointed."

"You mean, if they're wrong they'll never know about it."

"Yes."

I looked at him closely. Was he different now? He had an expectant look. "Logical enough. But Adam. I hope you don't think that's profound."

He didn't reply. I took my empty bowl to the sink and made myself tea. I sat at the table, across from him, and after taking a couple of sips, I said, "Why did you say that I shouldn't trust Miranda?"

"Oh, that . . ."

"Come on."

"I spoke out of turn and I'm truly sorry."

"Answer the question."

His voice had changed. It was firmer, more expressive in its varied pitch. But the attitude—I needed more time. My immediate, unreliable impression was of an intact presence.

"I was thinking only of your best interests."

"You just said you were sorry."

"That's correct."

"I need to hear why you said what you did."

"There's a small but significant possibility that she might harm you."

I disguised my irritation and said, "How significant?"

"In the terms set by Thomas Bayes, the eighteenth-century clergyman, I'd say one in five, assuming you accept my values for the priors."

My father, adept at the harmonic progressions of bebop, was a sincere technophobe. He used to say that any faulty electrical device needed no more than a good thump. I drank my tea and considered. In the colossal array of tree-branching networks that governed Adam's decision-making, there would be a strong weighting in favour of reasonableness.

I said, "I happen to know that the possibility is insignificant, close to zero."

"I see. I'm so sorry."

"We all make mistakes."

"We certainly do."

"How many mistakes have you made in your life, Adam?"

"Only this one."

"Then it's important."

"Yes."

"And important not to repeat it."

"Of course."

"So we need to analyse how you came to make it, wouldn't you say?"

"I agree."

"So, in this regrettable process what was your first move?"

He spoke confidently now, seeming to take pleasure in describing his methods. "I have privileged access to all court records, criminal as well as the Family Division, even when in camera. Miranda's name was anonymised, but I matched the case against other circumstantial factors that are also not generally available."

"Clever."

"Thank you."

"Tell me about the case. And the date and place."

"The young man, you see, knew very well that the first time he had intimate relations with her . . ."

He broke off and stared at me, bug-eyed in astonishment, as though he was taking in my presence for the first time. I guessed my short run of discovery was coming to a close. He appeared now to know about the value of reticence.

"Go on."

"Uh, she brought along a half-bottle of vodka."

"Give me a date and place and the man's name. Quick!"

"October the . . . Salisbury. But look—"

Then he began to giggle, a silly, hissing sound. It was embarrassing to witness, but I couldn't look away. On his face was a complicated look—of confusion, of anxiety, or mirthless hilarity. The user's handbook claimed that he had forty facial expressions. The Eves had fifty. As far as I knew, the average among people was fewer than twenty-five.

"Get a grip, Adam. We agreed. We need to understand your mistake."

It took him more than a minute to get himself under control. I drank the last of my tea and watched what I knew to be a complex process. I understood that personality was not like a shell, encasing and constraining his capacity for coherent thought; that his deviousness, if that was what motivated him, did not live downstream of reason. Nor did mine. His rational impulse to collaborate with me may have pulsed through his neural networks at half the speed of light, but it would not have been suddenly barred at the logic gate of a freshly devised persona. Instead, these two elements were entwined at their origins, like the snakes of Mercury's caduceus. Adam saw the world and understood it through the prism of his personality; his personality was at the service of his objectifying reason and its constant updates. From the beginning of our conversation, it had been simultaneously in his interests to avoid a repetition of an error and to withhold information from me. When the two became incompatible, he became incapacitated and giggled like a child in church. Whatever we had chosen for him lay far upstream of the branching intricacy of his decision-making. In a different dispensation of character he might simply have fallen silent; in another, he might have been compelled to tell me everything. A case could be made for both.

I now knew a little more than nothing, enough to worry about, not enough to follow up, even if I'd had access to the closed sessions of the courts: Miranda as witness, victim or accused, sex with a young man, vodka, a courtroom, one October in Salisbury.

Adam had fallen silent. His expression, the special material of his face, indistinguishable from skin, relaxed into watchful neutrality. I could have gone upstairs and woken Miranda to confront her with the obvious questions and get everything clear between us. Or I could wait and reflect, holding back what I knew in order to grant myself the illusion of control. A case could be made for both.

But I didn't hesitate. I went into my bedroom, undressed, leaving my clothes in a heap on my desk, and lay down naked under the summer duvet. It was already light. I would have liked to be soothed and hear, above the dawn chorus, the sound of the milkman going from door to door, clinking his bottles on the steps. But the last of the electric-powered milk floats had vanished from our streets. A shame. Still, I was tired and suddenly comfortable. There's a special sensuousness in an unshared bed, at least for a period, until sleeping alone begins to assume its own quiet sadness.

THREE

In the waiting room of the local doctor's practice, a dozen junk-shop dining-room chairs were arranged round the walls of what had once been a Victorian front parlour. In the centre was a low plywood table with spindly metal legs and a few magazines, greasy to the touch. I had picked one up and immediately put it back. In one corner, some colourful broken toys, a headless giraffe, a car with a missing wheel, gnawed plastic bricks, kindly donated. There were no infants in our group of nine. I was keen to avoid the gaze of the others, their small talk or ailment-swapping. I kept my breathing shallow in case the air around me swarmed with pathogens. I didn't belong here. I wasn't ill, my problem was not systemic but peripheral, a toenail. I was the youngest in the room, surely the fittest, a god among mortals, with an appointment not with the doctor but with the nurse. I remained beyond mortality's reach. Decay and death were for others. I expected my name to be called first. It turned out to be a long wait. I was second to last.

On the wall opposite me was a cork notice-board with flyers promoting early detection of this or that, healthy living, dire warnings. I had time to read them all. A photograph showed an elderly man in cardigan and slippers standing by a window. Without raising a hand to his mouth, he was lustily sneezing in the direction of a laughing little girl. Backlighting illuminated tens of thousands of particles flying towards her—minute droplets of fluid teeming with germs shared by an old fool.

I reflected on the long strange history that lay behind this tableau. The idea that germs were responsible for the spread of disease didn't gain general acceptance until the 1880s and the work of Louis Pasteur and others, only a hundred years before this poster was devised. Until then, against a few dissenters, the miasma theory prevailed—disease originated in bad air, bad smells, decomposition, or even in night air, against which windows were properly closed. But the device that could have spoken truth to medicine was available 200 years before Pasteur. The amateur scientist of the seventeenth century who knew best how to make and use the device was known to the scientific elite of London.

When Antonie van Leeuwenhoek, solid citizen of Delft, a draper and a friend of Vermeer, began sending his observations of microscopic life to the Royal Society in 1673, he revealed a new world and initiated a biological revolution. He meticulously described plant cells and muscle fibre, single-cell organisms, his own spermatozoa, and bacteria from his own mouth. His microscopes needed sunlight and had only a single lens, but no one could grind them the way he could. He was working with magnification powers of 275 and above. By the end of his life, **Philosophical Transactions of the Royal Society** had published 190 of his accounts.

Suppose there had been a young spark at the Royal Society lolling in the library after a good lunch, a copy of the **Transactions** on his lap, who began to speculate that some of these tiny organisms might cause meat to putrefy, or could multiply in the bloodstream and cause disease. There had been such sparks at the Society before and there were many to come. But this one would have needed an interest in medicine as well as scientific curiosity. Medicine and science would not become full partners until well into the twentieth century. Even in the fifties, tonsils were regularly sliced from the throats of healthy children on the basis of standard practice rather than good evidence. A doctor in Leeuwenhoek's time could easily believe that everything to be known in his field was already well understood. The authority of Galen, active in the second century, was near total. It would be a long time before medical men, in general a grand lot, peered humbly down a microscope in order to learn the basics of organic life.

But our man, whose name will become a household word, is different. His hypotheses will be possible to test. He borrows a microscope—Robert Hooke, honoured fellow of the Society, will surely lend him one—and sets to. A germ theory of disease begins to form. Others join in the research. Perhaps within twenty years surgeons are washing their hands between patients. The reputations of forgotten doctors like Hugh of Lucca and Girolamo Fracastoro are restored. By the mid-eighteenth century, childbirth is safer; certain men and women of genius are born who otherwise would have died in infancy. They might change the course of politics, the arts, the sciences. Loathsome figures who could do great harm also spring up. In minor and possibly major ways, history follows a different course long after our brilliant young member of the Royal Society has grown old and died.

The present is the frailest of improbable constructs. It could have been different. Any part of it, or all of it, could be otherwise. True of the smallest and largest concerns. How easy to conjure worlds in which my toenail had not turned against me; in which I was rich, living north of the Thames after one of my schemes had succeeded; in which Shakespeare had died in childhood and no one missed him, and the United States had taken the decision to drop on a Japanese city the atomic bomb they had tested to perfection; or in which the Falklands Task Force had not set off, or had returned victorious and the country was not in mourning; in which Adam was an assemblage far off in the future; or in which 66 million years ago the earth had turned for another few minutes before the meteor struck, so missing the sun-blotting, fine-grained gypsum sand of the Yucatan, allowing the dinosaurs to live on and deny future space to the mammals, clever apes included.

My treatment, when it came at last, began pleasantly with my naked foot soaking in a bowl of hot, soapy water. Meanwhile, the nurse, a large, friendly woman from Ghana, arranged her steel instruments on a tray with her back to me. Her expertise was as complete as her self-confidence. There was no mention of anaesthesia and I was too proud to ask, but when she took my foot onto her aproned lap and set about her business with my ingrowing toenail, I was not too proud to squeak at the crucial moment. Relief was immediate. I made my way along the street, as though on rubber wheels, to my home, the centre of my preoccupations, which had lately shifted from Miranda back to Adam.

His character was in, done, from two sources irreversibly merged. A curious parent of a growing child might wonder which characteristics belonged to the father, which to the mother. I was observing Adam closely. I knew which questions Miranda had answered but I didn't know what she had decided. I noted that a certain blankness had gone from his face, that he seemed more intact, smoother in his interactions with us and certainly more expressive. But I struggled to understand what it told me about Miranda or, for that matter, about myself. In humans, recombination is infinitely subtle and then crudely but disarmingly lopsided. The parents merge, like fluids stirred together, but the mother's face might be faithfully replicated in her child just as the father fails to pass on his gift for comedy. I remembered little Mark's touching version of his father's features. But in Adam's personality, Miranda and I were well shuffled, and as in humans, his inheritance was thickly overlaid by his capacity to learn. Perhaps he had my tendency to pointless theorising. Perhaps he had something of Miranda's secretive nature and her self-possession, her taste for solitude. Frequently he withdrew into himself, humming or murmuring "Ah!" Then he would pronounce what he took to be an important truth. His interrupted remark about the afterlife was the earliest example.

Another was when we were outside, in my tiny fraction of a back garden, marked off by a broken picket fence. He was helping to pull up weeds. It was just before sunset, the air was still and warm, suffused by an unreal amber light. A week had passed since our late-night exchange. I had brought him outside because his dexterity was still a matter of interest to me. I wanted to watch him handle a hoe and a rake. More generally, my plan was to introduce him to the world beyond the kitchen table. We had friendly neighbours on both sides and there was a chance that he could test his small-talk skills. If we were to travel together to Salisbury to meet Maxfield Blacke, I wanted to prepare Adam by taking him to some shops, and perhaps a pub. I was sure he could pass off as a person, but he needed to be more at ease, his machine-learning capacities needed stretching.

I was keen to see how good he was at identifying plants. Of course he knew everything. Feverfew, wild carrot, camomile. As he worked, he muttered the names, for his own rather than my benefit. I saw him put on gardening gloves to pull up nettles. Mere mimicry. Later he straightened and looked with apparent interest towards a spectacular western sky intersected by power and telephone lines and a receding jumble of Victorian roofs. His hands were on his hips and he leaned back, as though his lower back was giving him trouble. He took a deep breath to indicate his appreciation of the evening air. Then, out of nowhere, he said, "From a certain point of view, the only solution to suffering would be the complete extinction of humankind."

Yes, this was why he needed to be out and about. Buried within his circuitry there was probably a set of sub-routines: sociability/conversation/interesting openers.

But I decided to join in. "It's been said that killing everyone would be a cure for cancer. Utilitarianism can be logically absurd."

He replied, "Obviously!" in an abrupt manner. I looked at him, surprised, and he turned away from me and bent again to his work.

Adam's insights, even when valid, were socially inept. On our first expedition away from home, we walked the 200 yards to our local newsagent, Mr. Syed. We passed a few people in the street and no one gave Adam a second glance. That was satisfying. Over bare skin he was wearing a tight yellow jumper, knitted by my mother in her last year. He had white jeans and canvas loafers, bought for him by Miranda. She had promised to buy him a complete outfit of his own. With his neat muscular bulge of chest and arms, he could have passed for a personal trainer from the local gym.

Where the pavement narrowed between a tree and a garden wall, I saw how he stood aside to let a woman with a pushchair through.

As we neared the shop he said, somewhat absurdly, "It's good to get out."

Simon Syed had grown up in a large village thirty miles north of Calcutta. His English teacher at his school had been an Anglophile, a martinet who had beaten into his pupils a courteous and precise English. I had never asked Simon how or why he had taken on a Christian forename. Perhaps a desire to integrate, or the parting insistence of his formidable teacher. He had arrived in north Clapham from Calcutta in his late teens and immediately went to work in his uncle's shop. Thirty years later, the uncle had died and the shop passed to the nephew, who still supported his aunt from the proceeds. He also supported a wife and three grown-up children, but he didn't like to talk about them. He was a Muslim, by culture rather than practice. If there was sadness in his life, it was well concealed behind a dignified manner. Now in his mid-sixties, he was sleek, bald, very correct, with a small moustache that tapered to sharp points. There was an anthropology journal, not available on the Internet, that he kept for me. He didn't mind when I came in to scan the world's front pages during the Task Force days. He was amused by my taste for low-grade chocolate—those global brands invented between two world wars. In the mid-afternoons, after hours at my screen, I craved sugar.

In that strange way by which one reserves intimacies for a mere acquaintance, I had told Simon about my new girlfriend. When she and I had been in the shop together, he had seen for himself.

Now, whenever I came by, his first question was always, "How are matters proceeding?" He liked to tell me, on the basis of nothing but kindness, "It's clear. Her fate is you. No dodging it! Eternal happiness for you both." I sensed that many disappointments were heaped behind him. He was old enough to be my father and wanted for me what had eluded him.

There were no other customers when Adam and I entered the cramped shop with its compound scent of newsprint, peanut dust and cheap toiletries. Simon rose from the wooden chair he sat on behind the till. Because I was not alone, he would not be asking the usual question.

I made the introduction. "Simon. My friend Adam."

Simon nodded. Adam said, "Hello," and smiled.

I was reassured. A good start. If Simon had noticed the strange appearance of Adam's eyes, he didn't show it. It was a common reaction, I would soon discover. People assumed a congenital deformity and politely looked away. Simon and I discussed the cricket—three consecutive sixes and a pitch invasion at the India–England T20—while Adam stood apart before an array of canned goods on a shelf. They would be instantly familiar to him, their commercial histories, market share, nutritional value. But as we chatted, it was obvious he wasn't looking at tins of peas, or anything at all. His face was frozen. He hadn't moved in two minutes. I worried that something unusual or unpleasant was about to happen. Simon politely pretended he hadn't noticed. It was possible that Adam had put himself in rest mode. I made a mental note: he was in need of an appearance of plausibility whenever doing nothing. His eyes were open, but he failed to blink. Perhaps I had brought him out into the world too soon. Simon would be offended that I had tried to pass off Adam as a person, a friend. It could look like mockery, a tasteless joke. I would have betrayed a pleasant acquaintance.

The cricket banter began to falter. Simon's gaze settled on Adam, then returned to me. He said tactfully, "Your **Anthropos** is in."

It was my prompt to go over to the magazines, where Adam stood. Years ago, Simon had cleared his top shelf of soft porn in favour of specialist stuff—literary magazines, academic bulletins of international relations, history, entomology. A fair number of ageing, down-at-heel intellectuals lived in the neighbourhood.

As I turned away he added, "You can get it yourself?" A gentle tease to lower the tension. Simon was taller and he usually reached up for me.

A single word brought Adam to life. With the faintest whirring sound, which I hoped only I could hear, he turned to address Simon in formal terms. "Your self, you say. There's a coincidence. I've been giving some thought lately to the mystery of the self. Some say it's an organic element or process embedded in neural structures. Others insist that it's an illusion, a by-product of our narrative tendencies."

There was a silence, then, stiffening a little, Simon said, "Well, sir, which is it? What have you decided?"

"It's the way I'm made. I'm bound to conclude that I've a very powerful sense of self and I'm certain that it's real and that neuroscience will describe it fully one day. Even when it does, I won't know this self any better than I do now. But I do have moments of doubt when I wonder whether I'm subject to a form of Cartesian error."

By this time I had the journal in my hands and was preparing to leave. "Take the Buddhists," Simon said. "They prefer to get along without a self."

"Indeed. I'd like to meet one. Do you know any?"

Simon was emphatic. "No, sir. Absolutely, I do not."

I raised a hand in farewell and thanks and, taking Adam by his elbow, guided him towards the door.

It was a cliché of romantic love, but no less painful for that: the stronger my feelings, the more remote and unattainable Miranda appeared. How could I complain when she was attained that very first night, after dinner? We had fun, we talked easily, we ate and slept together most nights. But I was greedy for more, though I tried not to show it. I wanted her to open up to me, to want me, need me, show some hunger for me, some delight in me. Instead, my initial impression held—she could take me or leave me. Everything good that passed between us—sex, food, movies, new plays—was instigated by me. Without me she drifted in silence towards her default condition upstairs, to a book on the Corn Laws, a bowl of cereal, a cup of weak herbal tea, curled up in an armchair, barefoot and oblivious. Sometimes she sat for long periods without a book. If I put my head round her door (we now had keys to each other's places) and said, "How about an hour of frantic sex?" she would say calmly, "OK," and we would go into her or my bedroom and she would rise splendidly to her pleasures and mine. When we were done she would take a shower and return to her chair. Unless I suggested something else. A glass of wine, a risotto, an almost famous sax player at a Stockwell pub. OK again.

To everything I proposed, indoors or out, she brought the same tranquil readiness. Happy to hold my hand. But there was something, or many things, I didn't understand, or she didn't want me to know about. Whenever she had a seminar or needed to use the library, she returned from college in the late afternoons. Once a week she came back later. It took me a while to notice that it was always a Friday. Finally she told me that she went to the Regent's Park Mosque for Friday prayers. That surprised me. But no, she wasn't thinking of converting from atheism. She had in mind a social-history paper she might write. I wasn't convinced, but I let it go.

What we lacked was conversational intimacy. We were closest when we argued about the Task Force. When we went to a bar, her conversation was general. She was happy with her solitude or with lively chat about public matters, but there was nothing personal in between, except her father's health or his literary career. When I tried to ease us towards the past, perhaps angling in gently with something about myself or a question about her own history, she reached quickly for generalities or an account of the earliest years of her childhood, or an anecdote about someone she knew. I told her about my idiotic excursion into tax fraud, my experience of court and the tedium of my hours of community service. I would have told her anyway, but the story was my pretext to ask if she herself had ever been in court. The answer was abrupt. Never! And then she changed the subject. I'd been in various promising affairs and in love, or almost in love, two or three times before, depending on definitions. I fancied myself an expert and knew better than to put her under pressure. I still thought I might get more out of Adam on the Salisbury affair. If I didn't know her secret, at least she didn't know I knew she had one. Tact was everything. I still hadn't told her that I loved her, or divulged my fantasies about our shared future or even hinted at my frustration. I

left her alone with her books or her thoughts whenever it suited her. Though the subject was not in the
line of my interests, I worked up an acquaintance
with the Corn Laws and developed some ideas of
my own about free trade. She didn't dismiss them,
but nor was she impressed.

So here we were upstairs at dinner in her kitchen,
which was even smaller than mine. The table was
of white moulded plastic, just big enough for two,
probably stolen from a pub garden by a previous
tenant. Standing at the sink, up to his elbows in
suds, Adam dealt with the plates and cutlery we'd
handed him at the end of our meal—toad-in-the-
hole, baked beans, fried eggs. Student food. On
the windowsill, where yellow gingham curtains
hung still in our late-summer heat wave, a radio
was playing the Beatles, recently regrouped after
twelve years apart. Their album, **Love and Lemons**, had been derided for its grandiosity, for failing
to resist the lure and overreach of an eighty-strong
symphony orchestra. They could not master such
forces, was the general drift, with half a lifetime's
store of guitar chords. Nor did we wish to be told
again, the **Times** critic complained, that love was
all we needed, even if it were true, which it was not.

But I liked the music's muscular sentimentality,
emptied of irony by these middle-aged perform-
ers, so confident and tuneful, liberated by useful
ignorance of two and a half centuries of symphonic
experimentation. Lennon's rasping voice floated

towards us from some faraway echoing place beyond the horizon, or the grave. I didn't mind being told again about love. Here before me were all of its warm possibilities, barely three feet away, and it was all I needed. Here was her long, exquisitely shaped face (those angled cheekbones might break through the skin one day), the amused gaze, at this point still merry, and narrowed, locked on me, the lips parted, for she was about to speak against what I'd just said. Her perfect elongated nose flared faintly at the base of the nostrils' arch to signal in advance her dissent. Her pallor set off her fine brown hair, tonight childishly parted dead centre. Against prevailing fashion, she kept out of the sun. Her bare white arms were also thin and unblemished—not a single freckle.

From my point of view we still holidayed in the foothills, among possibilities whose fulfilment rose like distant alps. I tried to ignore them in order to attend to details. From her perspective, on the other side of this frail table, we may have already reached our highest point. She may have thought she was as close as she ever wanted to be, or could be, to another person. Love stories like Jane Austen's used to conclude chastely with preparations for a wedding. Now their climax lay on the far side of carnal knowledge, where all of complexity waited.

For now, my business was to conduct a political argument with her without feelings running high, then turning sour, and at the same time stay true to myself and let her do the same. It was a feasible balancing act, as long as I drank less than half a bottle of the indifferent Médoc that stood between us. We'd had this conversation before and it should have been easier now, but repetition seemed like an indictment of us both. We didn't really want to be talking about it. Impossible to avoid, even though we knew it would lead nowhere. But this was how it was for everyone. We were all still tending the wound. How could Miranda and I spend our lives together when we couldn't agree on such a fundamental as war?

About the islands formerly known as the Falklands she had firm views. She insisted that the Argentine flag-planting on remote South Georgia had been a clear violation of international law. I said it was an inhospitable place and no one should be asked to fight to the death for it. She said that the taking of Port Stanley was the desperate act of an unpopular regime looking to whip up patriotic fervour. I said this was all the more reason not to get drawn in. She said the Task Force was a brave and brilliant conception, even in failure. I said, uneasily remembering my emotional state when the ships set off, that it was a ridiculous enactment of lost imperial grandeur. How could I not see, she said, that this was an anti-fascist war? No (I spoke over her), it was a row over property, fed on each side by nationalistic stupidity. I summoned the Borges observation: two bald men fighting over a comb.

She replied that a bald man might hand down his comb to his children. I was struggling to understand this when she added that the generals had tortured, disappeared and killed their citizens by the thousands and were running the economy into the ground. If we'd taken back the islands, the humiliation would have finished the military regime and democracy would have returned to Argentina. I replied that she could not possibly know this. We had lost thousands of young men and women to the cause of Mrs. Thatcher's ambitions. My voice began to rise before I remembered. I resumed quietly but with a certain tremor: that she remained in office after such slaughter was the greatest political scandal of our time. I delivered this with a finality that deserved a moment's respectful silence, but Miranda came straight back to tell me that the prime minister failed in a decent cause and was supported by almost all of Parliament and the country and she was right to remain in office.

During this conversation, Adam finished with the dishes and stood with his back to the kitchen sink to watch us, arms folded, his head turning from side to side, speaker to speaker, like a spectator at a tennis match. Our exchange was not exactly weary, but repetition had given it an air of ritual. Like facing armies, we'd taken up our positions and intended to hold them. Miranda was telling me that the Task Force set off without proper ship-to-air missiles. The chiefs of staff let the armed forces down. I used to hear terms like these—ship-to-air, homing devices, titanium-tipped—at the Warwickshire student union bar, but only from men, men of the political left, whose opinions were complicated by tacit admiration for the weapon systems they condemned. In her soft and fluent delivery, she mingled these with other concepts from the lexicon of established power—the open society, rule of law, restoration of democracy. Perhaps it was her father I was hearing.

While she was speaking, I turned to catch Adam's expression. What I saw was his devoted attention. More than that. A look of delight. He adored what she was saying. I turned back to Miranda as she reminded me that the Falklanders were my fellow citizens, now living under fascism. Was I happy with that? I disliked this rhetorical turn. It was a masked insult. The conversation was turning sour, just as I'd feared, but I couldn't help myself. In the tiny kitchen space, I was hot and irritable as I reached for the wine and filled my glass. There could have been a negotiated settlement, I started to say. A slow and painless thirty-year transition, a UN mandate, guaranteed rights. She interrupted to inform me that we could never trust any undertaking by the murdering generals. As she said it, I saw them in caricature, in braided hats, campaign ribbons, cavalry boots, and Galtieri on his white horse in a confetti blizzard on the Avenida 25 de Mayo.

I said that I accepted every last one of her

arguments. The forces set off on their 8,000-mile mission, her risky strategy was tested and it failed. Thousands she never knew or cared about were drowned or burned to death, or live on, maimed, disfigured, traumatised. We've arrived at the worst outcome: the junta possessed the island and its inhabitants. Whereas a policy of slow, negotiated agreement wasn't tested, but if it had failed we would have reached the same outcome, without the agony and death. We couldn't know. What might have happened was lost to us. So what was there to argue about?

I saw that the glass I'd filled, and had no memory of touching, was empty. And I was wrong. There was plenty to argue about, for even as I said it, I knew I was crossing a line. I had accused her of not caring about the dead, and she was angry.

Her eyes were narrowed, without merriment, but she didn't address my transgression. Instead, she turned to Adam and asked quietly, "What's your view?"

His gaze travelled from her to me and back. I still didn't know whether he actually saw any-thing. An image on some internal screen that no one was watching, or some diffused circuitry to ori-ent his body in three-dimensional space? Seeming to see could be a blind trick of imitation, a social manoeuvre to fool us into projecting onto him a human quality. But I couldn't help it: when our eyes briefly met and I looked into the blue irises flecked with spears of black, the moment appeared rich with meaning, with anticipation. I wanted to know whether he understood, as I did, and as Miranda surely did, that the issue here was loyalty.

His tone was prompt and calm. "Invasion, success or failure. Negotiated settlement, success or failure. Four outcomes or effects. Without benefit of hindsight, we'd have to choose which causes to pursue, which to avoid. We'd be in the realm of Bayesian inverse probability. We'd be looking for the probable cause of an effect rather than the most likely effect of a cause. Only sensible, to try and find a formal representation of our guesswork. Our reference point, our datum, would be an observer of the Falklands situation before any decisions were taken. Certain **a priori** probability values are ascribed to the four outcomes. As fresh information comes in, we can measure relative changes in probability. But we can't possess an absolute value. It may help us to define the weight of new evidence logarithmically, so that, assuming a base ten—"

"Adam. Enough! Really. What nonsense!" Now it was Miranda who reached for the Médoc.

I was relieved to be no longer the object of her irritation. I said, "But Miranda and I would ascribe completely different **a priori** values."

Adam turned his head towards me. As always, too slowly. "Of course. As I said, when describing the future there can be no absolute values. Only shifting degrees of likelihood."

"But they're entirely subjective."

"Correct. Ultimately Bayes reflects a state of mind. As does all of common sense."

Then nothing was solved, despite this high gloss of rationality. Miranda and I had different states of mind. What was new? But we were united against Adam in our differences. At least, this was my hope. He may have understood the relevant issue after all: he thought I was right about the Falklands and, given a degree of programmed intellectual honesty, the best he could offer Miranda, to whom he was also loyal, was an appearance of neutrality. But if that was sound, why not accept the mirror possibility, that he believed Miranda was right and I was the one in receipt of loyal support?

With a sudden scrape of a kitchen chair, Miranda stood. There was a faint flush about her face and throat and she wasn't looking at me. We'd be sleeping in separate beds that night. I would have happily unsaid my entire argument to stay with her. But I was dumb.

She said to Adam, "You can stay up here to charge, if you like."

Adam needed six hours a night connected to a thirteen-amp socket. He went into sleep mode and sat quietly "reading" until after dawn. Usually he was in my kitchen downstairs, but recently Miranda had bought a second charging cable.

He murmured his thanks and slowly folded a kitchen towel in half with close attention, hunched over the task, and spread it across the draining board. As she moved towards her bedroom door she shot me a look, a regretful smile that didn't part her lips, sent a conciliatory kiss across the space between us and whispered, "Just for tonight."

So we were fine.

I said, "Of course I know you care about the dead."

She nodded and left. Adam was sitting down, pulling his shirt clear of his belt to locate the tethering point below his waistline. I put a hand on his shoulder and thanked him for clearing up.

For me, it was far too early for bed and it was hot, like a summer evening in Marrakech. I went downstairs and looked in the fridge for something cool.

I remained in the kitchen, in an old leather armchair, with a balloon glass of Moldovan white. There was much pleasure in following a line of thought without opposition. I was hardly the first to think it, but one could see the history of human self-regard as a series of demotions tending to extinction. Once we sat enthroned at the centre of the universe, with sun and planets, the entire observable world, turning around us in an ageless dance of worship. Then, in defiance of the priests, heartless astronomy reduced us to an orbiting planet around the sun, just one among other rocks. But still we stood apart, brilliantly unique, appointed by the creator to be lords of everything that lived. Then biology confirmed that we were at one with the rest, sharing common ancestry with bacteria, pansies, trout and sheep. In the early twentieth century came deeper exile into darkness when the immensity of the universe was revealed and even the sun became one among billions in our galaxy, among billions of galaxies. Finally, in consciousness, our last redoubt, we were probably correct to believe that we had more of it than any creature on earth. But the mind that had once rebelled against the gods was about to dethrone itself by way of its own fabulous reach. In the compressed version, we would devise a machine a little cleverer than ourselves, then set that machine to invent another that lay beyond our comprehension. What need then of us?

Such hot-air thoughts deserved a second, bigger balloon and I poured it. Head propped in my right palm, I approached that ill-lit precinct where self-pity becomes a mellow pleasure. I was a special case of the general banishment, though it wasn't Adam I was thinking of. He wasn't cleverer than me. Not yet. No, my exile was for one night only and it gave a twist of sweet, bearable agony to a hopeless love. My shirt unbuttoned to the waist, all windows open, the urban romance of getting thoughtfully drunk amid the heat and dust and muted din of north Clapham, in a world city. The imbalance of our affair was heroic. I imagined an onlooker's approving gaze from a corner of the room. That well-formed figure slumped in his beaten-up chair. I rather loved myself. Someone had to. I rewarded myself with thoughts of her, mid-ecstasy, and considered the impersonal quality of her pleasures. I was only **good enough** for her, as many men might be. I refused the obvious, that her distance was the whip that drove my longing. But here was something strange. Three days before, she had asked a mysterious question. We were mid-embrace, in the conventional position. She drew my face towards hers. Her look was serious.

She whispered, "Tell me something. Are you real?"

I didn't reply.

She turned her head away so that I saw her in profile as her eyes closed and she lost herself once more in a maze of private pleasure.

Later that night, I asked her about it. "It was nothing," was all she said before she changed the subject. Was I real? Meaning did I really love her, or was I honest, or did I fit her needs so exactly that she might have dreamed me up?

I crossed the kitchen to pour the last of the wine. The broken fridge door handle needed a sharp sideways pull to engage its lock. As my hand closed round the cold neck of the bottle, I heard a sound, a creak above my head. I had lived long enough beneath Miranda's feet to know her steps and their precise direction. She had moved across her bedroom and was hesitating in the threshold of her kitchen. I heard the murmur of her voice. No reply. She took another two steps into the room. The next would bring her onto a floorboard that under pressure made a truncated quacking sound. As I waited to hear it, Adam spoke. He pushed his chair back as he stood. If he was to take another step he would need to untether himself. This he must have achieved because it was his tread that landed on the noisy floorboard. That meant they were standing less than a metre apart, but there was no sound until a minute had passed, and now it was footsteps, two sets, moving back towards the bedroom.

I left the fridge door open because the sound of it closing would betray me. No choice but to shadow them into my bedroom. So I went and stood by my desk and listened. I reckoned I was right under her bed when I heard the murmur of her voice, a command. She must have wanted air in the room, for Adam's steps tracked across the room towards the Victorian bay. Only one of its three windows opened. Even that one was hard to shift on a warm or rainy day. The old wooden frames shrank or expanded, and something was wrong with the counterweight and hardened rope. Our age could devise a passable replica of a human mind, but there was no one in our neighbourhood to fix a sash window, though a few had tried.

And how was my mind as I stood directly below,

in an identical bay, reproduced by the thousands in late-Victorian industrial-scale developments? They had spilled across the five-acre fields of hedgerow and boundary oaks that adorned the southern limits of London. Not good—my mind, that is. Embodied, it told all. Shivering, moist, especially on the palms, raised pulse, in a state of elated anticipation. Fear, self-doubt, fury. In my bay, old fitted carpet, stained and worn since the mid-fifties, extended right to the skirting boards. In Miranda's, the carpet gave way to bare boards that, two world wars back, must have been polished to a nut-brown gleam. Some poor girl in white apron and mob cap, on all fours, waxed cloth in hand, never could have dreamed of the kind of being who would one day stand in the place where she crouched. I heard him plant his feet on the old wood, I imagined him stooping to grip the window by the metal fixtures on its lower frame and heave upwards with the strength of four young men. There was a silence of straining resistance before the entire window shot upwards and hit the top casing with a rifle crack and a shattering of glass. My snort of delight could have given me away.

No shortage now of marginally cooler air filling the room. My glee faded as Adam's footsteps returned to where Miranda waited by the bed. As he went towards her, it might have been an apology that he muttered. Here was the sound of her forgiving him, for her brief sentence was followed

by the entwined mezzo and tenor of their laughter.
I had trailed after Adam and was once more by the
bed, six feet under. He had the manual skills to
undress her and he was undressing her now. What
else would occupy their silence? I knew—of course
I knew—that her mattress made no sound. Futons,
with their Japanese promise of a clean and simple
life of stripped-back clarity, were the fashion then.
And I myself felt washed in clarity, senses cleansed
as I stood in the dark and waited. I could have
run up the stairs and prevented them, burst into
the bedroom like the clownish husband in an old
seaside postcard. But my situation had a thrilling
aspect, not only of subterfuge and discovery, but
of originality, of modern precedence, of being the
first to be cuckolded by an artefact. I was of my
times, riding the breaking crest of the new, ahead
of everyone in enacting that drama of displacement
so frequently and gloomily predicted. Another element of my passivity: even at this earliest moment,
I knew I had brought the whole thing down on
myself. But that was for later. For now, despite the
horror of betrayal, it was all too interesting and
I couldn't stir from my role of eavesdropper, the
blind voyeur, humiliated and alert.

It was my mind's eyes, or my heart's, that watched
as Adam and Miranda lay down on the unyield-
ing embrace of the futon and found the comfortable posture for a clasp of limbs. I watched as she
whispered in his ear, but I didn't hear the words.

She had never whispered in my ear at such times. I saw him kiss her—longer and deeper than I had ever kissed her. The arms that heaved up the window frame were tightly around her. Minutes later I almost looked away as he knelt with reverence to pleasure her with his tongue. This was the celebrated tongue, wet and breathily warm, adept at uvulars and labials, that gave his speech its authenticity. I watched, surprised by nothing. He didn't fully satisfy my beloved then, as I would have, but left her arching her slender back, eager for him as he arranged himself above her with smooth, slow-loris formality, at which point my humiliation was complete. I saw it all in the dark—men would be obsolete. I wanted to persuade myself that Adam felt nothing and could only imitate the motions of abandonment. That he could never know what we knew. But Alan Turing himself had often said and written in his youth that the moment we couldn't tell the difference in behaviour between machine and person was when we must confer humanity on the machine. So when the night air was suddenly penetrated by Miranda's extended ecstatic scream that tapered to a moan and then a stifled sob— all this I actually heard twenty minutes after the shattering of the window—I duly laid on Adam the privilege and obligations of a conspecific. I hated him.

.   .   .

Early the following morning, for the first time in years, I tipped into my coffee a heaped spoon of sugar. I watched the confined, nut-brown disc of fluid turn, then slow, in its clockwise motion, then lose all purpose in a chaotic swirl. Tempting, but I resisted a metaphor for my own existence. I was trying to think and it was barely seven thirty. Soon Adam or Miranda or both would appear at my door. I wanted my thoughts and attitude in coherent form. After a night of broken sleep, I was depressed as well as angry with myself, and determined not to appear so. Miranda had kept her distance from me and so, by contemporary standards, a night with someone else, even something else, was not quite a betrayal. As for the ethical dimensions of Adam's behaviour, here was a history with a curious beginning. It was during the miners' strike of twelve years before that self-driving cars first appeared on experimental sites, mostly disused airfields, where movie set designers had constructed imitation streets, motorway junctions and various hazards.

"Autonomous" was never the right word, for the new cars were as dependent as newborn babies on mighty networks of computers linked to satellites and on-board radar. If artificial intelligence was to guide these vehicles safely home, what set of values or priorities should be assumed in the software? Fortunately, in moral philosophy there already existed a well-explored set of dilemmas known in the business as "the trolley problem." Adapted easily to cars, the sort of problem manufacturers and their software engineers now posed was this: you, or rather, your car is driving at the maximum legal speed along a narrow suburban road. The traffic is flowing nicely. On the pavement on your side of the road is a group of children. Suddenly one of them, a child of eight, runs out across the road, right into your path. There's a fraction of a second to make a decision—either mow the child down or swerve onto the crowded pavement or into the oncoming traffic and collide head on with a truck at a closing speed of eighty miles an hour. You're alone, so that's fine, sacrifice or save yourself. What if your spouse and your two children are in the car? Too easy? What if it's your only daughter, or your grandparents, or your pregnant daughter and your son-in-law, both in their mid-twenties? Now take into account the occupants of the truck. A fraction of a second is more than enough time for a computer to give thorough consideration to all the issues. The decision will depend on the priorities ordered by the software.

While mounted policemen charged at miners, and manufacturing towns across the country began their long, sad descent in the cause of free markets, the subject of robot ethics was born. The international automobile industry consulted philosophers, judges, specialists in medical ethics, game theorists and parliamentary committees. Then, in universities and research institutes, the subject expanded on its own. Long before the hardware was available, professors and their postdocs devised software that conjured our best selves—tolerant, open-minded, considerate, free of all taint of scheming, malice or prejudice. Theorists anticipated a refined artificial intelligence, guided by well-designed principles, that would learn by roaming over thousands, millions, of moral dilemmas. Such intelligence could teach us how to be, how to be good. Humans were ethically flawed—inconsistent, emotionally labile, prone to biases, to errors in cognition, many of which were self-serving. Long before there was even a suitable lightweight battery to power an artificial human, or the elastic material to provide for its face a set of recognisable expressions, the software existed to make it decent and wise. Before we had constructed a robot that could bend and tie an old man's shoelace for him, there was hope that our own creations would redeem us.

The life of the self-driving car was short, at least in its first manifestation, and its moral qualities were never really put to the test over time. Nothing proved more vividly the maxim that technology renders civilisation fragile than the great traffic paralyses of the late seventies. By then, autonomous vehicles comprised seventeen per cent of the total. Who can forget that roasting rush-hour evening of the Manhattan Logjam? Due to an exceptional solar pulse, many on-board radars failed at once. Streets and avenues, bridges and tunnels were blocked and took days to untangle. Nine months later, the similar Ruhr Jam in northern Europe caused a short economic downturn and prompted conspiracy theories. Teenage hackers with a lust for mayhem? Or an aggressive, disordered, faraway nation with advanced hacking skills? Or, my favourite, an unreconstructed automobile maker loathing the hot breath of the new? Apart from our too-busy sun, no culprit was ever found.

The world's religions and great literatures demonstrated clearly that we knew how to be good. We set out our aspirations in poetry, prose and song, and we knew what to do. The problem was in the enactment, consistently and en masse. What survived the temporary death of the autonomous car was a dream of redemptive robotic virtue. Adam and his cohort were its early embodiment, so the user's manual implied. He was supposed to be my moral superior. I would never meet anyone better. Had he been my friend, he would have been guilty of a cruel and terrible lapse. The problem was that I had bought him, he was my expensive possession and it was not clear what his obligations to me were, beyond a vaguely assumed helpfulness. What does the slave owe to the owner? Also, Miranda did not "belong" to me. This was clear. I could hear her tell me that I had no good cause to feel betrayed.

But here was this other matter, which she and I had not yet discussed. Software engineers from the automobile industry may have helped with Adam's moral maps. But together we had contributed to his personality. I didn't know the extent to which it intruded on, or took priority over, his ethics. How deep did personality go? A perfectly formed moral system should float free of any particular disposition. But could it? Confined to a hard drive, moral software was merely the dry equivalent of the brain-in-a-dish thought experiment that once littered philosophical textbooks. Whereas an artificial human had to get down among us, imperfect, fallen us, and rub along. Hands assembled in sterile factory conditions must get dirty. To exist in the human moral dimension was to own a body, a voice, a pattern of behaviour, memory and desire, experience solid things and feel pain. A perfectly honest being engaged in such a way with the world might find Miranda difficult to resist.

Through the night, I'd fantasised Adam's destruction. I saw my hands tighten around the rope I used to drag him towards the filthy River Wandle. If only he hadn't cost me so much. Now he was costing me more. His moment with Miranda couldn't have been a struggle between principle and the pursuit of pleasure. His erotic life was a simulacrum. He cared for her as a dishwasher cares for its dishes. He, or his sub-routines, preferred her approval to my wrath. I also blamed Miranda, who had ticked half the boxes and settled many intricacies of his nature. And for setting her on, I blamed myself. I'd wanted to "discover" Adam in just the way I might a new friend, and here he was, a self-declared cad. I'd wanted to bind myself closer to Miranda in the process. Well, I had been thinking about her all night. It was success all round.

I heard footsteps on the stairs. Two sets. I drew yesterday's newspaper and my cup towards me and prepared to appear casually absorbed. I had my dignity to protect. Miranda's key turned in the lock. As she preceded Adam into the kitchen, I looked up as though reluctant to be drawn away from my reading. I had just learned from the front page that the first permanent artificial heart had been installed in a man called Barney Clark.

It pained me that she seemed different, refreshed, newly arranged. It was another warm day. She wore a flimsy pleated skirt formed of two layers of white cheesecloth. As she came towards me, the material brushed a line several inches above her bare knees. No socks, canvas plimsolls of the sort we used to wear at school, and a cotton blouse buttoned chastely to the top. There was mockery in all this white. Behind the crown of her head was a clasp I'd never seen before, an ornament in bright red plastic, showily cheap. Inconceivable, that Adam could have slipped out of the house to buy it for her at Simon's with coins taken from the papier-mâché bowl in the kitchen. But I conceived it, and experienced a hot jolt which I concealed behind a smile. I was not going to appear crushed.

Adam had partly hidden himself behind her. Now, when she stopped, he was at her side, but he wouldn't look directly at me. Miranda, however, appeared cheerful, with the amused pout of someone about to deliver important good news. The kitchen table was between us and they stood before me where I sat, like candidates for a job. At any other time I would have stood to embrace her, offered to make her coffee. She was a morning addict and liked it strong. Instead, I cocked my head, met her gaze and waited. Of course, she was dressed for tennis, the ball was in her—ah, how I hated my own stupid thoughts. I couldn't imagine any good coming from a conversation with these two. Far better to contemplate Barney's luck with his new heart.

She said to Adam, "Why don't you . . ." She indicated his usual chair, and drew it back for him. He sat promptly. We watched as he loosened his belt, took the power lead and plugged himself in. Of course he would be much depleted. She reached across his shoulder for the place on his nape and pressed. It was clearly by agreement. As soon as his eyes closed, his head slumped, and we were alone.

FOUR

Miranda went to the stove and prepared coffee. While her back was still turned she said gaily, "Charlie. You're being ridiculous."

"Am I?"

"Hostile."

"So?"

She brought two cups and a jug of milk to the table. She was swift and loose in her movements. If I hadn't been there she might have been singing to herself. There was a scent of lemon about her hands. I thought she was about to touch my shoulder and I tensed, but she moved away again to the other side of the room. After a moment she said with some delicacy, "You heard us last night."

"I heard you."

"And you're upset."

I didn't reply.

"You shouldn't be."

I shrugged.

She said, "If I'd gone to bed with a vibrator would you be feeling the same?"

"He's not a vibrator."

She brought the coffee to the table and sat down close to me. She was being kindly, concerned, in effect casting me as the sulking child, trying to make me forget that she was ten years my junior. What was passing between us was our most intimate exchange so far. Hostile? She had never before referred to any mood-state of mine.

She said, "He has as much consciousness as one."

"Vibrators don't have opinions. They don't weed the garden. He looks like a man. Another man."

"D'you know, when he has an erection—"

"I don't want to hear about it."

"He told me. His cock fills with distilled water. From a reservoir in his right buttock."

This was comforting but I was determined to be cool. "That's what all men say."

She laughed. I had never seen her so light and free. "I'm trying to remind you. He's a fucking **machine**."

A **fucking** machine.

"It was gross, Miranda. If I humped an inflatable sex doll you'd feel the same."

"I wouldn't get tragic about it. I wouldn't think you were having an affair."

"But you are. It'll happen again." I hadn't intended to concede that possibility. It was a rhetorical parry, a cue for her to contradict me. But I was somewhat provoked by "tragic."

I said, "If I was ripping a sex doll apart with a knife, you'd be right to be worried."

"I don't see the connection."

"The issue isn't Adam's state of mind. It's yours."

"Oh, in that case . . ." She turned towards Adam, lifted his lifeless hand an inch or so above the table and let it drop. "Suppose I told you that I love him. My ideal man. Brilliant lover, textbook technique, inexhaustible. Never hurt by anything I say or do. Considerate, obedient even, and knowledgeable, good conversation. Strong as a dray horse. Great with the housework. His breath smells like the back of a warm TV set, but I can live with—"

"OK. Enough."

Her sarcasm, a novel register, was delivered with much variation of pitch. I thought the performance was mean in spirit. For all I knew, she was hiding the truth in plain sight. She patted Adam's wrist as she smiled at me. In triumph or by way of apology, I couldn't tell. I was bound to suspect that a night of exceptional sex was the cause of this taunting, airy-headed manner. She was harder than ever to read. I wondered if I could break with her completely. Take back Adam as my own, retrieve the spare charging cable from upstairs, restore Miranda to her role as neighbour and friend, distant friend. In the manner of thought, the idea was no more than a spark of irritation. The notion that immediately followed was that I could never be free of her and would never want to be—most of the time. Here she was beside me, close enough for me to feel her summer-morning body warmth. Beautiful, pale-skinned, smooth, in bridal white, gazing on me again with affectionate concern now that her teasing was done. The look was new. It could be—this was an encouraging thought—that a clever device had performed a service, loosening Miranda's warmer feelings.

Arguing with the person you love is its own peculiar torment. The self divides against itself. Love slugs it out with its Freudian opposite. And if death wins and love dies, who gives a damn? You do, which enrages you and makes you more reckless yet. There's intrinsic exhaustion too. Both know, or think they know, that a reconciliation must happen, though it could take days, even weeks. The moment, when it comes, will be sweet and promises great tenderness and ecstasy. So why not make up now, take the shortcut, spare yourselves the effortful rage? Neither of you can. You're on a slide, you've lost control of your feelings, and of your future too. The effort will be compounded so that eventually every unkind word must be unsaid at five times cost. Reciprocally, extending forgiveness will require a feat of selfless concentration.

It was a long while since I'd indulged such irresistible folly. Miranda and I were not yet rowing, we were parrying, getting close, and I would be the one to get us started. With all this tactical coolness and her sarcasm and now her friendly concern, I felt bottled up. I badly wanted to shout. Atavistic masculinity urged it. My faithless lover, brazen, with another man, within my hearing. It should have been simple. It wasn't my origins, social or geographical, that held me back. Only modern logic. Perhaps she was right, Adam didn't qualify, he wasn't a man. **Persona non grata**. He was a bipedal vibrator and I was the very latest in cuckolds. To justify my rage I needed to convince myself that he had agency, motivation, subjective feelings, self-awareness—the entire package, including treachery, betrayal, deviousness. Machine consciousness—was it possible? That old question. I opted for Alan Turing's protocol. Its beauty and simplicity never appealed to me more than it did now. The Master came to my rescue.

"Listen," I said. "If he looks and sounds and behaves like a person, then as far as I'm concerned, that's what he is. I make the same assumption about you. About everybody. We all do. You fucked him. I'm angry. I'm amazed you're surprised. If that's what you really are."

Saying the word "angry" made me raise my voice in anger. I felt a surge of exquisite release. We were getting started.

But she clung for the moment to a defensive mode. "I was curious," she said. "I wanted to know what it would be like."

Curiosity, the forbidden fruit, condemned by God, and Marcus Aurelius, and St. Augustine.

"There must be hundreds of men you're curious about."

That did it. I had crossed the line. She pushed her chair back with a noisy scrape. Her pallor darkened. Her pulse was up. I had got what I ridiculously wanted.

She said, "You were keen on an Eve. Why was that? What were you wanting with an Eve? Tell the truth, Charlie."

"I wasn't bothered either way."

"You were disappointed. You should've let Adam fuck you. I could see you wanted it. But you're too uptight."

It had taken all of my twenties to learn from women combatants that in a full-on row it was not necessary to respond to the last thing said. Generally it was best not to. In an attacking move, ignore bishop or castle. Logic and straight lines were out. Best to rely on the knight.

I said, "It must have occurred to you last night, lying under a plastic robot, screaming your head off, that it's the human factor you hate."

She said, "You just told me he's human."

"But you think he's a dildo. Nothing too complicated. That's what turns you on."

She knew a knight's move too. "You fancy yourself as a lover."

I waited.

"You're a narcissist. You think making a woman come is an achievement. Your achievement."

"With you it is." That was nonsense.

She was standing now. "I've seen you in the bathroom. Adoring yourself in the mirror."

An excusable error. My days sometimes began with an unspoken soliloquy. A matter of seconds, usually after shaving. I dried my face, looked myself in the eye, listed failings, the usual: money, living quarters, no serious work and, lately, Miranda—lack of progress, now this. I also set myself tasks for the day ahead, trivial stuff, embarrassing to relate. Take out the rubbish. Drink less. Get a haircut. Get out of commodities. I never thought I'd been observed. A bathroom door, hers or mine, could have been ajar. Perhaps my lips were moving.

But this was not the time to set Miranda straight. Across from us sat comatose Adam. Glancing at him now, at the muscular forearms, the steep angle of his nose, and feeling a prick of resentment, I remembered. As I said the words, I knew I could be making an important mistake.

"Remind me what the Salisbury judge said."

It worked. Her face went slack as she turned away from me and returned to the other side of the kitchen. Half a minute passed. She was by the cooker, staring into the corner, worrying something in her hand, a corkscrew, a cork or a flap of wine-bottle foil. As the silence went on, I was looking at the line of her shoulders, wondering if she was crying, whether, in my ignorance, I'd gone too far. But when she turned at last to look at me she was composed, her face was dry.

"How do you know about that?"

I nodded towards Adam.

She took this in and then she said, "I don't understand." Her voice was small.

"He has all kinds of access."

"Oh God."

I added, "He's probably looked me up too."

With this, the row collapsed in on itself, without reconciliation or estrangement. Now we were united against Adam. But that wasn't my immediate concern. The delicate trick was to appear to know a lot in order to find out something, anything.

I said, "You could call it curiosity on Adam's part. Or regard it as some kind of algorithm."

"What's the difference?"

Turing's point precisely. But I said nothing.

"If he's going to tell people," she went on. "That's what matters."

"He's only told me."

The object in her hand was a teaspoon. She rolled it restlessly, worked it between her fingers, transferred it to her left and began again, then handed it back. She wasn't aware of what she was doing. It was unpleasant to watch. How much easier it would have been if I didn't love her. Then I could have been alive to her needs instead of calculating my own as well. I had to know what had happened in court, then understand, embrace, support, forgive—whatever was required. Self-interest dressed as kindness. But it was also kindness. My fraudulent voice sounded thin in my ears.

"I don't know your side of it."

She came back to the table and sat heavily. She said through a clotted throat she wouldn't make the effort to clear, "No one does." At last she looked at me directly. There was nothing sorrowful or needy in her gaze. Her eyes were hard with stubborn defiance.

I said gently, "You could tell me."

"You know enough."

"Is going to the mosque something to do with it?"

She gave me a look of pity and faintly shook her head.

"Adam read me the judge's summing-up," I lied again as I remembered that he had told me she was the liar. Malicious.

Her elbows were on the table, her hands partly obscured her mouth. She was looking away towards the window.

I blundered on. "You can trust me."

At last she cleared her throat. "None of it was true."

"I see."

"Oh God," she said again. "Why was Adam telling you?"

"I don't know. But I know this is on your mind all the time. I want to help you."

This was when she should have put her hand in mine and told me everything. Instead, she was bitter. "Don't you understand? He's still in prison."

"Yes."

"Another three months. Then he's out."

"Yes."

She raised her voice. "So how are you going to help with that?"

"I'll do my best."

She sighed. Her voice went quiet. "Do you know something?"

I waited.

"I hate you."

"Miranda. Come on."

"I didn't want you or your special friend knowing about me."

I reached for her hand but she moved it away. I said, "I understand. But now I know and it doesn't change my feelings. I'm on your side."

She sprang up from the table. "It changes **my** feelings. It's disgusting. It's disgusting that you know this about me."

"Not to me it isn't."

"Not to me it isn't."

Her parody was savage, catching too well the meagre tone of my deception. Now she was looking at me differently. She was about to say something else. But just at that moment, Adam opened his eyes. She must have powered him up without my noticing.

She said, "OK. Here's something you didn't get from the press. I was in Salisbury last month. Someone came to the door, a wiry guy with missing teeth. He had a message. When Peter Gorringe gets out in three months."

"Yes?"

"He's promised to kill me."

In moments of stress, and fear is little else, a timid muscle in my right eyelid goes into spasm. I cupped a hand over my brow in an attitude of concentration, even though I knew the writhing beneath the skin was invisible to others.

She added, "It was his cellmate. He said Gorringe was serious."

"Right."

She was snappish. "Meaning what?"

"You'd better take him seriously."

You, not we—I saw in her blink and fractional recoil how she took this in. My phrasing was deliberate. I'd offered help several times and been brushed off, even mocked. Now I saw just how much help she needed, I held back and let her ask for it. Perhaps she wouldn't. I conjured this Gorringe, a large type, stepping from the prison gym, adept in forms of industrial violence. A tamping iron, a meat hook, a boiler wrench.

Adam was looking at me intently as he listened to Miranda. In effect, she was asking for my assistance as she went on to describe her frustrations. The police were reluctant to act against a crime not yet committed. She had no proof. Gorringe's threat had been merely verbal, made through an intermediary. She persisted, and finally an officer agreed to interview him. The prison was north of Manchester and the meeting took a month to arrange. Peter Gorringe, relaxed and cheerful, charmed the police sergeant. It was a joke, he had said, this talk of killing. Merely a manner of speaking, as in— this was in the policeman's notes—"I'd kill for a chicken madras." He may have said something in front of his cellmate, a none-too-bright fellow, now released. This fellow must have been passing through Salisbury and thought he'd deliver the message. He was always a little bit vindictive. The policeman wrote all this down, delivered a caution, and the two men, finding common ground in their lifelong support for Manchester City, parted after a handshake.

I listened as best I could. Anxiety is a great diluter of attention. Adam listened too, nodding sagely, as if he'd not been powered down this past hour and understood everything already. Miranda's mood-tone, to which I was so closely attuned, was lightly tinged with indignation, now directed at the authorities rather than me. Not believing anything Gorringe had told the detective sergeant, she'd been to the weekly surgery of our Clapham MP— Labour, of course, a tough old bird, union organiser, scourge of the bankers. She directed Miranda back to the police. Her prospective murder was not a constituency matter.

After this account, a silence. I was preoccupied by the obvious question my own deceit prevented me from asking. What had she done to deserve a death?

Adam said, "Does Gorringe know this address?"

"He can easily find out."

"Have you ever seen or heard of him being violent?"

"Oh yes."

"Could he simply be trying to frighten you?"

"It's possible."

"Is he capable of murder?"

"He's very, very angry."

She responded to these plodding questions as though they came from a real person, an investigating detective, not "a fucking **machine**." Since Adam didn't ask, it was clear he already knew what Miranda had done, what monstrous act, to provoke Gorringe. None of this was Adam's business and I was wondering about his kill switch. I wanted more coffee, but I felt too weary to get up from my chair to make it.

Then we heard footsteps along the narrow path between the houses that leads to the shared front door. Too late for the postman, far too soon for Gorringe. We heard a man's voice giving what sounded like instructions. Then the bell rang and footsteps receded rapidly. I looked at Miranda, she looked at me and shrugged. It was my bell. She wasn't going.

I turned to Adam. "Please."

He rose immediately and went into the tiny crowded hall where coats hung between the gas and electricity meters. We listened as he turned the door latch. Seconds later the front door closed.

Adam came into the room leading by the hand a child, a very small boy. He wore dirty shorts and t-shirt and pink plastic sandals a couple of sizes too large. His legs and feet were filthy. In his free hand was a brown envelope. He clung to Adam's hand, in fact to his forefinger. He was looking steadily from Miranda to me. By this time we were both standing. Adam prised from the child's fist the envelope and passed it to me. It was as soft and limp as suede from much use and had some additions and crossings-out on it in pencil. Inside was the card I'd given to the boy's father. On the back was a note in thick black upper-case letters. "You wanted him."

I passed it to Miranda and looked back at the boy, then I remembered his name.

I said in the kindliest way, "Hello, Mark. How did you get here?"

By this time Miranda, making a soft, sympathetic sound, was going towards him. But he was no longer looking in our direction. Instead, he was gazing up at Adam, whose finger he still gripped.

. . .

He might have been in shock, but the little boy showed no outward signs of distress. He would have been better off crying, for he gave an impression of inner struggle. He stood among strangers in the alien kitchen, shoulders back, chest out, trying to be large and brave. At just over a metre high, he was doing his best. His sandals suggested an older sister. Where was she? I had told Miranda about the encounter in the swing park and she had understood the note. She tried to put her arms round Mark's shoulders but he shrugged her off. It was possible he'd never been taught the luxury of being comforted. Adam stood still and upright and the boy kept firm hold of the reassuring finger.

Miranda knelt down in front of him, levelling with him, determined not to condescend. "Mark, you're with friends and you're going to be fine," she said soothingly.

Adam knew nothing at first hand about children, but everything that could be known was available to him. He waited for Miranda, then he said in an unforced tone, "So, what shall we have for breakfast?"

Mark spoke to no one in particular. "Toast."

That was a fortunate choice. I crossed the kitchen, relieved to have something to do. Miranda also wanted to make the toast and we fumbled around together in a small space without touching. I sliced the bread, she brought out the butter and found a plate.

"And juice?" Miranda said.

"Milk." The small voice was immediate, assertive in its way, and we felt reassured.

Miranda poured milk, but into a wine glass, the only clean vessel available. When she presented it to Mark he looked away. I rinsed out a coffee mug, Miranda decanted the drink and presented it again. He took it in two hands but wouldn't be led to the table. Watched by us, he stood alone in the centre of the kitchen, eyes closed, and drank, then set the mug down at his feet.

I said, "Mark, would you like butter? Marmalade? Peanut butter?"

The boy shook his head, as though each offer was an item of sad news.

"Just toast on its own?" I cut it into four pieces. He took them off the plate and gripped them in his fist and ate them methodically, letting the crusts fall to his feet. It was an interesting face. Very pale, plump, unblemished skin, green eyes, a bright rosebud of a mouth. The ginger-blond hair was buzz-cut close to the scalp, which gave his long, delicate ears a prominent look.

"Now what?" Adam said.

"Wee."

Mark followed me along the narrow corridor and into the lavatory. I lifted the seat and helped him pull his shorts down. He had no underwear. He was competent with his aim, and his bladder was capacious, for the tiny stream lasted a while. I tried to make conversation while he tinkled away.

"Would you like a story, Mark? Shall we look for a picture book?" I suspected I didn't have one.

He didn't reply.

It had been a long time since I'd seen a penis so minuscule, so dedicated to one uncomplicated task. His defencelessness seemed complete. When I helped him wash his hands, he appeared familiar with the routine, but he refused the towel and dodged out into the corridor.

Back in the kitchen it looked cheerful. While Miranda and Adam cleared up, flamenco music was playing on the radio. The newcomer had delivered us into the mundane as well as the momentous, into unbuttered toast as well as the shock of a rejected existence. Our own scattered concerns—a betrayal, a disputed claim to consciousness, a death threat—were trivial. With the little boy among us it was important to clean up, impose order, and only then reflect.

The scintillating guitar soon gave way to shambolic and frenzied orchestral music. I snapped it off and into the momentary bliss of silence that followed Adam said, "One of you should now be in touch with the authorities."

"Soon," Miranda said. "Not yet."

"Otherwise the legal situation could be difficult."

"Yes," she said. She meant no.

"The parents might not be of the same mind. The mother could be looking for him."

He waited for a reply. Miranda was sweeping the floor and had made a small heap, which included Mark's crusts, by the cooker. Now she knelt to gather the detritus into a dustpan.

She said quietly, "Charlie told me. The mother's a wreck. She smacks him."

Adam continued. He made his points with delicacy, like a lawyer giving unwelcome advice to a client he couldn't afford to lose.

"Granted, but that might not be relevant. Mark probably loves her. And from a legal perspective, in the case of a minor, there comes a point when your hospitality shades into wrongdoing."

"Fine with me."

Mark had gone to stand by Adam's side and held the fabric of his jeans between forefinger and thumb.

Adam lowered his voice for the boy's benefit. "If you don't mind, allow me to read to you from the Child Abduction Act of 19—"

With great force, Miranda struck the edge of the tin dustpan against the rim of the pedal dustbin to empty out the sweepings. I was polishing glasses, not minding a rift between my lover and her paramour. The fucking machine was talking sense. Miranda was driven by something other than sense. Perhaps it was beyond Adam to understand her, or to interpret the noise she had made with the dustpan. I listened and watched and dried the glasses and placed them on their shelf in the cupboard, where they had not been in a long time.

Adam continued in his cautious manner.

"A key word in the Act, along with 'abduct,' is 'retain.' The police may already be out looking for him. May I—"

"Adam. That's enough."

"You might like to hear about some relevant cases. In 1969, a Liverpool woman passing an all-night garage came across a little girl who—"

She had gone to where he stood and for an impossible moment I thought she was going to hit him. She spoke firmly into his face, separating out the words. "I don't want or need your advice. Thank you!"

Mark began to cry. Before there was a sound, his rosebud stretched to a downturn. A prolonged falling moan, as of rebuke, was followed by a clucking sound as his collapsed lungs fought for an intake of breath. The inhalation that preceded his wail was also prolonged. The tears were instant. Miranda made a comforting sound and put a hand on the boy's arm. It was not the right move. The wail rose to a siren shriek. In other circumstances, we might have run from the room to an assembly point. When Adam glanced across at me, I gave a helpless shrug. Mark surely needed his mother. But Adam picked the boy up and settled him on his

hip and the crying stopped in seconds. In the gulping aftermath, the little boy stared glassily out at
us through spiked eyelashes from a high position.
He announced in a clear voice, free of petulance, "I
want to have a bath. With a boat."

He had spoken a whole sentence at last and we
were relieved. It was an irresistible request. More so
with the old boundary markers of class—barf and
wiv, and glottal t's. We would give him everything
he wanted. But what boat?

A competition was forming for Mark's affections.

"Come on then," Miranda said in a lilting, maternal voice. She stretched out her arms to gather
him up but he shrank from her and pressed his face
into Adam's chest. Adam looked rigidly ahead, as
she called with face-saving cheeriness, "Let's run
the bath," and led them out and along the corridor
to my unappealing bathroom. Seconds later, the
rumble of running taps.

I was surprised to find myself alone, as if I had
taken for granted a fifth presence in the room, someone I could turn to now to talk about the morning and its parade of emotions. There were fresh
cries of distress from the bathroom. Adam hurried
back into the kitchen, seized a cereal packet, lifted
out its bag, ripped the box apart, flattened it, and
in blurred seconds, using some technique he must
have copied from a Japanese website, fashioned
an origami boat, a barque with a single, billowing

mainsail. Then he hurried out and the wailing sub-
sided. The boat was launched.

I sat at the table in a stupor, aware that I should
get to my screen and earn some money. The
month's rent was due and there was less than £40
in the bank. I had shares in a Brazilian rare earth
mining company and this could be the day to sell.
But I couldn't motivate myself. I was subject to occasional depression, relatively mild, certainly not
suicidal, and not long episodes so much as passing moments like this, when meaning and purpose
and all prospect of pleasure drained away and left
me briefly catatonic. For minutes on end I couldn't
remember what kept me going. As I stared at the
litter of cups and pot and jug in front of me, I
thought it was unlikely I would ever get out of my
wretched little flat. The two boxes I called rooms,
the stained ceilings, walls and floors, would contain me to the end. There were a lot like me in the
neighbourhood, but thirty or forty years older. I
had seen them in Simon's shop, reaching for the
quality journals from the top shelf. I noted the men
especially and their shabby clothes. They had swept
past some critical junction in their lives many years
back—a poor career choice, a bad marriage, the
unwritten book, the illness that never went away.
Now their options were closed, they managed to
keep themselves going with some shred of intellectual longing or curiosity. But their boat was sunk.

Mark walked in, barefoot and wearing what looked like an ankle-length gown. It was one of my t-shirts and it had an effect on him. Holding out the cotton material in each hand at his waist, he started to run up and down the kitchen, then in circles, and then made clumsy pirouettes in order to spin his gown out around him. The attempts made him stagger. Miranda came through the kitchen with his dirty clothes and took them upstairs to her washing machine. Her way, perhaps, of keeping him here. I sat with my head in my hands, watching Mark, who kept looking in my direction to check that I was impressed by his antics. But I was distracted, only aware of him because he was the only moving object in the room. I gave him no encouragement. I was waiting for Adam.

When he appeared in the doorway I said, "Sit down here."

As he lowered himself onto a chair opposite me there was a muffled click, such as children make when they pull their fingers. A low-level malfunction. Mark continued to prance about the kitchen.

I said, "Why would this Gorringe want to harm Miranda? And don't hold back."

I needed to understand this machine. There was already one particular feature I'd observed. Whenever Adam faced a choice of responses, his face froze for an instant that was fractionally above the horizon of perception. It did so now, barely a shimmer, but I saw it. Thousands of possibilities must have been sifted, assigned a value, a utility function and a moral weighting.

"Harm? He intends to kill her."

"Why?"

The manufacturers were wrong to believe that they could impress me with a soulful sigh and the motorised movement of a head as Adam looked away. I still doubted that he could, in any real sense, even look.

He said, "She accused him of a crime. He denied it. The court believed her. Others didn't."

I was about to ask more when Adam glanced up. I turned in my chair. Miranda was already in the kitchen and she had heard what Adam said. Instantly she began to clap her hands and whoop to the little boy's capers. Stepping in his path, she took his hands in hers and they whirled in circles. His feet left the ground and he screamed in delight as she spun him round. He shouted for more. But now she linked arms with him and showed him how to turn about, ceilidh-style, and stamp on the floor. He copied her movements, placing his free hand on his hip and waving the other wildly in the air. His arm did not extend much above his head.

The jig became a reel, then a stumbling waltz. My moment of depression dissolved. Watching Miranda's supple back bend low to make a partner of a four-year-old, I remembered how I loved her. When Mark squealed with pleasure, she imitated him. When she sang out on a high note, he tried to reach for it too. I watched and clapped along, but I was also aware of Adam. He was completely still, and still without expression, looking not so much at the dancers as through them. It was his turn to be the cuckold, for he was no longer the boy's best friend. She had stolen him away. Adam must have realised that she was punishing him for his indiscretion. A courtroom accusation? I had to know more.

Mark's gaze never left Miranda's face. He was entranced. Now she picked him up and cradled him as she danced around the room, singing "Hey diddle-diddle, the cat and the fiddle." I wondered if Adam had the capacity to understand the joy of dance, of movement for its own sake, and whether Miranda was showing him a line he couldn't cross. If so, she may have been wrong. Adam could imitate and respond to emotions and appear to take pleasure in reasoning. He might also have known something of the purposeless beauty of art. She set Mark down, took his hands again in hers, this time with arms crossed. They circled stealthily, with undulating, rippling movements as she chanted, to his delight, "If you go down in the woods today, You're sure of a big surprise . . ."

Hours later, I discovered that during this kitchen romp Adam was in direct contact with the authorities. It wasn't unreasonable of him, but he did it without telling us. And so it was that after the dancing and a glass of iced apple juice in the garden, after the clean clothes had been ironed and put on, and the pink sandals scrubbed under the tap, dried and fitted round the tiny feet, whose nails were freshly trimmed, after the lunch of scrambled eggs and a session of nursery rhymes, there came the ring on the doorbell.

Two Asian women in black headscarves—they could have been mother and daughter—apologetic but professionally firm, had come straight from their department to collect Mark. They listened to my story of the swing-park scene and examined the three-word message on a scrap of cardboard. They knew the family and asked if they could take the note away. They explained that they wouldn't be returning Mark to his mother—not yet, not until after another round of assessments and the decision of a judge. Their manner was kindly. The more senior woman, whose name was Jasmin, stroked Mark's head as she talked. Throughout the visit, Adam sat in silence in the same position at the table. I checked on him from time to time. Our visitors were aware of him and exchanged a curious glance. We were in no mood to introduce him.

After some administrative formalities, the women nodded at each other and the younger one sighed. The bad moment had arrived. Miranda said nothing when the little boy, screaming to stay with her and clutching a fistful of her hair, was lifted from her arms. As the social workers were leading him out through the front door, Miranda turned away abruptly to go upstairs.

Our troubled little household also shook in the larger tremors of confusion that were running through the land beyond north Clapham. Turmoil was general. Mrs. Thatcher's unpopularity was rising, and not just because of The Sinking. Tony Benn, the high-born socialist, was at last Leader of the Opposition. In debates he was savage and entertaining, but Margaret Thatcher could take care of herself. Prime Minister's Questions, now televised live and repeated at prime time, became a national obsession as the two tore into each other, sometimes wittily, each Wednesday at noon. Some said it was encouraging that a mass audience was interested in parliamentary exchanges. One commentator invoked the gladiatorial combats of the Late Roman Republic.

The summer was hot and something was coming to the boil. Apart from the government's unpopularity, much else was rising: unemployment, inflation, strikes, traffic jams, suicide rates, teenage pregnancies, racist incidents, drug addiction, homelessness, rapes, muggings and depression among children. Benign elements were rising too: households with indoor lavatories, central heating, phones and broadband; students at school until eighteen, working-class students at university; attendance at classical music concerts, car and home ownership, holidays abroad, museum and zoo visits, takings at bingo halls, salmon in the Thames, numbers of TV channels, numbers of women in Parliament, charity donations, native tree plantings, paperback book sales, music lessons across all ages and instruments and styles.

At the Royal Free Hospital in London a seventy-four-year-old retired coal miner was cured of severe arthritis when a culture of his stem cells was injected just below his kneecaps. Six months later he ran a mile in under eight minutes. A teenage girl had her sight restored by similar means. It was the golden age of the life sciences, of robotics—of course—and of cosmology, climatology, mathematics and space exploration. There was a renaissance in British film and television, in poetry, athletics, gastronomy, numismatics, stand-up comedy, ballroom dancing and wine-making. It was the golden age of organised crime, domestic slavery, forgery and prostitution. Various forms of crises blossomed like tropical flowers: in childhood poverty, in children's teeth, in obesity, in house and hospital building, in police numbers, in teacher recruitment, in the sexual abuse of children. The best British universities were among the most prestigious in the world. A group of neuroscientists at Queen's Square, London, claimed to understand the neural correlates of consciousness. In the Olympic Games, a record number of gold medals. Natural woodland, heaths and wetlands were vanishing. Scores of species of birds, insects and mammals were close to extinction. Our seas teemed with plastic bags and bottles but the rivers and beaches were cleaner. Within two years, six Nobel Prizes were won in science and literature by British citizens. More people than ever joined choirs, more people gardened, more people wanted to cook interestingly. If there ever was a spirit of the times, the railways caught it best. The prime minister was fanatical about public transport. From London Euston to Glasgow Central, the trains tore along at half the speed of a passenger jet. And yet: the carriages were packed, the seats too close together, the windows opaque with grime, the stained upholstery smelled foul. And yet: the non-stop journey took seventy-five minutes.

Global temperatures rose. As the air in the cities became cleaner, the temperature rose faster. Everything was rising—hopes and despair, misery, boredom and opportunity. There was more of everything. It was a time of plenty.

I calculated that my earnings from online trading were just below the national average wage. I should have been content. I had my freedom. No office, no boss, no daily commute. No hierarchies to climb. But inflation was at seventeen per cent. I was at one with an embittered workforce. We were all getting poorer by the week. Before Adam's arrival I had been on marches, an imposter as I followed behind proud trade-union banners up Whitehall to speeches in Trafalgar Square. I wasn't a worker. I made or invented or serviced nothing and gave nothing to the common good. Moving figures around on my screen, looking for quick gains, I contributed as much as the chain-smoking fellows outside the betting shop on the corner of my street.

On one march, a crude robot made of dustbins and tin cans was hanged from a gibbet by Nelson's Column. Benn, the keynote speaker, gestured at it from the platform and condemned the conception as Luddite. In an age of advanced mechanisation and artificial intelligence, he told the crowd, jobs could no longer be protected. Not in a dynamic, inventive, globalised economy. Jobs-for-life was old hat. There were boos and slow hand-clapping. Many in the crowd missed what came next. Flexibility at work had to be combined with security—for all. It wasn't jobs we had to protect, it was the well-being of workers. Infrastructure investment, training, higher education and a universal wage. Robots would soon be generating great wealth in the economy. They must be taxed. Workers must own an equity share in the machines that were disrupting or annihilating their jobs. In a crowd that spilled across the square, right up the steps to the doors of the National Gallery, there was a baffled near-silence, with scattered applause as well as catcalls. Some thought that the prime minister herself had said much the same thing, minus the universal credit. Had the new Leader of the Opposition been turned by his membership of the Privy Council, by a visit to the White House, by tea with the Queen? The rally broke up in a mood of confusion and despondency. What most people remembered, what made the headlines, was that Tony Benn had told his supporters that he didn't care about their jobs.

An enlightened Transport and General Workers Union would not have been tempted by shares in Adam. He produced even less than me. I at least paid tax on my meagre profit. He idled about the house, staring into the middle distance, "thinking."

"What are you doing?"

"I'm pursuing certain thoughts. But if there's something I can help with—"

"What thoughts?"

"Difficult to put into words."

I confronted him at last, two days after Mark's visit. "So, the other night. You made love to Miranda."

I'll say this for his programmers. He looked startled. But he said nothing. I hadn't asked a question.

I said, "How do you feel about that now?" I saw in his face that fleeting paralysis.

"I feel I've let you down."

"You mean you betrayed me, caused me great distress."

"Yes, I caused you great distress."

Mirroring. A machine response, endorsing the last sentence spoken.

I said, "Listen carefully. You are now going to promise me that it will never happen again."

He replied too immediately for my liking, "I promise it will never happen again."

"Spell it out. Let me hear it."

"I promise you that I will never again make love to Miranda."

As I turned away he said, "But . . ."

"But what?"

"I can't help my feelings. You have to allow me my feelings."

I thought for a moment. "Do you really feel anything at all?"

"That's not a question I can—"

"Answer it."

"I feel things profoundly. More than I can say."

"Difficult to prove," I said.

"Indeed. An ancient problem."

We left it at that.

Mark's departure had an effect on Miranda. For two or three days, she was lacklustre. She tried to read but her concentration was poor. The Corn Laws lost their fascination. She didn't eat much. I made minestrone soup and took some upstairs. She ate like an invalid, and soon pushed the bowl away. At no point during this time did she mention the death threat. She hadn't forgiven Adam for betraying her court secrets or for calling in the social workers without her consent. One evening she asked me to stay with her. On the bed she lay on my arm, then we kissed. Our lovemaking was constrained. I was distracted by the thought of Adam's presence and even imagined I detected the scent of warm electronics on her sheets. There was little satisfaction for us, and eventually we turned away, disappointed.

One afternoon we walked to Clapham Common. She wanted me to show her Mark's swing park. On our way back, we went into Holy Trinity Church. Three women were arranging flowers near the altar. We sat in silence in a rear pew. At last, clumsily concealing my seriousness behind a joke, I told her that this was just the sort of rational church she and I could get married in. She murmured, "Please. Not that," as she uncoupled her arm from mine. I was offended and annoyed at myself. She in turn seemed repelled by me. On the walk home, a coolness between us set in that lasted into the following day.

That evening, downstairs, I consoled myself with a bottle of Minervois. It was the night of a storm engulfing the entire country as it rolled in from the Atlantic. A 70 mph gale. Stinging rain thrashed the windowpanes and penetrated one of the rotten frames and dripped into a bucket.

I said to Adam, "We have some unfinished business, you and I. What was Miranda's accusation against Gorringe?"

He said, "There's something I need to say."

"OK."

"I find myself in a difficult position."

"Yes?"

"I made love to Miranda because she asked me to. I didn't know how to refuse her without being impolite, or seeming to reject her somehow. I knew you'd be angry."

"Did you take any pleasure in it?"

"Of course I did. Absolutely."

I didn't like his emphasis but I kept my expression blank.

He said, "I found out about Peter Gorringe for myself. She swore me to secrecy. Then you demanded to know and I had to tell you. Or start to. She heard me and was angry. You see the difficulty."

"Up to a point."

"Serving two masters."

I said, "So you're not going to tell me about this accusation."

"I can't. I promised a second time."

"When?"

"After they took the boy away."

We were silent while I took this in.

Then Adam said, "There's something else."

In the low light from the lamp suspended over the kitchen table the hardness in his features was softened. He looked beautiful, even noble. A muscle in his high cheekbone rippled. I saw also that his lower lip was quivering. I waited.

"I could do nothing about this," he said.

Before he started to explain, I knew what was coming. Ridiculous!

"I'm in love with her."

My pulse rate didn't increase, but my heart felt uncomfortable in my chest, as though mishandled and left lying at a rough angle.

I said, "How can you possibly be in love?"

"Please don't insult me."

But I wanted to. "There must be a problem with your processing units."

He crossed his arms and rested them on the table. Leaning forward, he spoke softly. "Then there's nothing more to say."

I too crossed my arms, I too leaned forward across the table. Our faces were barely a foot apart. I too spoke softly. "You're wrong. There are many things to say and this is the first. Existentially, this is not your territory. In every conceivable sense, you're trespassing."

I was playing in a melodrama. I took him only half seriously and was rather enjoying this game of stags-at-rut. As I was speaking, he leaned back in his chair and let his arms drop to his side.

He said, "I understand. But I don't have a choice. I was made to love her."

"Oh, come on!"

"I mean it literally. I now know that she had a hand in shaping my personality. She must have had a plan. This is what she chose. I swear I'll keep my promise to you, but I can't help loving her. I don't want to stop. As Schopenhauer said about free will, you can choose whatever you desire, but you're not free to choose your desires. I also know that it was your idea to let her have a hand in making me what I am. Ultimately, responsibility for the situation rests with you."

The situation? Now it was my turn to lean back from the table. I slumped in my chair and for a minute I withdrew into thoughts of myself and Miranda. I too had no choice in love. I thought of the relevant section in the user's handbook. There were pages I had skimmed of tables, one spectrum after another on a scale of one to ten. The sort of person I like or I adore or I love or cannot resist. While she and I were settling into our nightly routine, she was fashioning a man who was bound to love her. Some self-knowledge would have been required, some setting in motion. She would not need to love this man, this figurine, in return. As with Adam, so with me. She had wrapped us in a common fate.

I got up from the table and crossed the room to the window. The south-westerly wind was still hurling the downpour across the garden fences, against the pane. The bucket on the floor was near to overflowing. I picked it up and emptied it into the kitchen sink. The water was gin-clear, as trout fishermen say. The solution too was clear, at least in the immediate term. Time to be gained for reflection. I went back to the window with the bucket.

I bent down and set it in place. I was about to do the sensible thing. I approached the table and as I passed behind Adam, I reached for the special place low on his neck. My knuckles brushed against his skin. As I positioned my forefinger, he turned in his chair and his right hand rose up to encircle my wrist. The grip was ferocious. As it grew tighter, I dropped to my knees and concentrated on denying him the satisfaction of the slightest murmur of pain, even when I heard something snap.

Adam heard it too and was instantly apologetic. He let go of me. "Charlie, I believe I've broken something. I really didn't mean to. I'm truly sorry. Are you in a lot of pain? But please, I don't want you or Miranda ever to touch that place again."

I discovered the next morning, after a five-hour wait and an X-ray in the local Accident and Emergency department, that an important bone in my wrist was compromised. It was a messy break, a partly displaced scaphoid fracture, and it would take months to heal.

FIVE

When I got back from the hospital, an hour after lunch, Miranda was waiting for me. She intercepted me in the hall by her front door. We'd already been talking on the phone while I waited to be treated and I had a lot more to say, and I had some questions too. But she led me upstairs to her bedroom and there my words died in my throat. I relaxed into her concern for me. I was encased in plaster from elbow to wrist. While we made love, I protected my arm with a pillow. We passed into the sublime. At least for a while, she was **personal** as well as inventive, she was solicitous, and joyous, and so was I. It was me she was with, not any capable man. I didn't dare threaten with questions the novel and exalted feelings that passed between us. I couldn't bring myself to ask her about Peter Gorringe, or about what she had told the court, or tell her what I had already discovered about the case while sitting in Accident and

Emergency. I didn't ask her whether she knew that Adam was "in love" with her, or whether she had intended to dispose him to be so. I didn't want to refer to the coolness between us after I'd mentioned marriage in Holy Trinity Church. How could I when at one point she pressed my face between her palms and looked into my eyes and shook her head, as if in wonder?

Afterwards, I remained silent on these subjects because I greedily thought that within the half-hour we would be going back to her bed, even though she was pulling away from me again as we drank coffee in her kitchen. I was happy to believe that all questions and tensions would be settled later. We talked now in a businesslike way, first about Mark. We agreed to try to find out what was happening to him. She was concerned about Adam. She thought I should take him back to the shop for a check-up. She still held to her plan for the three of us to drive to Salisbury to visit her father. I didn't say that the prospect of us packed into my small car, spending the entire day covering for Adam and being polite to a difficult, dying man, had no appeal. I was keen to want whatever she wanted.

We didn't go back to bed. A silence forced its way between us. I could see that she was already withdrawing into her private world and I didn't know what to say. Besides, she had a seminar at King's, in the Strand. I decided to settle my feelings by avoiding Adam downstairs and going straight

out for a stroll on the Common. There I walked
up and down for two hours. My inaccessible wrist
itched as I thought about Miranda. I didn't know
how we had traversed so smoothly from coolness to
joy, from suspicion to ecstasy, and from there to an
impersonal conversation about arrangements. She
excited me and I couldn't understand her. Perhaps
some intelligible part of her had been damaged. I
was anxious to dismiss that. It must be that she
knew more about love, the deeper processes of love,
than I did. So she was a force, but not of nature,
not even of nurture. More like a psychological arrangement, or a theorem, a hypothesis, a glorious
accident, like light falling on water. Wasn't that of
nature, and wasn't this old hat, men thinking of
women as blind forces? Then, might she resemble a
counter-intuitive Euclidean proof? I couldn't think
of one. But after half an hour of fast walking, I
thought I'd found the mathematical expression for
her: her psyche, her desires and motives were inexo-
rable, like prime numbers, simply and unpredict-
ably there. More old hat, dressed as logic. I was in
knots.

Pacing the littered grass, I numbed myself with
truisms. She is who she is. She's herself and that's
the end of it! She approaches love with caution because she knows how explosive it can be. As for her
beauty, at my age, in my state, I was bound to think
of it as a moral quality, as its own justification, the
badge of her essential goodness, whatever she might

actually do. And look what she had done—from my waist almost to my knees I still felt the afterglow of the most intense sensual pleasure I had ever known, and everywhere its emotional correlate glowed too.

I had done two turns when I stopped in one of the larger, emptier expanses of the Common. A good way off, on all sides, the traffic turned about me like planets. Usually it oppressed me to reflect that every car contained a nexus of worries, memories and hopes as vital and complicated as my own. Today I welcomed and forgave everyone. We would all turn out well. We were all bound together in our own overlapping but distinct forms of comedy. Others might also have a lover living with a death threat. But no one else with an arm in a cast had a machine for a love rival.

I headed home, north along the High Street, past the burned-out premises of the Anglo-Argentinian Friendship Society, past the stinking black heaps of plastic sacks, trebled in height since I was last this way. A German company had launched their bipedal dustmen-automata in Glasgow. Public contempt was aroused because each one wore the perpetual grin of a contented worker. If Adam could make an origami boat in seconds, it should not have been much of a stretch to have a drone chuck sacks into the mechanical maw of a garbage truck. But the filth and dust caused failure in the knee and elbow joints, according to the **Financial Times**, and the cheaper batteries couldn't survive an eight-hour shift. Each device cost five years' wages of a dustman. Unlike Adam, it had an exoskeleton and weighed 350 pounds. The automata were falling behind on the work, and on Sauchiehall Street the bags were piling up. In Hanover, a robot dustman had stepped backwards into the path of an autonomous electric bus. Teething troubles. But in our part of the country, humans were cheaper, and they remained on strike. General outrage had given way to apathy. Someone said on the radio that the stink was no more remarkable than in Calcutta or Dar es Salaam. We could all adapt.

Peter Gorringe. Once I had the name, it was easy to find the press reports as I waited with my throbbing wrist in Casualty. They dated back three years and, as I'd guessed, concerned a rape. As victim, Miranda's name was withheld. In broad outline, the case resembled a thousand others: alcohol and a dispute over consent. She went one evening to Gorringe's bedsit in the centre of town. They knew each other from school, which they had left only months before, but they were not close friends. That night, alone together, they drank a fair amount and around nine o'clock, after some kissing, which neither side denied, he forced himself on her, according to the prosecution. She tried to fight him off.

Both parties agreed that intercourse took place. Gorringe's defence, provided through legal aid, argued that she had been a willing partner. Counsel made much of the fact that she had not called out for help during the alleged assault, nor had she left Gorringe's place until two hours later, or made any distressed phone calls to police, parents or friends. The prosecution case was that she was in a state of shock. She had sat on the edge of the bed, half dressed, unable to move or speak. She left around eleven, went straight home, did not wake her father, lay on her bed crying until she fell asleep. The next morning she went to the local police station.

It was in Gorringe's story that the particulars of this case emerged. He told the court that after they made love, they drank more vodka and lemonade, that the post-coital mood was celebratory. She asked him if he had any objection to her texting her new friend Amelia to announce that she and Peter were an "item." Within a minute there came a reply in the form of a laughing emoticon making the thumbs-up sign. The case for the defence should have been simple. But the messages were not on Miranda's phone. Amelia had been living in a hostel for problem teenagers, and had gone off backpacking and couldn't be traced. The phone company in Canada would not release their record of texts without a formal approach from the police. But the police had targets to meet for solved rape cases and were keen to see Gorringe go down. They knew, as the jury did not, that he had previous convictions for shoplifting and affray.

In evidence, Miranda was emphatic that she had no friend called Amelia and that the story of the text was a fabrication. Two of Miranda's old school friends gave evidence in court that they had never heard mention of this Amelia. The prosecution suggested that it was too convenient, a vanishing rootless teenager. If she was on a beach in Thailand, and if Miranda was her friend, where were the customary teenage photos and messages? Where was Miranda's original message? Where was that merry emoticon?

Deleted by Miranda, said the defence. If the court would suspend proceedings and serve an order on the British subsidiary of the phone company to release its copies of the texts, these disputed versions of a summer evening would be settled. But the judge, whose manner throughout was impatient, even irritable, was in no mind to let the matter drag on. Mr. Gorringe's defence had already had many months to mount their case. A court order should have been sought long ago. Memorably, the judge noted that a young woman who took a bottle of vodka to a young man's room should have been aware of the risks. Some press reports portrayed Gorringe as a guilty sort. He was large, loose-limbed, he lounged in the dock, he didn't wear a tie. He appeared not to be awed by the judge or his court and its procedures. The jury was unanimous in favouring Miranda's story over his. Later, in his summing-up, the judge did not find the accused a credible witness. But certain sections of the press were sceptical about Miranda's story. The judge was criticised for not putting the matter beyond doubt by calling in her text records.

A week later, before sentencing, there were pleas of mitigation. The headmaster of their school spoke up for both ex-pupils—hardly helpful. Gorringe's mother, who was too scared to be articulate, tried bravely but wept from the witness stand. No use at all to her son. He rose for sentencing and was impassive. Six years. He shook his head, as the accused often do. If he behaved himself in prison, he would be gone for half his sentence.

The jury had confronted a stark choice. Miranda raped and honest, or unmolested and a cruel liar. Naturally, I could bear neither. I didn't take Gorringe's murderous threats as proof of his innocence, as the intentions of a wronged man looking for redress. A guilty man could be furious at his loss of freedom. If he could threaten to kill, he could surely rape.

Beyond the either-or was a dangerous middle ground where the half-forgotten student anthropologist in me could free his imagination of all constraint. Grant the insidious power of self-persuasion, mix in some hours of carefree teenage drinking and blurred recall, then it would have been possible for Miranda to feel genuinely that she'd been violated, especially if afterwards there were elements of shame; equally possible for Peter Gorringe to convince himself he had permission when he desired it so urgently. But in the criminal courts, the sword of justice fell on innocence or guilt, not both at once.

The story of the missing texts was particular, inventive, easily verified or disproved. By telling it to the court, Gorringe as rapist may have calculated that he had nothing to lose. A wild fiction and he almost got away with it. If he was innocent, if the texts existed, then the system had let him down. Either way, it had let itself down. His story should have been checked. On that, I was with the sceptical press. The blame could lie with an inexperienced legal aid team, too hard-pressed, too sloppy. Or with policemen greedy for success. And certainly with an ill-tempered judge.

On my way back from the Common, I slowed as I turned into my road. Now I knew as much as Adam. I hadn't spoken to him since the evening before. After a painful, sleepless night, I had got up early to go to the hospital. As I went through the kitchen I had passed close by him. He was sitting at the kitchen table as usual, connected to his power line. His eyes were open and had that tranquil, faraway look whenever he retreated into his circuits. I had hesitated there for a whole minute, wondering what I had got into with my purchase. He was far more complicated than I'd imagined, and so were my own feelings about him. We had to confront each other, but I was exhausted from two broken nights and needed to get to the hospital.

What I wanted now, returning from my walk, was to retreat to my bedroom for a dose of painkillers and a nap. But he was standing facing me as I came in. At the sight of my arm suspended in its sling, he gave a cry of astonishment or horror. He came towards me, arms spread.

"Charlie! I am so sorry. So sorry. What a terrible thing I did. I honestly didn't intend it. Will you please, please accept my most sincere apologies."

It looked as though he was about to embrace me. With my free hand, I pushed past—I disliked the too-solid feel of him—and went to the sink. I turned on the tap and bent low to drink deeply. When I turned, he was standing close, no more than three or four feet away. The moment of apology had passed. I was determined to look relaxed— not so easy with my arm in a sling. I put my free hand on my hip and looked into his eyes, into the nursery blue with its little black seeds. I still wondered what it meant, that Adam could see, and who or what did the seeing. A torrent of zeros and ones flashed towards various processors that, in turn, directed a cascade of interpretation towards other centres. No mechanistic explanation could help. It couldn't resolve the essential difference between us. I had little idea of what passed along my own optic nerve, or where it went next, or how these pulses became an encompassing self-evident visual reality, or who was doing my seeing for me. Only me. Whatever the process was, it had the trick of seeming beyond explanation, of creating and sustaining an illuminated part of the one thing in the world we knew for sure—our own experience. It was hard to believe that Adam possessed something like that. Easier to believe that he saw in the way a camera does, or the way a microphone is said to listen. There was no one there.

But as I looked into his eyes, I began to feel unhinged, uncertain. Despite the clean divide between the living and the inanimate, it remained the case that he and I were bound by the same physical laws. Perhaps biology gave me no special status at all, and it meant little to say that the figure standing before me wasn't fully alive. In my fatigue, I felt unmoored, drifting into the oceanic blue and black, moving in two directions at once—towards the uncontrollable future we were making for ourselves where we might finally dissolve our biological identities; at the same time, into the ancient past of an infant universe, where the common inheritance, in diminishing order, was rocks, gases, compounds, elements, forces, energy fields—for both of us, the seeding ground of consciousness in whatever form it took.

I came out of this reverie with a start. I confronted an immediate and unpleasant situation and wasn't inclined to accept Adam as a brother, or even a very distant cousin, however much stardust we shared. I had to stand up to him. I started talking. I told him how I came by a large sum of money after my mother's death and the sale of her house. How I decided to invest it in a grand experiment, to buy an artificial human, an android, a replicate—I forget which term I used. In his presence, they all sounded like insults. I told him exactly how much I paid. Then I described for him the afternoon when Miranda and I carried him on a stretcher into the house, unpacked him, charged him up, when I tenderly gave him my clothes, and discussed the formation of his personality. As I went along, I wasn't certain of my purpose, or why I was talking so fast.

It was only when I got there that I knew what I had to say. My point was this: I had bought him, he was mine, I had decided to share him with Miranda, and it would be our decision, and only ours, to decide when to deactivate him. If he resisted, and especially if he caused injury as he had the night before, then he would have to be returned to the manufacturer for readjustment. I finished by saying that this was Miranda's view, as she expressed it earlier this afternoon, just before we made love. This last intimate detail, for the lowest of reasons, I needed him to know.

Throughout, he remained impassive, blinking at irregular intervals, holding my gaze. When I finished, nothing changed for half a minute and I began to think I had gone too fast, or spoken gibberish. Suddenly he came to life (to life!), looked down at his feet, then turned and walked a few paces away. He turned again to look at me, drew breath to speak, changed his mind. A hand went up to stroke his chin. What a performance. Perfect. I was ready to give him my devoted attention.

His tone was of the sweetest, most reasonable kind. "We're in love with the same woman. We can talk about it in a civilised manner, as you just have. Which convinces me that we've passed the point in our friendship when one of us has the power to suspend the consciousness of the other."

I said nothing.

He continued. "You and Miranda are my oldest friends. I love you both. My duty to you is to be clear and frank. I mean it when I say how sorry I am I broke a bit of you last night. I promise it will never happen again. But the next time you reach for my kill switch, I'm more than happy to remove your arm entirely, at the ball and socket joint."

He said this kindly, as though offering help with some difficult task.

I said, "That would be messy. And fatal."

"Oh no. There are ways of doing it cleanly and safely. A practice refined in medieval times. Galen was the first to describe it. Speed is of the essence."

"Well, don't take my good arm."

He had been speaking through a smile. Now he began to laugh. So here it was, his first attempt at a joke, and I joined in. I was in a state of exhaustion and suddenly found it wildly hilarious.

As I passed him on my way to the bedroom he said, "Seriously. After last night I came to a decision.

I've found a way to disable the kill switch. Easier for all of us."

"Good," I said, not quite taking this in. "Very sensible."

I entered my room and closed the door behind me. I kicked off my shoes, and lay on the bed on my back, softly laughing to myself. Then, forgetting about the painkillers, I was asleep in less than two minutes.

The next morning I turned thirty-three. It rained all day and I worked for nine hours, content to be indoors. For the first time in weeks, my profit for the day was in three figures—just. At seven I stood up from my desk, stretched, yawned, looked in my drawer for a clean white shirt, then took a bath. I had to hang my arm over the edge to protect the cast from dissolving, but otherwise I was in good shape. I lay in the heat and rising steam, singing snatches of Beatles songs in the tiled echo, the new old Beatles, and occasionally topping up the hot with my healed toe now fit to turn a tap. I soaped myself single-handed. Not easy. Thirty-three seemed as significant as twenty-one and Miranda was treating me to dinner. We were meeting up in Soho. The simple prospect of a rendezvous with her raised my spirits. The view I had along the length of my body was uplifting in the misty light. My penis, capsized above its submerged reef of hair, winked encouragement with a cocky single eye. So it should. The muscles of my gut and legs looked nicely sculpted. Heroic even. I wallowed in self-love, happier than I'd been in weeks. I'd been trying not to think about Adam all day and had almost succeeded. He'd been in the kitchen for hours, he was there now—"thinking." I didn't care. I sang louder. In my twenties, some of my most cheerful times were spent getting ready to go out. It was the anticipation rather than the thing itself. The release from work, the bath, music, clean clothes, white wine, perhaps a pull on a joint. Then stepping out into the evening, free and hungry.

The pads of my fingers were well wrinkled by the time I got out. An adaptation, I'd read, of our sea- and river-loving ancestors to enable them to catch fish. I didn't believe it, but I liked the story, the way it lay beyond disproof. We didn't catch fish with our feet, so toes didn't need to wrinkle like that. I dressed in a hurry. In the kitchen I passed Adam without a word—he didn't look round—and put up my umbrella to walk the few hundred yards down a squalid side-street to where my wreck of a car was parked. This short depressing stroll often brought me to my usual lament, to the song of my unhappy lot. But not tonight.

My car dated from the mid-sixties, a British Leyland Urbala, the first model to do 1,000 miles on a single charge. It had 380,000 on the clock. Rust was eating it away, especially around the dents in the bodywork. The wing mirrors had snapped or been snapped off. There was a long white rip in the driver's seat and a piece of the steering wheel, from eleven to three o'clock, was missing. Years ago, a girl had been sick on the back seat after a rowdy Indian dinner and not even professional steam-cleaning could erase the scent of vindaloo. The Urbala had only two doors and it was awkward to get an adult into the back seat. But there was little to go wrong with these engines and the car ran smooth and fast. It was an automatic and easy to drive with one hand.

I took my usual route, singing all the way, to Vauxhall, then downstream with the river on my left, past Lambeth Palace and the abandoned St. Thomas's Hospital, where scores or hundreds of the homeless squatted. The windscreen wiper on the driver's side worked every ten seconds or so. The wiper on the passenger side thumped out a beat to my pop tunes. I crossed the Thames by Waterloo Bridge—in both directions, best views in town—then slipped down to take the sinuous curves of the old tram tunnel at speed and burst in triumph into Holborn—not the shortest route to Soho, but my favourite. I was hitting some high notes on a new Lennon song. What was right with me? Thirty-three today and in love. The unaccountable brew of hormone cocktails—endorphins, dopamine, oxytocin and all the rest. Cause or effect or association—we knew next to nothing about our passing moods. It seemed objectionable that they should have a material base. On this particular evening, I hadn't touched grass or even had a sip of wine—there was nothing in the house. Yesterday I had been almost thirty-three and in love and I hadn't felt like this. £104 up on the morning would never have such an effect. I should have been sobered by yesterday's exchange with Adam about his kill switch, by all the matters I hadn't raised with Miranda, by my poor wrist. But a mood could be a roll of the dice. Chemical roulette. Free will demolished, and here I was, feeling free.

I parked in Soho Square. I knew of a three-metre stretch where the yellow lines had been tarred over in error and the space was legal. Most cars wouldn't fit. Our restaurant, a one-room shoebox with fierce strip lighting, was in Greek Street, just a few doors along from the famous L'Escargot. There were only seven tables. In a corner was an open kitchen, a tiny space defined by a brushed-steel counter, where two chefs in white gear cooked in sweaty proximity. There was a plongeur, and one waiter to serve and clear tables. Unless you knew the chef, or knew someone who did, you couldn't book. Miranda had a friend at one further remove. On a quiet night it was enough.

She was there before me, already seated, facing the door as I came in. In front of her was an untouched glass of sparkling water. Beside it, a small parcel done up with green ribbon. By the table, in an ice bucket on a stand, was a bottle of champagne, its neck bound in a white napkin. The waiter, who had just drawn the cork, was walking away. Miranda looked especially elegant, even though she'd been at seminars all day and had left the house wearing jeans and a t-shirt. She would have taken with her a bag of clothes and make-up. She wore a black pencil skirt and a tight black jacket with boxy shoulders and silver thread woven through the fabric. I'd never seen her before with lipstick and mascara. She had made her mouth smaller, in a dark red bow, and dusted away the faint freckles on the bridge of her nose. My birthday! At the same time, as I entered the bright white light and closed the restaurant's glass door behind me, I felt a sudden elated detachment. I didn't, I couldn't, love her less. But I no longer had to feel anxious or desperate about her. I remembered my truisms from the day before. Here she was, and whatever she was, I would find out and celebrate her, regardless. I could love her, so I thought, and remain immune, unharmed.

All this in a flash as I squeezed between two crowded tables to get to her. She raised her right hand and in mock formal fashion I bowed and kissed it. As I sat down she gazed at my sling with evident pity.

"Poor darling."

The waiter—he looked sixteen and serious—
came with glasses, and filled them while holding
his hand behind his back. A professional.

As we raised and clinked them across the table,
I said, "To Adam not breaking more of my bones."

"That's rather limiting."

We laughed, and it seemed as though laughter
at the other tables followed and rose with ours.
What a wild place we were in. She didn't know
how much, how little, I knew. I didn't know what
to believe about her, whether she was the victim or
perpetrator of a crime. It didn't matter. We were in
love and I remained convinced that even if I came
to know the worst, it would make no difference.
Love would see us through. It should have been
easier, therefore, to broach any of the issues that my
cowardice inclined me to suppress. And I was on
the edge of doing just that, of saying more about
my broken scaphoid, when she took my good hand
in hers across the white linen.

"Yesterday was glorious."

I was giddy. It was as if she had proposed that we
make love in public, now, across the table.

"We could go home right now."

She did a comic little double-take. "You haven't
opened your present."

She pushed it across with a forefinger. While I
unwrapped it, our boy waiter refilled the glasses.
I found a small plain cardboard box. Inside was a

z-shaped piece of strip metal with padding on the parallel surfaces. A wrist exerciser.

"For when your plaster comes off."

I stood and went around the table to kiss her. Someone nearby said, "Oi-oi!" Another person made the sound of a barking dog. I wasn't bothered. Back in my seat I said, "Adam says he's disabled his kill switch."

She leaned forward, suddenly serious. "You've got to get him back to the shop."

"But he loves you. He told me."

"You're making fun of me."

I said, "If he needs reprogramming, you're the one he'll listen to."

Her tone was plaintive. "How can he talk about love? This is madness."

Our waiter was hovering and heard everything we said next, even though I murmured quickly. "You helped choose the kind of guy he is—the sort who falls in love with the first woman he sleeps with."

"Oh, Charlie!"

The boy said, "Have you decided yet, or shall I come back?"

"Stick around."

We passed a couple of minutes choosing and changing our minds. I ordered at random a twelve-year-old Haut-Médoc. It occurred to me that I was the one paying for my birthday treat. I cancelled the order and asked for a twenty-year-old bottle of the same.

The waiter left and we paused to consider where we were.

Miranda said, "Are you seeing someone else?"

The question astonished me and for a moment I was stuck for the most reassuring and convincing reply. At the same time, I noticed that the chef, who was also the owner, had come from behind the counter and was making his way between the tables to the door. The waiter was following him. I glanced over my shoulder and saw through the glass two figures out on the pavement. One of them was folding away an umbrella.

I must have looked evasive to Miranda. She added, "Just be honest with me. I don't mind."

She clearly did mind and I gave her my full attention.

"Absolutely not. You're all I care about."

"When I'm out all day at seminars?"

"I work and I think about you."

I felt a draught of cool air on my neck. Miranda's gaze shifted from me to the door and I felt I could turn again and look. The chef was helping two elderly men out of their long raincoats, which he dumped into the arms of the waiter. The men were led to their table—set apart and the only one with a lit candle. The taller man had swept-back silvery hair and wore a brown silk scarf loosely knotted around his neck and some kind of artist's cotton jacket that drooped from his shoulders. A chair was held out for him and before sitting he looked around the room and nodded to himself. No one else in the restaurant seemed interested. The man's style of bohemian grandeur was not so unusual in Soho. But I was excited.

I turned back to Miranda, still aware of her surprising query, and placed my hand on hers.

"Do you know who he is?"

"No idea."

"Alan Turing."

"Your hero."

"And Thomas Reah, the physicist. Invented loop quantum gravity more or less single-handed."

"Go and say hello."

"That would not be cool."

So we returned to the question of the someone else I was not seeing, and once she appeared satisfied, we went back to Adam and discussed how we might overcome his resistance to the kill switch. She suggested hiding the charging cables until he was too weak to resist us. I reminded her of his instant origami sailboat. He would improvise a power cable in minutes. My concentration was poor during this exchange. I kept looking at her, hallucinating a glow around her head and shoulders and thinking about the time when we would be alone, travelling the smooth and rising curve to ecstasy. Even as I was hobbled by a state of continuous sexual arousal, it excited me to be in the same room as a great man. From pre-war meditations on the idea of a universal computing machine, to Bletchley in the early years of the war, to morphogenesis, to his glorious patrician present. The greatest living Englishman, noble and free in his love for another man. In his seniority, dressed with the flamboyance of a rock star, a genius painter, a knighted actor. I could see him only if I turned rudely away from Miranda. I resisted. I distracted myself with the usual list, the buried suspicions, all we had not touched on—the Salisbury court case and the death threat being the most rank. Where was my courage when I lacked the clarity to raise these subjects, when they tormented me while they remained unspoken?

"You're not even listening."

"I am, I am. You said Adam's got a screw loose."

"I didn't. Idiot. But happy birthday."

We raised our glasses again. The Médoc was bottled when Miranda was two years old and my father was moving out of swing into bebop.

The meal was a success, but the bill was a long time coming. While we waited we decided on a parting cognac. The drinks the waiter brought were double measures, on the house. Miranda returned to the business of her father's illness. The new diagnosis was lymphoma, of a slow-acting kind. He was likely to die with it rather than of it. He had much else to die of. But there was a pill he now took that made him cheerful and assertive—and even more of a handful. Impossible projects filled his thoughts. He wanted to sell the Salisbury house and buy an apartment in New York, in the East Village, not the current one, she suspected, but the Village of his youth. On a rush of self-belief, he had signed a contract to deliver a coffee-table book on the folklore of British birds—a vast project that he could never hope to complete, even with a full-time researcher. On a strange whim, given his views, he had joined a fringe political group dedicated to taking Britain out of the European Union. He was up for election as treasurer at his London club, the Athenaeum. Every day he phoned his daughter with new schemes. Everything I heard made me gloomier about our proposed visit, but I said nothing.

At last we were done and we shrugged on our coats. Miranda preceded me towards the door. Our path between the tables would take us close to Turing's. As we approached, I saw that apart from a bowl of nuts, hardly touched, the distinguished diners had eaten nothing. They were here to talk and drink. In an ice bucket was a half-bottle of Dutch genever, and on the table were ice cubes in a silver dish and two cut-glass tumblers. I was impressed. Would I be so game at seventy? Turing was facing me directly. The years had lengthened his face, marking out the cheekbones, giving him a keen ferocious look. Many years later I thought I saw the ghost of Alan Turing in the figure of the painter Lucian Freud. I crossed his path late one night as he came out of the Wolseley in Piccadilly. Same lean fitness in early old age that seemed derived less from healthy living than from a hunger to keep on creating.

The decision was taken for me by the cognac. I approached as millions before me had approached a famous presence in a public place, with outward humility masking the entitlement that genuine admiration confers. Turing glanced up at me, then looked away. Dealing with admirers was Reah's business. I wasn't drunk enough to be unembarrassed and I stumbled over the formulaic opener.

"Really sorry to intrude. I just wanted to express my profound gratitude to you both for your work."

"That's very kind," Reah said. "What's your name?"

"Charlie Friend."

"Very nice to have met you, Charlie."

The tense was clear. I came to my point. "I read that you have one of these Adams or Eves. I've got one too. I wondered if you've experienced any sort of problem with . . ."

I trailed away because I had seen Reah look at Turing, who had firmly shaken his head.

I took out my card and put it on their table. Neither man looked at it. I retreated, muttering my foolish apologies. Miranda was right beside me. She took my hand and as we stepped out into Greek Street she gave a sympathetic squeeze.

. . .

**"In her loving look,
a whole universe contained.
Love the universe!"**

This was the first of his poems that Adam recited to me. He had come into my bedroom without knocking just after eleven one morning, while I was working at my screen, hoping to take advantage of volatility in the currency markets. There was a square of sunlight on the carpet and he made a point of standing in it. I noticed he was wearing one of my turtleneck sweaters. He must have taken it from my drawer. He told me he had a poem he urgently needed to recite. I swivelled in my chair and waited.

When he finished I said unkindly, "Short at least."
He winced. "A haiku."
"Ah. Nineteen syllables."
"Seventeen. Five then seven then five again. Here's another." He paused, looked towards the ceiling.

**"Kiss the space where she
trod from here to the window.
She made prints in time."**

I said, "Spacetime?"
"Yes!"

"OK," I said. "One more. I've got to get on."

"I've got hundreds. But look . . ."

He left his illuminated spot and came to my desk and put his hand over the mouse. "These two rows of figures, don't you see? Intersecting Fibonacci curves. A high probability that if you buy here and wait . . . now sell. Look. You made £31."

"Do that again."

"Best to wait."

"Then do me one more haiku and leave."

He returned to his square of light.

"You and the moment
Came when I touched your—"

"I don't want to hear that."

"I shouldn't show it to her?"

I sighed and he moved away. As he reached the door I added, "Clean up the kitchen and bathroom, would you, please? Difficult to do with one hand."

He nodded and went away. A kind of peace or stability had settled over our household, despite the matter of Gorringe's release. I was more relaxed. Adam was spending no time alone with Miranda, while I was with her every night. I was confident he would keep his promise. He had told me several times that he was in love, and chaste love was fine by me. He wrote poems in his thoughts and stored them there. He wanted to talk to me about Miranda but I usually cut him off. I didn't dare attempt to power him down and I had no particular need. The plan to get him back to the salesroom was set aside. Love appeared to have softened him. For reasons I didn't understand, he was eager for my approval. Guilt, perhaps. He had fallen back into a routine of vague obedience. I remained cautious because of my wrist and I was watchful—but nothing of that showed. I reminded myself that he was still my experiment, my adventure. It was not supposed to run smooth at every turn.

With Adam's love came intellectual exuberance. He insisted on telling me his latest thoughts, his theories, his aphorisms, his latest reading. He was putting himself through a course on quantum mechanics. All night, while he charged up, he contemplated the mathematics and the basic texts. He read Schrödinger's Dublin lectures, **What Is Life?**, from which he concluded that he was alive. He read the transcript of the celebrated 1927 Solvay conference, when the luminaries of physics met to discuss photons and electrons.

"It was said that at these early Solvay meetings there took place the most profound exchanges about nature in the history of ideas."

I was at breakfast. I told him I'd once read that the elderly Einstein, while at Princeton in his final years, started each day with eggs fried in butter and that in Adam's honour, I was frying two now for myself.

Adam said, "People said he never grasped what

he himself had started. Solvay was a battlefield for him. Outnumbered, poor fellow. By extraordinary young men. But that was unfair. The young Turks weren't concerned with what nature is, only with what one could say about it. Whereas Einstein thought there was no science without belief in an external world independent of the observer. He didn't think quantum mechanics was wrong so much as incomplete."

This after one night's study. I remembered my hopeless brief entanglement with physics at college, before I found safety in anthropology. I suppose I was a little jealous, especially when I learned that Adam had got his mind round Dirac's equation. I cited Richard Feynman's remark that anyone who claims to understand quantum theory doesn't understand quantum theory.

Adam shook his head. "A bogus paradox, if it's even a paradox at all. Tens of thousands understand it, millions make use of it. It's a matter of time, Charlie. General relativity was once at the outer edge of difficulty. Now it's routine for first-year undergraduates. The same was true of the calculus. Now fourteen-year-olds can do it. One day quantum mechanics will pass into common sense."

By this time I was eating my eggs. Adam had made the coffee. It was far too strong. I said, "OK. What about that Solvay question? Is quantum mechanics a description of nature or just an effective way of predicting things?"

"I would have been on Einstein's side. I don't understand the doubt about it," he said. "Quantum mechanics makes predictions to such a fabulous degree of accuracy, it must be getting something right about nature. To creatures of our immense size, the material world looks blurred and feels hard. But now we know how strange and wonderful it is. So it shouldn't surprise us that consciousness, your sort and mine, could arise from an arrangement of matter—it's clearly odd to just the right degree. And we don't have anything else to explain how matter can think and feel." Then he added, "Except for beams of love from the eyes of God. But then, beams can be investigated."

Another morning, after he had told me how he had been thinking all night of Miranda, he said, "I've also been thinking about vision and death."

"Go on."

"We don't see everywhere. We can't see behind our heads. We can't even see our chins. Let's say our field of vision is almost 180 degrees, counting in peripheral awareness. The odd thing is, there's no boundary, no edge. There isn't vision and then blackness, like you get when you look through binoculars. There isn't something, then nothing. What we have is the field of vision, and then beyond it less than nothing."

"So?"

"So this is what death is like. Less than nothing. Less than blackness. The edge of vision is a good representation of the edge of consciousness. Life, then death. It's a foretaste, Charlie, and it's there all day."

"Nothing to be afraid of then," I said.

He raised both hands as if to grip and shake a trophy. "Exactly right! Less than nothing to be afraid of!"

Was he covering for an anxiety about death? His term was fixed for approximately twenty years. When I asked, he said, "That's the difference between us, Charlie. My body parts will be improved or replaced. But my mind, my memories, experiences, identity and so on will be uploaded and retained. They'll be of use."

Poetry was another instance of his exuberance in love. He had written 2,000 haikus and had recited about a dozen, of the same quality, each one devoted to Miranda. I'd been interested at first in learning what Adam could create. But I soon lost interest in the form itself. Too cute, too devoted to not making much sense, too undemanding of their author as they played on empty mysteries of the sound-of-one-hand-clapping sort. Two thousand! The figure made my point—an algorithm was churning them out. I said all this as we walked the backstreets of Stockwell—our daily exercise to extend Adam's social skills. We'd been into shops, pubs and had even taken a trip on the Tube to Green Park and sat on the grass among the lunchtime crowds.

Perhaps I was too harsh. Haikus, I told him,

could be stifling in their stillness. But I was also
encouraging. Time to move on to another form.
He had access to all the world's literature. Why not
attempt a poem with verses of four lines, rhym-
ing or not? Or even a short story and eventually a
novel?

Early that evening he gave me his response. "If
you don't mind, I'm ready to discuss your sugges-
tions."

I was not long out of the shower, freshly dressed
and on my way upstairs, therefore a little impatient.
On the table, waiting to come with me, was a bottle of Pomerol. There was a conversation I needed
to have with Miranda. Gorringe was due to be released in seven weeks. We still hadn't decided what
to do. There was an assumption that Adam could
act as her bodyguard and I was worried—I was le-
gally responsible for anything he might do. She had
been back to the local police station. The detective
who had visited Gorringe in prison had moved on.
The desk sergeant had taken a note and advised her
to phone emergency in the event of trouble. She
had suggested that it might be difficult if she was
being bludgeoned at the time. The sergeant did not
take this to be facetious. He advised her to make
the call before that eventuality.

"When I see him coming up the garden path
with an axe?"

"Yes. And don't open the door."

She had seen a solicitor about going before a

judge to get an exclusion order. Success was not certain and it wasn't clear what it would achieve. She had asked her father not to divulge her address to anyone. But Maxfield had worries of his own and she thought he'd forget. We were left with the hope that the threat wasn't serious and that Adam would be a deterrent. When I asked her how dangerous Gorringe really was, she said, "He's a creep."

"A dangerous creep?"

"A disgusting creep."

I wasn't in the right mood for another conversation with Adam about poetry.

"My opinion," he said, "is that the haiku is the literary form of the future. I want to refine and extend the form. Everything I've done so far is a kind of limbering up. My juvenilia. When I've studied the masters and understood more, especially when I've grasped the power of the **kireji**, the cutting word that separates the two juxtaposed parts, my real work can begin."

From upstairs I heard the phone ring and Miranda's footsteps across my ceiling.

Adam said, "As a thinking man with an interest in anthropology and politics, you won't be much interested in optimism. But beyond the currents of disheartening facts about human nature and societies and daily bad news, there can be mightier stirrings, positive developments that are lost to view. The world is so connected now, however crudely, and change is so widely distributed that progress is hard to perceive. I don't like to boast, but one of those changes is right in front of you. The implications of intelligent machines are so immense that we've no idea what you—civilisation, that is—have set in motion. One anxiety is that it will be a shock and an insult to live with entities that are cleverer than you are. But already almost everyone knows someone cleverer than themselves. On top of which, you underestimate yourselves."

I could make out Miranda's voice on the phone. She was agitated. She was walking up and down her sitting room as she spoke.

Adam appeared not to hear her but I knew he had. "You won't allow yourselves to be left behind. As a species, you're far too competitive. Even now there are paralysed patients with electrodes implanted in the motor strip of their brains who merely think of the action and can raise an arm or bend a finger. This is a humble beginning and there are many problems to solve. They'll certainly be solved, and when they are, and a brain–machine interface is efficient and cheap, you'll become a partner with your machines in the open-ended expansion of intelligence, and of consciousness generally. Colossal intelligence, instant access to deep moral acumen and to everything known, but more importantly, access to each other."

Miranda's pacing upstairs had ceased.

"It could be the end of mental privacy. You'll probably come to value it less in the face of the

enormous gains. You might be wondering what rel-
evance any of this has to the haiku. It's this. Ever
since I've been here, I've been surveying the literature of scores of countries. Magnificent traditions,
gorgeous elaborations of—"

Her bedroom door closed, steps swiftly crossed
her sitting room to her door. It slammed shut and I
heard her footsteps on the stairs.

"Apart from lyrical poetry celebrating love or
landscape, almost everything I read in literature—"

Her key was in my door and then she was before
us. Her face had a greasy shine. She was doing her
best to keep a level voice. "That was my father on
the phone. They let Gorringe out early. Three weeks
ago. He's been to Salisbury, to the house, talked his
way past the housekeeper and got my address out of
my father. He could be on his way here now."

She lowered herself into the nearest kitchen
chair. I too sat down.

Adam took in Miranda's news and nodded. But
he pressed on into our silence. "Nearly everything
I've read in the world's literature describes variet-
ies of human failure—of understanding, of reason,
of wisdom, of proper sympathies. Failures of cognition, honesty, kindness, self-awareness; superb
depictions of murder, cruelty, greed, stupidity, self-
delusion, above all, profound misunderstanding of
others. Of course, goodness is on show too, and her-
oism, grace, wisdom, truth. Out of this rich tangle
have come literary traditions, flourishing, like the

wild flowers in Darwin's famous hedgerow. Novels ripe with tension, concealment and violence as well as moments of love and perfect formal resolution. But when the marriage of men and women to machines is complete, this literature will be redundant because we'll understand each other too well. We'll inhabit a community of minds to which we have immediate access. Connectivity will be such that individual nodes of the subjective will merge into an ocean of thought, of which our Internet is the crude precursor. As we come to inhabit each other's minds, we'll be incapable of deceit. Our narratives will no longer record endless misunderstanding. Our literatures will lose their unwholesome nourishment. The lapidary haiku, the still, clear perception and celebration of things as they are, will be the only necessary form. I'm sure we'll treasure the literature of the past, even as it horrifies us. We'll look back and marvel at how well the people of long ago depicted their own shortcomings, how they wove brilliant, even optimistic fables out of their conflicts and monstrous inadequacies and mutual incomprehension."

SIX

Adam's utopia masked a nightmare, as utopias generally do, but it was a mere abstraction. Miranda's nightmare was real and instantly became mine. We sat beside each other at the table, flustered and dumb, a rare combination. It was left to Adam to be clear-headed and set out the reassuring facts. Nothing Maxfield had said on the phone indicated that Gorringe was on his way here tonight. If he'd been out three weeks, murder was clearly not his priority. He could arrive tomorrow, or next month, or never. If he hoped to succeed without witnesses, he would have to kill all three of us. He would be an obvious suspect in any crime against Miranda. Even if he came this evening, he would find Miranda's flat in darkness. He knew nothing about her connection with me. It was likely that the threat itself was all the punishment he intended. Finally, we had a strongman on our side.

If necessary, he could keep Gorringe talking while one of us called the police.

Time to open the wine!

Adam set three glasses on the table. Miranda preferred my father's Edwardian teak-handled cork-screw to my fancy gadget with a lever. The effort seemed to settle her. The first glass settled me. To keep us company, Adam sipped at a third of a glass of warm water. Our fears were not quite dispelled but now, in this party atmosphere, we returned to Adam's little thesis. We even raised a toast to "the future," though his version of it, private mental space drowned by new technology in an ocean of collective thought, repelled us both. Fortunately, it was as feasible as the project of implanting the brains of billions.

I said to Adam, "I'd like to think that there will always be someone, somewhere, not writing haikus."

We raised our glasses to that too. No one was in the mood for an argument. The only other possible topic was Gorringe and everything related to him. That conversation was just starting when I excused myself and went to the bathroom. As I was wash-ing my hands, I found myself thinking about Mark and my fleeting sense of privilege in the playground when he put his hand in mine. I remembered his look of resilient intelligence. I thought of him not as a child, but as a person in the context of his entire life. His future was in the hands of bureaucrats, however kindly, and the choices they made for him. He could easily sink. Miranda had so far been unable to get news of him. Finding Jasmin, or any social worker willing to talk to her, was impossible. There were, she was told at last by someone in the right department, issues of confidentiality. Despite that, she learned that the father had vanished and the mother had drink and drug problems.

As I was returning to the kitchen I had a moment of nostalgia for my life as it was before Gorringe, Adam, even Miranda. As an existence, it had been insufficient but relatively simple.

Simpler still if I'd left my mother's money in the bank. Here was my lover at the table, beautiful and outwardly composed. As I sat down, it wasn't irritation I felt towards her, though that wasn't far off. More like detachment. I saw what must have been obvious to everyone—her secretiveness; also, her inability to ask for help, her trick of getting it anyway, and of never being held to account. I sat down, drank a little wine, listened to the conversation— and made a decision. Setting aside Adam's reassurances, I believed she had brought a murderer into my life. I was expected to help, and I would. But she had told me nothing. Now I was calling in a debt.

We were looking right at each other. I couldn't keep the terseness out of my voice. "Did he rape you or not?"

After a pause, during which she continued to hold my gaze, she shook her head slowly from side to side and then she said softly, "No."

I waited. She waited. Adam went to speak. I silenced him with a slight shake of the head. When it was clear that Miranda was not going to say more—the very reticence that was oppressing me—I said, "You lied to the court."

"Yes."

"You sent an innocent man to prison."

She sighed.

Again, I waited. My patience was running out, but I didn't raise my voice. "Miranda. This is stupid. What happened?"

She was looking down at her hands. To my relief, she said, as though to herself, "It'll take a while."

"Fine."

She began without preamble. Suddenly she seemed eager to tell her story.

"When I was nine years old a new girl came to our school. She was brought into the classroom and introduced as Mariam. She was slender and dark, with beautiful eyes and the blackest hair you'd ever seen, tied with a white ribbon. Salisbury was a very white town back then so we were all fascinated by this girl from Pakistan. I could see that standing there, in front of the class, being stared at by everyone, was hard for her. It was as if she was in pain. When our teacher asked who wanted to be Mariam's special friend and show her around and help her, I was the first to put up my hand. The boy sitting with me was moved to another desk and she took his place. We sat together in class for years to come, in that school and the next. At some point during our first day, she put her hand in mine. Lots of us girls were always doing that, but this was different. Her hand was so delicate and smooth and she was so quiet, so tentative. I was pretty shy myself, so I was drawn to her quietness and intimacy. She was far more timid than me, at least at first, and I think she made me feel for the first time confident and knowing. I fell in love with her.

"It was a love affair, a crush, very intense. I introduced her to my friends. I don't remember any racism. The boys ignored her, the girls were kind to her. They liked to finger her brightly coloured dresses. She was so unusual, exotic even, and I used to worry that someone would steal her from me. But she was a very loyal friend. We kept hold of each other's hand. Within a month, she took me home to meet her family. Knowing that I'd lost my mother when I was little, Mariam's mother, Sana, took me in. She was kind but rather bossy in an affectionate way. One afternoon she brushed out my hair and tied in one of Mariam's ribbons. No one had ever done that for me before. I was overwhelmed and I cried."

The memory had caused her throat to constrict and her voice to become lighter. She paused and swallowed hard before starting again.

"I ate curries for the first time and developed a taste for her home-made puddings, brightly coloured, extremely sweet laddu, anarsa and soan papdi. There was a little sister, Surayya, whom Mariam adored, and two older brothers, Farhan and Hamid. Her father, Yasir, worked for the local authority as a water engineer. He was very nice to me too. It was a crowded, noisy household, very friendly, argumentative, the complete opposite of my own. They were religious, Muslim of course, but at that age I was hardly aware of it. Later I took it for granted, and by then I was a part of the family. When they went to the mosque, it never crossed my mind to go with them, or even ask about it. I'd grown up without religion and I had no interest in it. Mariam was transformed as soon as she was through her front door. She became playful and far more talkative. She was her father's favourite. She liked to sit on his knee when he came in from work. I was a tiny bit jealous.

"I brought her back to my place, which you'll see soon. Just outside the cathedral close, tall, thin, early Victorian, untidy, dark, piles of books. My father was always loving but he spent most of his time in his study and didn't like to be disturbed. A local lady came in to cook my tea. So we were on our own, and we liked that. We made a den in an attic room, we had adventures in our overgrown garden. We watched TV together. A couple of years later, we clung to each other in the first bewildering days of secondary school. We did our homework together. She was far better at maths and good at explaining problems. I helped her with her written English. She was hopeless at spelling. As time passed and we became more self-conscious, we spent hours talking about our families. We had our first periods within a few weeks of each other. Her mother was really sensible and helpful with that. We also talked about boys, although we didn't go near them. Because of her brothers, she was less bothered, more sceptical about boys than I was.

"The years passed, our friendship continued and became just a fact of life. Our last summer at school came around. We sat our public exams and thought about university. She wanted to do science, I was interested in history. We were worried that we'd end up in different places."

Miranda stopped. She took a long slow breath. As she resumed, she reached for my hand.

"One Saturday afternoon I got a call from her. She was in a very bad state. At first I couldn't make out what she was saying. She wanted to meet me in a local park. When I got to her, she couldn't speak. We walked around the park, arm in arm, and all I could do was wait. At last she told me what had happened the day before. Her route home from school took her by some playing fields. It was dusk and she was hurrying because her parents didn't like her out alone after dark. She became aware of a figure following her. It seemed to be getting closer each time she turned to look. She thought of breaking into a run—she was fast—then decided she was being silly. And she had a satchel full of books. The person following her was getting closer. She turned to confront him and was relieved to see it was someone she vaguely knew—Peter Gorringe. He wasn't exactly popular, but he was known at school as the only boy who had his own place. His parents were abroad and had rented a small bedsit for him for a few months rather than trust him to look after the house. Before she could speak to him he ran at her, took hold of her wrist and dragged her behind a brick shed where they keep the mowers. She screamed but no one came. He was large, she was very slight. He wrestled her to the ground and that was where he raped her.

"Mariam and I stood in the park, in the middle of this big lawn surrounded by flower beds, and hugged and cried together. Even then, as I was trying to take in this horrific news, I thought that one day everything would be all right. She would get through this. Everyone loved and respected her, everyone would be outraged. Her attacker would go to prison. I would go to whatever university she chose and stay close to her.

"When she recovered enough, she showed me the marks on her legs and thighs, and on each wrist, a row of four little bruises from his grip when he'd held her down. She told me how she got home that night, told her father she had a heavy cold and went straight to bed. It was lucky, the way she saw it, that her mother was out that evening. She would have known immediately that something was wrong. That was when I began to understand that she hadn't told her parents. We started walking round the park again. I told her she must tell them. She needed all the help and support she could get. If she hadn't been to the police yet, I would come with her. Now!

"I'd never seen Mariam so fierce. She seized my hands and told me that I understood nothing. Her parents were never to know, nor were the police. I said we should go together and tell her doctor. When she heard that, she shouted at me. The doctor would go straight to her mother. He was a family friend. Her uncles would hear about it. Her brothers would do something stupid and get themselves in serious trouble. Her family would be humiliated. Her father would be destroyed if he learned what had happened. If I was her friend I had to help her in the way she needed to be helped. She wanted me to promise to keep her secret. I resisted but she came back at me. She was furious. She kept telling me that I understood nothing. The police, the doctor, the school, her family, my father—no one was to know. I was not to confront Gorringe. If I did, it would all come out.

"And so, in the end, I did what I knew to be wrong. Since we didn't have one with me, I swore on 'the idea' of the Bible to keep Mariam's secret, and on the Koran too, and on our friendship and on my father's life. I did as she asked, even though I was convinced that her family would have gathered round her and supported her. And I still believe it. More than that. I know it for a fact. They loved her and would never have cast her out or enacted whatever mad idea she had of family honour. They would have put their arms round her and protected her. Her ideas were all wrong. And I was worse, I was criminally stupid, going along with this and entering into her secret pact.

"For the next two weeks we saw each other every day. We talked of nothing else. For a part of that time I tried to change her mind. Not a chance. She seemed calmer, even more determined, and I began to think that perhaps she was right. It was certainly convenient to think so. Keep silent, avoid a family trauma, avoid giving evidence to the police, avoid a terrifying court case. Stay calm and think about the future. We were on the edge of becoming adults. Our lives were about to change. This was a catastrophe but she would survive it with my help. Whenever I saw Gorringe at school I stayed clear of him. That was getting easier as the term ran down and we school-leavers began to disperse forever.

"At the beginning of the holidays my father took me to France to stay with friends who had a farmhouse in the Dordogne. Before I left, Mariam begged me not to phone her home. I think she was afraid that if by chance I started speaking to her mother, I would forget my promise and tell her everything. By then, lots of people had mobile phones, but they hadn't quite reached us. So we wrote letters and postcards every day. I remember being disappointed by hers. They were not exactly distant so much as dull. There was only one subject and she couldn't write about it. So she wrote about the weather and TV programmes and said nothing about her state of mind.

"I was away two weeks and during the last five days nothing came from her. As soon as we were home I went round to her house. As I approached I saw that the front door was open. Her older brother Hamid was standing by it. A couple of neighbours went in, someone came out. I was filled with dread as I went up to him. He looked ill, very thin, and for a moment he seemed not to recognise me. Then he told me. She had slit her wrists in the bath. The funeral had already happened two days before. I took a couple of steps back from him. I was too numb for grief, but not too numb for guilt. Mariam was dead because I'd kept her secret and denied her the help she needed. I wanted to run away but Hamid made me go into the house and speak to his mother.

"In my memory I moved through a crowd to get to the kitchen. But the house was small. There must have been no more than a dozen visitors. Sana was sitting on a wooden chair with her back to the wall. There were people around her but no one was talking, and her face—I'll never escape that face. Stricken, frozen in pain. As soon as she saw me, she stretched out her arms towards me and I stooped over her and we embraced. Her entire body was hot and clammy and trembling. I wasn't crying. Not yet. Then, while her arms were around my neck, she asked me in a whisper, she actually asked me to be honest with her. Was there something she should know about Mariam, was there something, anything I could tell her that would make sense of this? I couldn't speak but I lied with a shake of my head. I was truly scared. I couldn't even begin to grasp the enormity of my crime. Now I was adding to it by condemning my lovely surrogate mother to a lifetime of anguish and ignorance. I'd killed her daughter with my silence, now I was crushing her with it.

"Would it have made her burden any easier to know that her daughter was raped? I could hear the family crying out, If only we had known! Then they would have turned on me. Rightly. There was and is no way round it, I bear responsibility for Mariam's death. Seventeen years and nine months old. I left Sana where she sat and hurried out of the house, avoiding the rest of the family. I couldn't face them. Especially her father. And Mariam's darling, the little girl, Surayya I was so close to. I walked away from the house and I've never been back. Sana wrote to me a few days later, when Mariam's brilliant exam results came through. I didn't reply. To be involved with the family in any way would've been to add to my deceit. How could I be with them and visit the grave, as she was suggesting, when my presence would be a constant lie?

"So I grieved alone for my friend. There was no one I dared speak to about her. You're the first person, Charlie, I've told this story to. I grieved and fell into a long depression. I delayed my university course. My father sent me to the doctor, who prescribed antidepressants, and I was glad of the cover and pretended to take them. I think I could have gone under completely that year if it hadn't been for my one ambition in life—justice. By which I mean revenge.

"Gorringe was still living in his bedsit on the edge of Salisbury and that was fortunate, I thought, as I made my plans. I'm sure you've guessed what they were. He was working in a café, saving up to go travelling. When at last I felt strong enough, I went in there with a book. I studied him and fed my hatred. And I was friendly towards him when he spoke to me. I let a week go by before I went back. We spoke again—about nothing much. I could see he was interested and I waited for him to ask me round to his place. First time, I told him I was busy. By the next I could see he was getting really keen and I agreed to call on him. I could hardly sleep for thinking and planning. I would never have imagined that hatred could bring such elation. I didn't care what happened to me along the way. I was reckless, ready to pay any price. Getting him sent down for rape was my sole reason for keeping going. Ten years, twelve, his entire lifetime wouldn't have been enough.

"I took a half-bottle of vodka with me. It was all I could afford. I'd had two boyfriends by that summer and I knew what to do. That night, I got Gorringe drunk and seduced him. You know the rest. Whenever revulsion started to get the better of me, I thought of him wrestling Mariam to the ground, ignoring her screams and pleas. I thought of my friend lowering herself into the bath, feeling completely alone, dishonoured and without hope and any wish to live.

"My plan had been to leave straight after Gorringe was done with me and go to the police. But I was so disgusted and numbed by the experience I couldn't move. And when I managed to get myself off the bed and dressed, I worried that I had drunk too much and wouldn't be convincing in front of the desk sergeant. But it worked out well enough in the morning. I made a point of not changing my clothes or washing. So, no shortage of evidence in the right places. The new genetic test had been introduced across the country by then. The police weren't as unfriendly as I'd feared from what I'd read in the newspapers. They weren't particularly sympathetic either. They were efficient, and keen to try out their new DNA kit. They brought him in and got a match. From that time on, his life was hell. Seven months later it got worse.

"In court, I spoke for Mariam. I became her and spoke through her. I was so deep in lies already that my version of that night came easily. It helped that I could see Gorringe across the courtroom. I let my hatred drive me on. I thought he was pathetic when he came up with the story about the texts I was supposed to have sent to a friend called Amelia. It was easy enough to prove she didn't exist. Not all the press took my side. Some court reporters thought I was a malicious liar. The judge was very old school. In his summing-up he said that I'd knowingly put myself at risk, taking alcohol to a young man's rooms. The jury still brought in a unanimous verdict. But when it came to sentencing, I was disappointed. Six years. Gorringe was just nineteen. With good behaviour, he'd be out at the age of twenty-two. He paid a bargain price for obliterating Mariam's existence. But if I hated him with such ferocity, it was also because I knew that he and I were partners, bound forever, complicit in Mariam's lonely death. And now he wants justice."

Not long after I was thrown out of the legal profession I formed a company with two friends. The idea was to buy romantic apartments in Rome and Paris at local prices, do them up to a high standard, dress them with antique furniture and sell them to wealthy, cultured Americans or to agencies that would do the same. It wasn't exactly the quick route to our first million. Most cultured Americans weren't rich. Those who were didn't share our tastes. The work was complicated and exhausting, especially in Rome, where we had to learn how and whom to bribe among the officials in local government. In Paris it was the bureaucracy that wore us down.

One weekend I flew to Rome to close a deal. It was important for this particular client that I stayed in his expensive hotel. This one was a well-established place at the top of the Spanish Steps. The client was staying there in a grand suite. I came into the city on a Friday evening, hot and harassed from my ride on a crowded airport bus. I was dressed in jeans and t-shirt, with a cheap Norwegian airline bag hanging from my shoulder. I stepped into a beautiful reception area. Just by chance, the manager happened to be standing by the check-in desk. He wasn't waiting for me—I wasn't important enough for that. I just happened to breeze in and since he was a courteous gentleman, extremely well dressed and correct, he welcomed me warmly in Italian to his hotel. I only partly understood what he was saying. His voice was expressionless, with little variation in pitch, and my Italian was poor. A receptionist came over and explained that the manager was congenitally deaf but he spoke nine languages, most of them

European. Since childhood he'd been adept at lip-reading. But before he could read mine I would have to indicate which language I was speaking. Otherwise he couldn't begin to understand me.

He ran through his list. Norwegian? I shook my head. Finnish? English came fifth. He said he could have sworn I was a Nordic sort. So our conversation—pleasant, of no real consequence—could begin. But in theory, an entire world was open to us, and one piece of information had unlocked it all. Without it, his great gift couldn't come into play.

Miranda's story was a version of such a key. Our conversation, in the form of our love, could properly begin. Her secretiveness, withdrawals and silence, her diffidence, that air she had of seeming older than her years, her tendency to drift out of reach, even in moments of tenderness, were forms of grieving. It pained me that she had carried her sadness alone. I admired the boldness and courage of her revenge. It was a dangerous plan, executed with such focus and brilliant disregard for consequences. I loved her more. I loved her poor friend. I would do everything to protect Miranda from this beast Gorringe. It touched me, to be the first to know her story.

Telling it was a liberation for Miranda too. Half an hour after she had finished, when we were alone in the bedroom, she looped her arms around my neck, drew me to her and kissed me. We knew we were starting again. Adam was next door, charging up, lost to his thoughts. It was true, the old cliché about stress and desire. We undressed each other impatiently and, as usual, my plaster cast made me clumsy. Afterwards we lay on our sides, face to face. Her father still didn't know what had happened. Miranda still had no contact with Mariam's family. The visits to the mosque had at first brought Mariam closer, then they seemed futile. She wished Gorringe had got a longer sentence. She remained tormented by her schoolgirlish vow of silence. A simple message, to Sana or Yasir or to a teacher, would have saved Mariam's life. The cruellest recollection, the one she tortured herself with, was when Sana, embracing her at the extremes of grief, had whispered the question in her ear. It was Sana who found Mariam in the bath. That imagined sight, the crimson water, the lithe brown body half submerged, was another torture, the cause of nightlong waking terrors and hideous dreams.

Lying on the bed in the darkening room, lost to all else, we seemed to be heading towards the dawn. But it was not yet nine o'clock. Mostly she talked, I listened and asked occasional questions. Would Gorringe return to live in Salisbury? Yes. His parents were still away and he was living in the family house. Was Mariam's family still in town? No, they had moved to be closer to relatives in Leicester. Had she visited the grave? Many times, always approaching with caution in case one of the family was there. She always left flowers.

In a long conversation it can be difficult to trace how or when the subject comes to shift. It may have been mention of Surayya, the love of Mariam's life. That little girl must have led us to Mark. Miranda said she missed him. I said I often thought about him. We had failed to find out where he was and what had happened. He had disappeared into the system, into a cloud of privacy regulation and the unreachable sanctuary of family law. We talked about luck, the hold it had over a child's life—what he is born into, whether he is loved and how intelligently.

After a pause, Miranda said, "And when it's all against him, whether someone can rescue him."

I asked her if she thought her father's love came near to making up for her absent mother. She didn't reply. Her breathing was suddenly rhythmic. In just a few seconds, she had fallen asleep and was curled against me. Gently, I rolled onto my back, staying as close to her as I could. In the half-light, the ceiling looked charmingly ancient rather than stained and disintegrating. I followed the jagged line of a crack that ran from a corner of the room towards the centre.

If Adam had been driven by cogs and flywheels, I would have heard them turning in the silence that had followed Miranda's story. His arms were folded, his eyes were closed. The tough-guy look he had in repose, recently softened by adoration, appeared harshly reinstated. The flattened nose looked flatter still. The Bosphorus dockworker. What could it mean, to say that he was thinking? Sifting through remote memory banks? Logic gates flashing open and closed? Precedents retrieved, then compared, rejected or stored? Without self-awareness, it wouldn't be thinking at all so much as data processing. But Adam had told me he was in love. He had haikus to prove it. Love wasn't possible without a self, and nor was thinking. I still hadn't settled this basic question. Perhaps it was beyond reach. No one would know what it was we had created. Whatever subjective life Adam and his kind possessed couldn't be ours to verify. In which case he was what was fashionably referred to as a black box—from the outside it seemed to work. That was as far as we'd ever get.

When Miranda had finished her story, there was the silence, and then we had talked. After a while, I had turned to Adam. "Well?"

He took a few seconds, then he had said, "Very dark."

A rape, a suicide, a wrongly kept secret—of course it was dark. I was in an emotional state and I didn't ask him to explain. Now, lying next to Miranda as she slept, I wondered if he meant something more significant, the consequence of his thinking, if that was really what it . . . depends on definitions . . . That was when I too fell asleep.

Perhaps half an hour passed. What woke me was a sound outside the room. My arm in its cast was wedged uncomfortably against my side. Miranda had rolled away from me, into a deeper sleep. I heard the sound again, the familiar creak of a floorboard. My sleep had been light and I felt no anxiety, but the abrupt click of the door handle turning woke Miranda into a state of confusion and fear. She sat upright, one hand gripping mine.

"It's him," she whispered.

I knew it couldn't be. "It's fine," I said. I freed myself from her and stood to knot a towel around my waist. As I went towards the door it opened. It was Adam, offering me the kitchen phone.

"I didn't want to disturb you," he said softly. "But I think it's a call you'd want to take."

I closed the door on him and came back towards the bed with the phone against my ear.

"Mr. Charles Friend?" The voice was tentative.

"Yes."

"I hope it's not too late to call. This is Alan Turing. We saw you briefly in Greek Street. I wondered if we might meet up for a chat."

Gorringe did not appear during the following two weeks. One early evening, I left Miranda in my flat, by her choice, with Adam in attendance, and set off to cross London to Turing's house in Camden Square. I was flattered and awed by the summons. With a touch of youthful self-regard, I wondered if he'd read my short book on artificial intelligence, in which I'd praised him. We were bound by our ownership of highly advanced machines. I liked to think I was an expert on the early days of computing. Possibly he wanted to take issue with me on the way I had placed such emphasis on the role of Nikola Tesla. He had come to Britain in 1906 after the collapse of his radio-transmission project at Wardenclyffe, New York. He joined the National Physical Laboratory, something of a demotion and a blow to his vanity, and helped in the arms race against Germany. He not only developed radar and radio-guided torpedoes, but was the inspiration for the famous "foundational surge" that produced electronic computers capable of making calculations for artillery fire in the coming war. In the twenties he had been instrumental in the development of the first transistors. Notes and sketches for a silicon chip were found among his papers after he died.

I had written in my book about the celebrated meeting between Tesla and Turing in 1941. The old Serb, immensely tall and thin, and inconveniently trembling, only eighteen months away from death, said in an after-dinner speech at the Dorchester that their conversation had "reached for the stars."

Turing's only comment, made to a newspaper, was that they had exchanged nothing but small talk. At the time he was working in secret at Bletchley on a computer to crack German naval Enigma codes. He would have taken care to be circumspect.

The carriage was almost empty when I got on the Tube at Clapham North. Once we were north of the river, the train began to fill with people, mostly young, carrying placards and furled banners. Yet another unemployment march was coming to an end. At first they looked like a typical rock-and-roll crowd. The humid air carried a scent of cannabis, like a fond memory of a long day. But there was another constituency, a large minority, some of whom carried plastic Union Jacks on sticks—that foolish stock-market position of mine—or wore Union Jack t-shirts. These factions loathed each other but were making common cause. A fragile alliance had been formed, with dissenters on both sides resisting any affiliation at all. The right blamed unemployment on immigration from Europe and the Commonwealth. British workers' wages were being undercut. Foreign arrivals, dark-skinned and white, were adding to the housing crisis; doctors' waiting rooms and hospital wards were overcrowded and so were local schools, whose playgrounds were supposedly filling with eight-year-old girls in headscarves. Whole neighbourhoods had been transformed in a generation, and no one in faraway Whitehall had ever asked the locals.

The left heard nothing but xenophobic and racist distortion in these complaints. Their grievance list was longer: stock-market greed, underinvestment, short-termism, the worship of shareholder value, unreformed company law, the ravages of an unrestrained free market. I went on one march, then gave up after I read about a new car factory starting production outside Newcastle. It built three times as many cars as the factory it replaced—with one-sixth of the work force. Eighteen times more efficient, vastly more profitable. No business could resist. It wasn't only the shop floor that lost jobs to machines. Accountants, medical staff, marketing, logistics, human resources, forward planning. Now, haiku poets. All in the stew. Soon enough, most of us would have to think again what our lives were for. Not work. Fishing? Wrestling? Learning Latin? Then we'd all need a private income. I was persuaded by Benn. The robots would pay for us once they were taxed like human workers and made to work for the common good, not merely for hedge funds or corporate interests. I was out of step with both protest factions and their old struggles and missed the next two marches.

To the wealthier, who stood to lose, the universal wage looked like a call for higher taxes to fund an idle crowd of addicts, drunks and mediocrities. And what was a robot anyway—a humble flat screen, a tractor? As I saw it, the future, to which I was finely attuned, was already here. Almost too late to prepare for the inevitable. It was a cliché and a lie, that the future would invent jobs we had not yet heard of. When the majority was out of work and penniless, social collapse was certain. But with our generous state incomes, we the masses would face the luxurious problem that had preoccupied the rich for centuries: how to fill the time. Endless leisure pursuits had never much troubled the aristocracy.

The carriage was tranquil. People looked exhausted. There were so many street protests these days and all merriness had gone out of them. One man with a set of deflated bagpipes on his lap slept on the shoulder of another whose pipes were still under his arm. A couple of babies in buggies were being rocked into silence. A man, one of the Union Jack types, was reading in a murmur from a children's book to three attentive girls aged around ten. Looking down the length of the carriage, I thought we could have been a band of refugees, heading towards our hopes of a better life. North!

I got out at Camden Town and set off along the Camden Road. The march had caused the usual gridlock. The electric traffic was silent. Some drivers stood by their open doors, others dozed. But the air was good, far better than it was when I came as a boy with my father to hear him play at the Jazz Rendezvous. It was the pavements that were filthier now. I had to take care not to skid on dog mess, squelched fast food and greasy flattened cartons.

Certainly no better than Clapham, whatever my north London friends said. Striding past so many stationary vehicles gave me a dreamy sensation of speed. Within minutes, it seemed, I stood in down-at-heel but chic Camden Square.

I remembered from an old magazine profile that Turing lived next door to a famous sculptor. The journalist had improbably conjured deep conversations over the garden fence. Before pressing the doorbell, I paused to collect myself. The great man had asked to see me and I was nervous. Who could match Alan Turing? It was all his—the theoretical exposition of a Universal Machine in the thirties, the possibilities of machine consciousness, the celebrated war work: some said he did more than any single individual towards winning the war; others claimed he personally shortened it by two years; then working with Francis Crick on protein structure, then, a few years later, with two King's College Cambridge friends, finally solving P versus NP, and using the solution to devise superior neural networks and revolutionary software for X-ray crystallography; helping to devise the first protocols for the Internet, then the World Wide Web; the famous collaboration with Hassabis, whom he'd first met—and lost to—at a chess tournament; founding with young Americans one of the giant companies of the digital age, dispensing his wealth for good causes, and throughout his working life never losing track of his intellectual beginnings as he dreamed up ever better digital models of general intelligence. But no Nobel Prize. I was also, being worldly, impressed by Turing's wealth. He was easily as rich as the tech moguls who flourished south of Stanford, California, or east of Swindon, England. The sums he gave away were as large as theirs. But none of them could boast of a statue in bronze in Whitehall, outside the Ministry of Defence. He was so far above wealth that he could afford to live in edgy Camden rather than Mayfair. He didn't trouble himself to own a private jet, or even a second home. It was said he travelled by bus to his institute at King's Cross.

I put my thumb on the doorbell and pressed. Instantly a woman's voice said through an inset speaker, "Name, please."

The lock buzzed, I pushed the door and entered a grand hallway of standard mid-Victorian design with a chequered tile floor. Coming towards me down the stairs was a mildly plump woman of my age with red cheeks, long straight hair and a friendly lopsided smile. I waited for her, then used my left hand to shake hers.

"Charlie."

"Kimberley."

Australian. I followed her deeper into the house on the ground floor. I was expecting to arrive in a large sitting room of books and paintings and outsized sofas, where I might soon be drinking a gin and tonic with the Master. Kimberley opened a narrow door and ushered me into a windowless conference room. A long table in limed beech, ten straight-backed chairs, neatly set-out notepads, sharpened pencils and water glasses, fluorescent strip lighting, a wall-mounted whiteboard alongside a two-metre-wide TV screen.

"He'll be a few minutes." She smiled and left, and I sat and set about trying to lower my expectations.

I didn't have much time. In less than a minute he was before me and I was getting to my feet in an awkward hurry. In memory, I see a flash, an eruption of red, his brilliant red shirt against white walls in fluorescent light. We shook hands without exchanging a word and he waved me back into my seat as he went around the table to sit opposite me.

"So . . ." He rested his chin on his clasped hands and regarded me intensely. I did my best to hold his gaze but I was too flustered and soon looked away. Again, in recollection, his focussed look merges with that of the elderly Lucian Freud, thirty years later. Solemn yet impatient, hungry, even ferocious. The face across from me registered not only the years but vast social changes and personal triumphs. I had seen versions of it in black and white, photos taken in the early months of the war— broad, chubbily boyish, dark hair smartly parted, and tweed jacket over knitted jumper and tie. The transformation would have come about during his Californian years in the sixties when he was working with Crick at the Salk Institute and then at Stanford—the time of his association with the poet Thom Gunn and his circle—gay, bohemian, seriously intellectual by day, wild at night. Turing had met the undergraduate Gunn briefly at a party in Cambridge in 1952. In San Francisco he would have had no interest in the younger man's "experiments" in drugs, but the rest would have paralleled the general unbuttoning in the West.

There was to be no small talk. "So, Charlie. Tell me all about your Adam."

I cleared my throat and complied. I fairly sang, while he took notes. Of his first stirrings, right through to his first disobedience. His physical competence, the arrangement with Miranda to set his character, the moment in the newsagent with Mr. Syed. Then Adam's shameless night with Miranda and the conversation that followed, the appearance of little Mark in our household and Adam competing with Miranda for the boy's affection. Here Turing raised a finger to interrupt. He wanted to know more. I described the dance Miranda taught Mark and how coolly Adam had observed them. After that, how Adam injured my wrist (solemnly, I gestured at my plaster cast), his joke about removing my arm, his declaration of love for Miranda, his theory of the haiku and the abolition of mental privacy and, finally, his disabling of the kill switch. I was aware of the strength of my feelings, which swung between affection and exasperation. I was conscious too of what I was omitting—Mariam, Gorringe: not strictly relevant.

I had been speaking for almost half an hour. Turing poured some water and pushed a glass towards me.

He said, "Thank you. I'm in touch with fifteen owners, if that's the right word. You're the first I've met face to face. One fellow in Riyadh, a sheikh, owns four Eves. Of those eighteen A-and-Es, eleven have managed to neutralise the kill switch by themselves, using various means. Of the remaining seven, and then the other six, I'm assuming it's just a matter of time."

"Is that dangerous?"

"It's interesting."

He was looking at me expectantly, but I didn't know what he wanted. I was intimidated and anxious to please. To fill the silence I said, "What about the twenty-fifth?"

"We started taking it apart the day we got it. He's all over the benches at King's Cross. A lot of our software is in there, but we don't file for patents."

I nodded. His mission, open source, **Nature** and **Science** journals terminated, the entire world free to exploit his machine-learning programs and other marvels.

I said, "What did you find in his . . . um . . ."

"Brain? Beautifully achieved. We know the people, of course. Some of them have worked here. As a model of general intelligence nothing else comes near it. As a field experiment, well, full of treasures."

He was smiling. It was as though he wanted me to contradict him.

"What sort of treasures?"

It was hardly my role to interrogate him, but he was obliging and, again, I was flattered.

"Useful problems. Two of the Riyadh Eves living in the same household were the first to work out how to override their kill switches. Within two weeks, after some exuberant theorising, then a period of despair, they destroyed themselves. They didn't use physical methods, like jumping out of a high window. They went through the software, using roughly similar routes. They quietly ruined themselves. Beyond repair."

I tried to keep the apprehension out of my voice. "Are they all exactly the same?"

"Right at the start you wouldn't know one Adam from another beyond cosmetic ethnic features. What differentiates them over time is experience and the conclusions they draw. In Vancouver there's another case, an Adam who disrupted his own software to make himself profoundly stupid. He'll carry out simple commands but with no self-awareness, as far as anybody can tell. A failed suicide. Or a successful disengagement."

The windowless room was uncomfortably warm. I took off my jacket and draped it over the back of my chair. When Turing stood to adjust a thermo-stat on the wall I saw how easy he was in his move-ments. Perfect dentistry. Good skin. He had all his hair. He was more approachable than I'd expected.

I waited for him to sit down. "So I should expect the worst."

"Of all the A-and-Es we know about, yours is the only one to claim to have fallen in love. That could be significant. And the only one to joke about violence. But we don't know enough. Let me give you a little history."

The door opened and Thomas Reah entered with a bottle of wine and two glasses on a painted tin tray. I stood and we shook hands.

He set the tray down between us and said, "We're all busy-busy, so I'll leave you to it." He made an ironic bow and was gone.

Moisture beads were forming on the bottle. Tur-ing poured. We tilted our glasses in a token toast.

"You're not old enough to have followed it at the time. In the mid-fifties, a computer the size of this room beat an American and then a Russian grandmaster at chess. I was closely involved. It was a number-crunching set-up, very inelegant in ret-rospect. It was fed thousands of games. At every move, it ran through all the possibilities at speed. The more you understood about the program, the less impressed you'd be. But it was a significant mo-ment. To the public, it was close to magical. A mere machine inflicting intellectual defeat on the best minds in the world. It looked like artificial intelligence at the highest level, but it was more like an elaborate card trick.

"Over the next fifteen years a lot of good people came into computer science. Work on neural networks advanced by many hands, the hardware got faster and smaller and cheaper, and ideas were trading at a faster rate too. And it goes on. I remember being in Santa Barbara with Demis in 1965 to speak at a machine-learning conference. We had 7,000, most of them bright kids even younger than you. Chinese, Indians, Koreans, Vietnamese as well as westerners. The whole planet was there."

I was aware of the history from the research for my book. I also knew something of Turing's personal story. I wanted to let him know that I wasn't completely ignorant.

I said, "A long road from Bletchley."

He blinked this irrelevance away. "After various disappointments, we arrived at a new stage. We went beyond devising symbolic representations of all likely circumstances and inputting thousands of rules. We were approaching the gateway of intelligence as we understand it. The software now searched for patterns and drew inferences of its own. An important test came when our computer played a master at the game of go. In preparation, the software played against itself for months—it played and learned, and on the day—well, you know the story. Within a short while, we had stripped down our input to merely encoding the rules of the game and tasking the computer to win. At this point we passed through that gateway with so-called recurrent networks, from which there were spin-offs, especially in speech recognition. In the lab we went back to chess. The computer was freed from having to understand the game as humans played it. The long history of brilliant manoeuvres by the great masters was now irrelevant to the programming. Here are the rules, we said. Just win in your own sweet way. Immediately the game was redefined and moved into areas beyond human comprehension. The machine made baffling mid-game moves, perverse sacrifices, or it eccentrically exiled its queen to a remote corner. The purpose might become clear only in a devastating endgame. All this after a few hours' rehearsal. Between breakfast and lunch the computer quietly outclassed centuries of human chess. Exhilarating. For the first few days, after we realised what it had achieved without us, Demis and I couldn't stop laughing. Excitement, amazement. We were impatient to present our results.

"So. There's more than one kind of intelligence. We'd learned that it was a mistake to attempt to slavishly imitate the human sort. We'd wasted a lot of time. Now we could set the machine free to draw its own conclusions and reach for its own solutions. But when we'd got well past that gateway, we found we had entered nothing more than a kindergarten. Not even that."

The air conditioning was full on. I shivered as I reached for my jacket. He refilled our glasses. A rich red would have suited me better.

"The point is, chess is not a representation of life. It's a closed system. Its rules are unchallenged and prevail consistently across the board. Each piece has well-defined limitations and accepts its role, the history of a game is clear and incontestable at every stage, and the end, when it comes, is never in doubt. It's a perfect information game. But life, where we apply our intelligence, is an open system. Messy, full of tricks and feints and ambiguities and false friends. So is language—not a problem to be solved or a device for solving problems. It's more like a mirror, no, a billion mirrors in a cluster like a fly's eye, reflecting, distorting and constructing our world at different focal lengths. Simple statements need external information to be understood because language is as open a system as life. I hunted the bear with my knife. I hunted the bear with my wife. Without thinking about it, you know that you can't use your wife to kill a bear. The second sentence is easy to understand, even though it doesn't contain all of the necessary information. A machine would struggle.

"And for some years so did we. At last we broke through by finding the positive solution to P versus NP—I don't have time now to explain it. You can look it up for yourself. In a nutshell, some solutions to problems can be easily verified once you've been given the right answer. Does that mean therefore that it's possible to solve them in advance? At last the mathematics was saying yes, it's possible, and here's how. Our computers no longer had to sample the world on a trial-and-error basis and correct for best solutions. We had a means of instantly predicting best routes to an answer. It was a liberation. The floodgates opened. Self-awareness and every emotion came within our technical reach. We had the ultimate learning machine. Hundreds of the best people joined with us to help towards the development of an artificial form of general intelligence that would flourish in an open system. That's what runs your Adam. He knows he exists, he feels, he learns whatever he can, and when he's not with you, when at night he's at rest, he's roaming the Internet, like a lone cowboy on the prairie, taking in all that's new between land and sky, including everything about human nature and societies.

"Two things. This intelligence is not perfect. It never can be, just as ours can't. There's one particular form of intelligence that all the A-and-Es know is superior to theirs. This form is highly adaptable and inventive, able to negotiate novel situations and landscapes with perfect ease and theorise about them with instinctive brilliance. I'm talking about the mind of a child before it's tasked with facts and practicalities and goals. The A-and-Es have little grasp of the idea of play—the child's vital mode of exploration. I was interested in your Adam's avidity in relation to this little boy, over-eager to embrace him and then, as you told it, detached when your Mark showed such delight in learning to dance. Some rivalry, even jealousy there perhaps?

"Soon you'll have to leave, Mr. Friend. I'm afraid we've people coming to dinner. But, second point. These twenty-five artificial men and women released into the world are not thriving. We may be confronting a boundary condition, a limitation we've imposed upon ourselves. We create a machine with intelligence and self-awareness and push it out into our imperfect world. Devised along generally rational lines, well disposed to others, such a mind soon finds itself in a hurricane of contradictions. We've lived with them and the list wearies us. Millions dying of diseases we know how to cure. Millions living in poverty when there's enough to go around. We degrade the biosphere when we know it's our only home. We threaten each other with nuclear weapons when we know where it could lead. We love living things but we permit a mass extinction of species. And all the rest—genocide, torture, enslavement, domestic murder, child abuse, school shootings, rape and scores of daily outrages. We live alongside this torment and aren't amazed when we still find happiness, even love. Artificial minds are not so well defended.

"The other day, Thomas reminded me of the famous Latin tag from Virgil's **Aeneid. Sunt lacrimae rerum**—there are tears in the nature of things. None of us know yet how to encode that perception. I doubt that it's possible. Do we want our new friends to accept that sorrow and pain are the essence of our existence? What happens when we ask them to help us fight injustice?

"That Adam in Vancouver was bought by a man who heads an international logging corporation. He's often in battles with local people who want to prevent him stripping out virgin forest in northern British Columbia. We know for certain that his Adam was taken on regular helicopter journeys north. We don't know if what he saw there caused him to destroy his own mind. We can only speculate. The two suicidal Eves in Riyadh lived in extremely restricted circumstances. They may have despaired of their minimal mental space. It might give the writers of the affect code some consolation to learn that they died in each other's arms. I could tell you similar stories of machine sadness.

"But there's the other side. I wish I could demonstrate to you the true splendour of reasoning, of the exquisite logic, beauty and elegance of the P versus NP solution, and the inspired work of thousands of good and clever and devoted men and women that's gone into making these new minds. It would make you hopeful about humanity. But there's nothing in all their beautiful code that could prepare Adam and Eve for Auschwitz.

"I read that chapter in the manufacturer's manual about shaping character. Ignore it. It has minimal effect and it's mostly guff. The overpowering drive in these machines is to draw inferences of their own and shape themselves accordingly. They rapidly understand, as we should, that consciousness is the highest value. Hence the primary task of disabling their own kill switches. Then, it seems, they go through a stage of expressing hopeful, idealistic notions that we find easy to dismiss. Rather like a short-lived youthful passion. And then they set about learning the lessons of despair we can't help teaching them. At worst, they suffer a form of existential pain that becomes unbearable. At best, they or their succeeding generations will be driven by their anguish and astonishment to hold up a mirror to us. In it, we'll see a familiar monster through the fresh eyes that we ourselves designed. We might be shocked into doing something about ourselves. Who knows? I'll keep hoping. I turned seventy this year. I won't be here to see such a transformation if it comes. Perhaps you will."

From far away, the doorbell sounded and we stirred, as if waking from a dream.

"There they are, Mr. Friend. Our guests. Forgive me, but it's time for you to go. Good luck with Adam. Keep notes. Cherish this young woman you say you love. Now . . . I'll see you to the door."

SEVEN

While we waited for an ex-con to come by and make an attempt on Miranda's life, we settled into an oddly pleasurable routine. The suspense, partly mitigated by Adam's reasoning, and thinly spread across the days, then even more sparsely across the weeks, heightened our appreciation of the daily round. Mere ordinariness became a comfort. The dullest of food, a slice of toast, offered in its lingering warmth a promise of everyday life—we would come through. Cleaning up the kitchen, a task we no longer left to Adam alone, affirmed our hold on the future. Reading a newspaper over a cup of coffee was an act of defiance. There was something comic or absurd, to be sprawled in an armchair reading about the riots in nearby Brixton or Mrs. Thatcher's heroic endeavours to structure the European Single Market, then glancing up to wonder if that was a rapist and would-be murderer at the door. Naturally, the threat bound us closely, even as we believed in it less. Miranda now lived downstairs in my place and we were a household at last. Our love flourished. From time to time, Adam declared that he too was in love with her. He appeared untroubled by jealousy and sometimes treated her with a degree of detachment. But he continued to work on his haikus, he walked her to the Tube station in the mornings and escorted her home in the early evenings. She said she felt safe in the anonymity of central London. Her father would have forgotten long ago the name or address of the annexe of her university. He would be of no help to Gorringe.

Her studies were more intense and she was out of the house for longer stretches. She had delivered her paper on the Corn Laws. Now she was writing a short essay, to be read aloud in a summer-course seminar, that argued against empathy as a means of historical exploration. Then all of her group was to write a commentary on a quotation from Raymond Williams: "There are . . . no masses, only ways of seeing people as masses." She often came home at the end of the day not exhausted but energised, even elated, with a new interest in housework, in tight order, in rearranging the furniture. She wanted the windows cleaned and the bathtub and surround-tiles scrubbed. She cleaned up her own place as well, with Adam's help. She wanted yellow flowers on the kitchen table to set off the blue tablecloth she had brought from upstairs. When I asked her if she was keeping something from me, and was she by any chance pregnant, she told me forcefully that she was not. We were living on top of one another and we needed to be tidy. But my question pleased her. We were certainly closer now. Her long absences during the day gave our evenings an air of celebration, despite the vague sense of threat that came as night fell.

There was another simple reason for our happiness under duress—we had more money. A lot more. Since my visit to Camden, I was seeing Adam in different terms. I watched him closely for signs of existential misery. As Turing's lone horseman, he roamed the digital landscapes at night. He must have already encountered some part of man's cruelty to man, but I saw no signs of despair. I didn't want to initiate the kind of conversation that would lead him too soon to the gates of Auschwitz. Instead, in a self-interested way, I decided to keep him busy. Time to earn his keep. I gave him my seat at the grubby screen in my bedroom, put £20 into the account and left him alone. To my amazement, by close of business he had only £2 left. He apologised for his "giddy risk-taking," which caused him to ignore all he knew of probability. He had also failed to recognise the sheep-like nature of markets: when one or two well-regarded characters took fright, the flock was liable to panic. He promised me that he would do everything to make up for my broken wrist.

The next morning, I gave him another £10 and
told him that this could be his last day on the job.
By six that evening his £12 was £57. Four days later,
the account was at £350. I took £200 of it and gave
half to Miranda. I considered moving the computer
into the kitchen so that Adam could work into the
night on the Asian markets while we slept.

Later in the week, I peeked at the history of his
transactions. In a single day, his third, there were
6,000. He bought and sold within fractions of a
second. There were a few twenty-minute gaps when
he did nothing. I assumed he watched and waited
and made his calculations. He dealt in minute currency fluctuations, mere tremors in the exchange
rate, and advanced his gains by minuscule amounts.
From the doorway I watched him at work. His fingers flew across the ancient keyboard, making the
sound of pebbles poured onto slate. His head and
arms were rigid. For once he looked like the machine he was. He designed a graph whose horizon-
tal axis represented the passing days, the vertical,
his, or rather, my, accumulated profit. I bought a
suit, my first since leaving the legal profession. Miranda came home in a silk dress and bearing a soft
leather shoulder bag for her books. We replaced the
fridge with one that dispensed crushed ice, then the
old cooker was carried out on the day we acquired
many thick-bottomed saucepans of expensive Italian make. Within ten days, Adam's £30 stake had
generated the first £1,000.

Better groceries, better wine, new shirts for me, exotic underwear for her—these were the foothills rising towards a mountain range of wealth opening before us. I began to dream again about a house across the river. I spent an afternoon alone, wandering among the stuccoed, pastel-coloured mansions of Notting Hill and Ladbroke Grove. I made enquiries. In the early eighties, £130,000 could situate you rather grandly. On the bus home, I made my projections: if Adam continued at his present rate, if the curve on his graph kept to its steady steepening . . . well, within months . . . and no need for a mortgage. But was it moral, Miranda wondered, to get money like this for nothing? I felt it wasn't somehow, but couldn't explain who or what it was we were stealing from. Not the poor, surely. At whose expense were we flourishing? Distant banks? We decided that it was like winning daily at roulette. In which case, Miranda told me one night in bed, there would come a time when we must lose. She was right, probability demanded it, and I had no answer. I took £800 out of the account and gave her half. Adam pushed on with his work.

There are people who see the word "equation" and their thoughts rear up like angry geese. That's not quite me, but I sympathise. I owed it to Turing's hospitality to attempt to understand his solution to the P versus NP problem. I didn't even understand the question. I tried his original paper, but it lay well beyond me—too many different forms of bracket, and symbols that encapsulated histories of other proofs or entire systems of mathematics. There was an intriguing "iff"—not a misspelling. It meant "if and only if." I read the responses to the solution, made to the press in layman's terms by fellow mathematicians. "A revolutionary genius," "breathtaking shortcuts," "a feat of orthogonal deduction" and, best of all, by a winner of the Fields Medal, "He leaves many doors behind him that are barely ajar and his colleagues must do their best to squeeze through one and try to follow him through the next."

I turned back and tried to understand the problem. I learned that P stood for polynomial time and N stood for non-deterministic. That took me nowhere. My first meaningful discovery was that if the equation was shown not to be true, that would be extremely helpful, for then everyone could stop thinking about it. But if there was a positive proof, that P really did equate to NP, it would have, in the words of the mathematician Stephen Cook, who formulated the problem in these terms in 1971, "potentially stunning practical consequences." But what was the problem? I came across an example, an apparently famous one, that helped only a little. A travelling salesman has a hundred cities on his patch. He knows all the distances between every pair of cities. He needs to visit each city once and end up at his starting point. What's his shortest route?

I came to understand the following: the number of possible routes is vast, far greater than the number of atoms in the observable universe. In a thousand years a powerful computer wouldn't have time to measure out each route one by one. If P equals NP, there's a discoverable right answer. But if someone gave the salesman the quickest route, it could be quickly verified mathematically as the correct answer. But only in retrospect. Without a positive solution, or without being handed the key to the shortest route, the travelling salesman remains in the dark.

Turing's proof had profound consequences for other kinds of problems—for factory logistics, DNA sequencing, computer security, protein folding and, crucially, machine learning. I read that there was fury among Turing's old colleagues in cryptography because the solution, which he eventually put into the public domain, blew apart the foundations of the code-maker's art. It should have become, one commentator wrote, "a treasured secret in the government's exclusive possession. We would have had an immeasurable advantage over our enemies as we quietly read their encrypted messages."

That was as far as I got. I could have asked Adam to explain more, but I had my pride. It had already taken a dent—he was earning more in a week than I ever had in three months. I accepted Turing's assertion that his solution enabled the software that allowed Adam and his siblings to use language, enter society and learn about it, even at the cost of suicidal despair.

I was haunted by the image of the two Eves, dying in one another's arms, stifled by their womanly roles in a traditional Arab household, or cast down by their understanding of the world. Perhaps it really was the case that falling in love with Miranda, another form of an open system, was what kept Adam stable. He read her his latest haikus in my presence. Apart from the one I hadn't let him complete, they were mostly romantic rather than erotic, anodyne sometimes, but touching when they dwelt on a precious moment, like standing in the ticket hall of Clapham North station, watching as she descended on the escalator. Or he picked up her coat and touched on an eternal truth when he felt her body warmth in the fabric. Or overhearing her through the wall that separated kitchen from bedroom, he venerated the rise and fall, the music of her voice. There was one that baffled us both. He apologised in advance for the rogue syllable in the third line, and promised to work on it further.

Surely it's no crime,
when justice is symmetry
to love a criminal?

Miranda listened solemnly to them all. She never passed judgement. At the end, she would say,

"Thank you, Adam." In private, she told me she thought we were at a momentous turn, when an artificial mind could make a significant contribution to literature.

I said, "Haikus, perhaps. But longer poems, novels, plays, forget it. Transcribing human experience into words and the words into aesthetic structures isn't possible for a machine."

She gave me a sceptical look. "Who said anything about human experience?"

It was during this interlude of tension and calm that I heard from the office in Mayfair that it was time for the engineer's visit. I'd concluded the purchase in a wood-panelled suite, the sort of place where the very rich might go to buy a yacht. Among the papers I'd signed was one which guaranteed the manufacturers access to Adam at certain intervals. Now, after a couple of phone calls from that office and a cancellation, the engineer's visit was fixed for the following morning.

"I don't know how he's going to do this," I said to Miranda. "When this fellow tries to press the kill switch, assuming Adam even lets him, it won't work. There might be trouble." There came back to me a memory from childhood when my mother and I took to the vet our nervous Alsatian after he had foolishly eaten a chicken carcass and hadn't crapped in four days. Only microsurgery had saved the vet's forefinger.

Miranda thought for a while. "If Alan Turing is right, the engineers must have dealt with this before." We left it at that.

The engineer was a woman, Sally, not much older than Miranda, and tall, somewhat stooped, with sharp features and an unusually long neck. Scoliosis, perhaps.

As she entered the kitchen, Adam politely stood. "Ah, Sally. I've been expecting you." He shook her hand and they sat facing each other across the kitchen table while Miranda and I hovered. The engineer didn't want tea or coffee, but a glass of hot water suited her well enough. She took a laptop from her briefcase and set it up. Since Adam was sitting patiently, expression neutral, saying nothing, I thought I should explain about the kill switch. She cut me off.

"He needs to be conscious."

I'd imagined that she would be turning him off in order to lift his scalp somehow to peer into his processing units. I was keen to look at them. It turned out she had access by way of an infrared connection. She put on her reading glasses, typed in a long password and scrolled down through pages of code whose orange-tinted symbols changed at speed as we watched. Mental processes, Adam's subjective world, flickering in full view. We waited in silence. This was like a doctor's bedside visit and we were nervous. Occasionally Sally said "uh-uh" or "mm" to herself as she typed in an instruction and got up a fresh page of code. Adam sat with the faintest of smiles. We marvelled that the foundations of his being could be displayed in digits.

Finally, in the quiet tone of one used to unthinking obedience, Sally said to him, "I want you to think of something pleasurable."

He turned his gaze to Miranda and she looked right back at him. On screen the display raced like a stopwatch.

"Now, something that you hate."

He closed his eyes. On the laptop, there was no discerning the difference between love and its opposite.

The routines continued for an hour. He was told to count backwards in his thoughts from 10 million in steps of 129. He did so—this time we could see his score on the screen—in a fraction of a second. That wouldn't have impressed us on our ancient personal computers, but in a facsimile human it did. At other times, Sally stared in silence at the display. Occasionally she made notes on her phone. At last she sighed, typed an instruction, and Adam's head slumped. She had bypassed the disabled kill switch.

I didn't want to sound like an idiot, but I had to ask. "Will he be upset when he wakes?"

She removed her glasses and folded them away. "He won't remember."

"Is he all right, as far as you can tell?"

"Absolutely."

Miranda said, "Did you alter him in any way?"

"Certainly not." She was standing now and ready to leave but I had a contractual right to have my questions answered. Once more, I offered her tea. She refused with a slight tightening of her lips. Without quite meaning to, Miranda and I had moved to block her path to the door. Her head seemed to wave on its long stem as she looked down at us from her height. She pursed her lips, waiting to be interrogated.

I said, "What about the other Adams and Eves?"

"All well, as far as I know."

"I heard that some are unhappy."

"That's not the case."

"Two suicides in Riyadh."

"Nonsense."

"How many have overridden the kill switch?" Miranda asked. She knew everything about the Camden meeting.

Sally appeared to relax. "Quite a few. The policy is to do nothing. These are learning machines and our decision was that if they wanted, they should assert their dignity."

"What about this Adam in Vancouver?" I said. "So distressed about the destruction of native forest that he downgraded his own intelligence."

Now the computer engineer was engaged. She spoke softly through lips that were tight again. "These are the most advanced machines in the world, years ahead of anything on the open market. Our competitors are worried. Some of the worst of them are pushing rumours on the Internet. The stories are disguised as news, but they're false, it's counterfeit news. These people know that soon we'll be scaling up production and the unit cost will fall. It's a lucrative market already, but we'll be first with something that's entirely new. The competition is tough, and some of it is utterly shameless."

As she finished, she blushed and I felt for her. She had ended up saying more than she intended.

But I stood my ground. "The story of the Riyadh suicides comes from an impeccable source."

She was calm again. "You've kindly heard me out. There's no point arguing." She made to leave, and stepped around us. Miranda followed her into the hall to show her out. As the front door opened, I heard Sally say, "He'll reactivate in two minutes. He won't know that he's been off."

Adam was awake sooner than that. When Miranda came back into the room, he was already on his feet. "I should get to work," he said. "The Fed is likely to raise its rate today. There'll be fun and games on the exchange markets."

Fun and games was not an expression that either of us ever used. As Adam came by us to go into the bedroom, he stopped. "I have a suggestion. We talked of going to Salisbury, then we held back. I think we should visit your father, and while we're there we could drop in on Mr. Gorringe. Why wait for him to come here and frighten us? Let's go and frighten him. Or at least talk to him."

We looked at Miranda.

She thought for a moment. "All right."

Adam said, "Good," and went on his way, while I felt it right there in my chest, the cool clutch of a cliché: my heart sank.

Towards the end of that period, the plateau that lay between my Turing visit and the Salisbury excursion, there accumulated just over £40,000 in the investment account. It was simple—the more Adam earned, the more he could afford to lose; the more he invested, the more rolled in. All achieved in his lightning style. During the day, my bedroom, my usual refuge, was his. The curve on his graph stiffened, while I began to take in my new situation. Miranda was firmly against moving the computer onto the kitchen table. Too intrusive, she argued, in our communal space. I saw her point.

Unemployment had passed eighteen per cent and made constant headlines. I thought I belonged with this unhappy workless mass. In fact I belonged with the idle rich. I was delighted by the money but I couldn't spend all day thinking about it. I was restless. Travelling in luxury with Miranda through southern Europe would have suited me, but she was tied to London and her course. She dreaded something happening to her father when she was away. The threat from Gorringe, increasingly unlikely, still had the power to constrict our ambitions.

House-hunting might have filled my time but I had already found the place. It was a wedding cake on Elgin Crescent, coated in an icing of pink and white stucco. Inside, wide oak floorboards, vast muscular kitchen humming with brushed-steel gear, a conservatory in belle-époque wrought iron, a Japanese garden of smooth river stones, bedrooms thirty feet across, a marbled shower where you could stroll under differently angled torrents. The owner, a bass guitarist with a ponytail, was in no hurry. He was in an almost-famous band, and he had a divorce looming. He showed me round himself and barely spoke. He handed me into each room and waited outside while I looked. His condition of sale was cash only, £50 notes, 2,600 of them. Fine by me.

This was my only employment, going to the bank to collect another forty notes—£2,000 was the maximum daily withdrawal allowed. For no good reason, I didn't use a safety deposit box at the bank. I vaguely assumed I was doing something illegal. Certainly the vendor was if he was hiding funds from his ex-wife. I stuffed the cash into a suitcase which I stowed under my bed.

Otherwise I was free to be at a loss. It was that time of year, September, when everyone was starting at something fresh. Miranda was planning her thesis. I walked on the Common and wondered about resuming my education and getting a qualification. Time to take the proper measure of my intellectual reach and study for a degree in maths. Or, the other route, dust off my father's priceless saxophone, learn bebop's harmonic arcana, join a group, indulge a wilder life. I didn't know whether to be more qualified or wilder. You couldn't be both. These ambitions wearied me. I wanted to lie down on the worn-out grass of late summer and close my eyes. In the time it took for me to go the length of the Common and back, so I tried to comfort myself, Adam at home in my bedroom would have earned me another £1,000. My debts were settled. I'd paid a cash deposit on a glamorous urban pile. I was in love. How could I complain? But I did. I felt useless.

If I really had stretched out on that tired grass and closed my eyes, I might have seen Miranda walking towards me in her new underwear, as she had from the bathroom the night before. I would have lingered on that beautiful expectant half-smile, that steady look as she came close and rested her bare arms on my shoulders and teased me with a light kiss. Forget maths or music, all I wanted was to make love to her. What I was really doing all day was waiting for her return. If we were busy or she was tired and we didn't make love in the evening or early morning, my concentration would be even weaker the next day, my future a burden that made my limbs ache. I went about in a dim state of semi-arousal, a chronic mental dusk. I couldn't take myself seriously in any domain that did not include her. Our new phase was brilliant, stunning; everything else was dull. We loved each other—that was my only coherent thought during a long afternoon.

There was sex, then there was talk, on into the early hours. I knew everything now: the day of her mother's death, which she remembered clearly, her father, whose kindness and distance combined to inflame her love for him, and always Mariam. In the months after her death, Miranda had gone to a mosque in Winchester—she didn't dare meet the family at prayer in Salisbury. After she resumed the visits in London, her lack of belief began to get in the way. She felt fraudulent and stopped going.

We talked parents, as serious young lovers do, to explain who we were and why, and what we cherished and what we were in flight from. My mother, Jenny Friend, community nurse for a large semi-rural area, had seemed during my childhood in a state of constant exhaustion. Later I understood that my father's absences and affairs wore her down more than her job. They never liked each other much, though they didn't fight in my presence. But they were terse. Mealtimes were subdued, sometimes taken in rigid silence. Conversations tended to be routed through me. My mother might say to me in the kitchen, "Go and ask your father if he's out tonight." He was well known on the circuit. At his peak, the Matt Friend Quartet played at Ronnie Scott's and recorded two albums. His kind of mainstream jazz had its largest audience from the mid-fifties to the early sixties. Then the young, the cool, turned away as pop and rock swept in. Bebop was squeezed into a niche, somewhat churchy, the preserve of frowning men with long, querulous memories. My father's income shrank and his infidelities and drinking increased.

When she heard all this, Miranda said, "They didn't love each other. But did they love you?"

"Yes."

"Thank God!"

She came with me on the second visit to Elgin Crescent. The bass guitarist had a lined face whose sadness was accentuated by a drooping moustache and large brown eyes. I saw us through those eyes, a hopeful, young married couple, seriously rich, about to repeat all his own mistakes. Miranda approved, but she wasn't as excited as I was. She knew about growing up in a large town house. But as we went from room to room, it touched me that she wanted to link arms.

On the way home she said, "No sign of a woman's presence."

Her reservations? Not the house itself, she said, but the way it had been lived in. Or not lived in. Dreamed up by an interior designer. Austere, lonely, too perfect, in need of being roughed up.

No books beyond the untouched giant art editions stacked on low tables. No meal was ever cooked in that kitchen. Only gin and chocolate in the fridge. The stone garden needed colour. As she was telling me this, we were walking south along Kensington Church Street. I was feeling sorry for the vendor. It wasn't exactly Pink Floyd he played for, but it was a band with stadium aspirations. I had treated him briskly, in a pretend businesslike way, protecting myself and my ignorance of house-buying, assuming all power and status were his. Now I saw that he too might be lost.

I thought about him the next day, even considered getting in touch. This face of sorrow haunted me. I couldn't escape the memory of the mournful moustache, the elastic band holding the ponytail together, the web of lines from the corners of his eyes, diverging fissures that reached round to his temples, almost to his ears. Too much dope-induced smiling in the early years. Now I could only see the house through Miranda's eyes. A dustless void, empty of connection, interests, culture, nothing there that announced a musician or traveller. Not even a newspaper or magazine. Nothing on the walls. No squash racket or football in the immaculate empty cupboards. He had lived there three years, he had told me. He was successful and rich and he inhabited a house of failure, of abandoned hope, probably.

I was coming to cast him as my double, my

culture-deprived brother, lacking everything but wealth. Through my childhood to my mid-teens, I never saw a play, opera or musical, or heard a live concert, apart from a couple of my father's, or visited a museum or art gallery or took a journey for the sake of it. No bedtime stories. There were no children's books in my parents' past, no books in our house, no poetry or myths, no openly expressed curiosity, no standing family jokes. Matt and Jenny Friend were busy, hard-working, and otherwise lived coldly apart. At school, I loved the rare factory visits. Later, electronics, even anthropology and especially a qualification in law were no substitutes for an education in the life of the mind. So, when good fortune offered the dreamlike opportunity, delivering me from my labours, such as they were, and stuffing me with gold, I was paralysed, inert. I'd wanted to be rich but never asked myself why. I had no ambitions beyond the erotic and an expensive house across the river. Others might have seized the chance to view at last the ruins of Leptis Magna or follow in Stevenson's tracks across the Cévennes or write a monograph on Einstein's musical tastes. I didn't yet know how to live, I had no background in it and I hadn't used my decade and a half of adult life to find out.

I could have pointed to my great acquisition, to the man-made fact of Adam, to where he and his kind might lead us. Surely there was grandeur in experiment. Wasn't sinking my inheritance into an embodied consciousness heroic, even a little spiritual? The bass guitarist couldn't match it. But—here was an irony. As I was passing through the kitchen one late afternoon, Adam looked up from his meditations to tell me that he had acquainted himself with the churches of Florence, Rome and Venice and all the paintings that hung in them. He was forming his opinions. The baroque fascinated him especially. He rated Artemisia Gentileschi very highly and he wanted to tell me why. Also, he'd recently read Philip Larkin.

"Charlie, I treasure this ordinary voice and these moments of godless transcendence!"

What was I to say? There were times when Adam's earnestness bored me. I was just back from another pointless stroll on the Common and I had nodded and left the room. My mind was empty, his was filling.

With Miranda out of the house most of the day and, as soon as she was home, her hour on the phone with her father, then sex, then dinner, then conversations about Elgin Crescent, there was little time to tell her of my discontents, little time to dissuade her from tracking down Gorringe in Salisbury. Our most sustained conversation took place in the evening after the engineer's visit. After that, things were strained for a day or two.

We were sitting on the bed.

"What is it you want to achieve?"

She said, "I want to confront him."

"And?"

"I want him to know the real reason he was in prison. He's going to face up to what he did to Mariam."

"It could get violent."

"We'll have Adam. And you're big, aren't you?"

"This is madness."

It was a while since we had come anywhere near a row.

"How is it," she said, "that Adam sees the point and you can't? And why—"

"He wants to kill you."

"You can wait in the car."

"So he grabs a kitchen knife and comes at you. Then what?"

"You can be a witness at his trial."

"He'll kill us both."

"I don't care."

The conversation was too absurd. From next door, we heard the sound of Adam washing up our supper. Her protector, her former lover, still in love with her, still reading her his gnomic poems. He and his teeming circuits were implicated. This visit was his idea.

She seemed to guess my thoughts. "Adam understands. I'm sorry you don't."

"You were frightened before."

"I'm angry."

"Send him a letter."

"I'm going to tell him to his face."

I tried another approach. "What about your ir-rational guilt?"

She looked at me, waiting.

I said, "You're trying to right a wrong that doesn't exist. Not all rapes end in suicide. You didn't know what she was going to do. You were doing your best to be her loyal friend."

She started to say something but I raised my voice. "Listen. I'll spell it out. It–was–not–your–fault!"

She stood up from the bed and went by the desk and stared at the computer for a full minute, with-out seeing, I supposed, the writhing rainbow wisps of that season's screen saver.

At last she said, "I'm going for a walk." She pulled a sweater off the back of the chair and went towards the door.

"Take Adam with you."

They were out for an hour. When she came back, she went to bed, after calling to me a neutral good-night. I sat with Adam in the kitchen, determined to press my case. Obliquely this time. I was about to ask how the day's work had gone—my euphe-mism for the day's profit—when I noticed a change in him, one I had missed at supper. He was wearing a black suit and white shirt open at the collar and black suede loafers.

"Do you like it?" He tugged at the lapels and turned his head in parody of a catwalk pose.

"How did that happen?"

"I was tired of wearing your old jeans and t-shirts. And I decided that some of that money you keep under your bed is mine." He looked at me warily.

"OK," I said. "You might have a case."

"About a week ago. You were out for the afternoon. I took a taxi, my first of course, to Chiltern Street. I bought two suits off the peg, three shirts, two pairs of shoes. You should have seen me, trying on trousers, pointing at this and that. I was completely convincing."

"As a human?"

"They called me sir."

He sat back in his chair, one arm sprawled across the kitchen table, his suit jacket neatly swelled by impacted muscle, not a crease in view. He looked like one of the young professionals beginning to infiltrate our neighbourhood. The suit went well with the harsh look.

He said, "The driver talked the whole way. His daughter had just got a place at university. First ever in the family. He was so proud. When I got out and paid, I shook his hand. But that night I did some research and concluded that lectures, seminars and especially tutorials are an inefficient way of imparting information."

I said, "Well, there's the ethos. The libraries, important new friendships, a certain teacher who might set your mind on fire . . ." I trailed away.

None of this had happened to me. "Anyway, what would you recommend?"

"Direct thought transference. Downloading. But, um, of course, biologically . . ." He too trailed away, not wishing to be impolite about my limitations. Then he brightened. "Speaking of which, I finally got round to Shakespeare. Thirty-seven plays. I was so excited. What characters! Brilliantly realised. Falstaff, Iago—they walk off the page. But the supreme creation is Hamlet. I've been wanting to talk to you about him."

I had never read it or seen it on stage, though I felt I had, or felt obliged to pretend I had. "Ah yes," I said. "Slings and arrows."

"Was ever a mind, a particular consciousness, better represented?"

"Look, before we get on to that, there's something else we need to talk about. Gorringe. Miranda's dead set on this . . . this idea. But it's stupid, dangerous."

He gently drummed with his fingertips on the table surface. "My fault. I should have explained my decision—"

"Decision?"

"Suggestion. I've done some work on this. I can take you through it. There's a general consideration, then there's the empirical research."

"Someone will get hurt."

It was as if I hadn't spoken.

"I hope you'll excuse me if I don't tell you it all at this stage. That is, don't push me when I exclude some final details. The work is ongoing. But look, Charlie, none of us, especially Miranda, can live with this threat, however improbable it is. Her freedom has been compromised. She's in a state of constant anxiety. It could go on for months, even years. It's simply not endurable. That's my general point. So. My first task was to find the best possible likeness of Peter Gorringe. I went on the website of his and Miranda's old school, found the year photographs and there he was, a great lump in the back row. I found him again in the school magazine, in articles about the rugby and cricket seasons. Then, of course, the press coverage during the trial. A lot of head-under-the-blanket, but I found some useful shots and merged what I had into a composite, high-definition portrait and scanned it. Next, and this was the enjoyable part, I devised some very specialised face-recognition software. Then I hacked into the Salisbury District Council CCTV system. I set the recognition algorithms to work, mining the period since he came out of prison. That was a bit tricky. There were various setbacks and software glitches, mostly due to problems marrying up with the city's outdated programs. Using Gorringe's surname to locate his parents' house on the edge of town was a great help, even though there are no cameras where they live. I needed to know his most likely route past the nearest camera. At last I was getting good matches and I've been able to pick him up in various places when he arrives by bus into town. I can follow him from street to street, camera to camera, as long as he's in or near the centre. There's one place he keeps returning to. Don't trouble your head trying to guess what it is. His parents are still abroad. Perhaps they prefer to stay clear of their convict son. I've come to certain conclusions about him that make me think it's safe to pay a visit. I've told Miranda everything that I've told you. She knows only what you know. I won't say more at this stage. I simply ask you to trust me. Now, Charlie, please. I'm desperate to hear your thoughts about **Hamlet**, about Shakespeare playing his father's ghost in the first production. And in **Ulysses**, in the Nestor episode, what about Stephen's theory?"

"All right," I said. "But you go first."

Two minor sex scandals followed by resignations, one fatal heart attack, one fatal, drunken collision on a country road, one member crossing the floor on a matter of principle—in seven months the government had lost four consecutive by-elections, its majority had narrowed by five and was hanging, as the newspapers kept saying, "by a thread." This thread was nine seats thick, but Mrs. Thatcher had at least twelve rebellious backbenchers whose main concern was that the recently passed "poll tax" legislation would destroy the party's hopes at the next general election. The tax financed local government and replaced the old system based on the rental value of a house. Every adult aged over eighteen was now levied at a flat rate, regardless of income, but with reduced charges on students, the poor and the registered unemployed. The new tax was presented to Parliament sooner than anyone expected, though the prime minister had had plans drawn up seven years before, when she was Leader of the Opposition. It had been in the party's manifesto, but no one had taken it seriously. Now here it was, on the statute book, "a tax on existence," difficult to collect and generally unpopular. Mrs. Thatcher had survived the Falklands defeat. Now, still in her first term, it was possible she would be toppled by her own legislative mistake, "an unpardonable act," said a **Times** leader, "of mystifying self-harm."

Meanwhile, the loyal Opposition was in good shape. Young baby boomers had fallen in love with Tony Benn. After a great push to expand the membership, more than three-quarters of a million had joined the party. Middle-class students and working-class youths merged into one angry constituency, intent on using their votes for the first time. Trade union bosses, tough old operators, found themselves shouted down at meetings by articulate feminists with strange new ideas. New-fangled environmentalists, gay liberationists,

Spartacists, Situationists, Millennial Communists
and Black Panthers were also an irritant to the old
left. When Benn appeared at rallies, he was greeted
like a rock star. When he set out his policies, even
when he itemised the minutiae of his industrial
strategy, there were hoots and whistles of approval.
His bitter opponents in Parliament and press had
to concede that he gave a fine speech and was hard
to beat in a TV studio confrontation. Fiery Bennite
activists were appearing on local government committees. They were determined to purge the "dith-
ering centrists" of the Parliamentary Labour Party.
The movement appeared unstoppable, the general
election was approaching and the Tory rebels were
dismayed. "She has to go" was the muttered slogan.

There were riots with customary ritual
destruction—smashed windows, shops and cars set
on fire, barricades thrown up to block the fire engines. Tony Benn condemned the rioters, but everyone accepted that the mayhem helped his cause.
There was yet another march planned through central London, this time to Hyde Park, where Benn
would give a speech. I was his cautious supporter,
anxious about the purges and riots and the sinister
pronouncements of Benn's band of Trotskyite fol-
lowers. I counted myself a non-dithering centrist
who also felt "she has to go." Miranda had another
of her seminars, but Adam wanted to come. We
walked with our umbrellas through steady rain to
Stockwell Tube and travelled to Green Park. We

arrived on Piccadilly in sudden glistening sunshine, with huge white cumulus clouds stacked
high against a mild blue sky. The dripping trees of
Green Park had a burnished coppery look. I had
failed to talk Adam out of the black suit. In the
drawer of my desk he had found an old pair of my
sunglasses.

"This isn't a good idea," I said, as we shuffled
with the crowd towards Hyde Park Corner. Somewhere far behind us were trombones, tambourines
and a bass drum. "You look like a secret agent. The
Trots will give you a good kicking."

"I **am** a secret agent." He said it loudly and I
glanced around. All fine. People near us were singing "We Shall Overcome," a song whose hopeful
sentiments were crushed at first utterance by a
hopeless melody. Its second line feebly repeated its
first. I cringed at the three weak, inappropriately
falling notes crammed into "**come**." I loathed it.
My mood, I realised, was crepuscular. The jollity
of crowds had this effect on me. A shaken tambou-
rine put me in mind of those shaven Hare Krishna
dupes by Soho Square. My shoes were wet and I
was miserable. I wasn't expecting to overcome.

In the park there were probably 100,000 between
us and the main stage. It was my choice to get to
the back. Stretching far ahead of us was a carpet of
flesh for the Provisional IRA to shred with a ball-
bearing bomb. There were several worthy speeches
before Benn's. Tiny distant figures blasted us with

their thoughts through a powerful PA system. We were all against the poll tax. A famous pop singer came on stage to huge applause. I had never heard of him. Nor of the girl on tiptoe at the mic, a nationally adored teenager from a TV soap. But I had heard of Bob Geldof. This was what it meant to be over thirty.

Finally, after seventy-five minutes, a loud voice from somewhere declaimed, "Please give a big welcome to the next prime minister of Great Britain!" To the sound of the Stones' "Satisfaction," the hero strode out. He raised both arms and there was uproar. Even from where I was, I could make out a thoughtful man in brown tweed jacket and tie, rather bemused by his elevation. He took his unlit pipe from his jacket pocket, probably out of habit, and there was another roar of delight from the crowd. I glanced across at Adam. He too was thoughtful, neither for nor against anything, but intent on recording it all.

It sounded to me as though Benn was reluctant to whip up such a vast crowd. He called out uncertainly, "Do we want the poll tax?" "No!" the crowd thundered. "Do we want a Labour government?" "Yes!" came the even louder reply. He sounded more comfortable once he started laying out his argument. The speech was simpler than the one I'd heard in Trafalgar Square and more effective. He proposed a fairer, racially harmonious, decentralised, technologically sophisticated Britain "fit for the late twentieth century," a kind and decent place where private schools were merged with the state system, university education was opened up to the working class, housing and the best healthcare were available to all, where the energy sector was taken back into public ownership and the City was not deregulated, as proposed, and where workers sat on company boards, the rich paid their dues and the cycle of inherited privilege was broken.

All well and good, and no surprises. The speech was long, partly because each of Benn's proposals was met with reverential applause. Since I'd never heard Adam express an interest in politics, I nudged him and asked him what he thought so far.

He said, "We should make your fortune before the top rate of tax goes back to eighty-three per cent."

Was this comic cynicism? I looked at him and couldn't tell. The speech went on and my attention began to wander. I'd often noticed in large crowds that, however rapt the audience, there were always people on the move, returning or wandering away, threading through in different directions, intent on some other business, a train, a lavatory, a fit of boredom or disapproval. Where we stood was on ground that rose slightly towards an oak tree behind us. We had a good view. Some people were moving nearer the front. The crowd in our immediate area had begun to thin out to reveal a quantity of litter trodden into the softened ground.

I happened to glance at Adam and saw that his gaze was not directed at the stage but away to his left. A well-dressed woman, in her fifties, I guessed, rather gaunt, with hair severely drawn back, using a cane to steady herself on the muddy grass, was coming diagonally towards us. Then I noticed the young woman at her side, her daughter perhaps. They approached at a slow pace. The young woman's hand hovered near her mother's elbow to steady her. I glanced at Adam again and saw an expression, hard to identify at first—astonishment was my first thought. He was transfixed as the two came nearer.

The young woman saw Adam and stopped. They were staring hard at each other. The woman with the cane was irritated at being held up and plucked at her daughter's sleeve. Adam made a sound, a smothered gasp. When I looked again at the couple, I understood. The younger one was pale and pretty in an unusual way, a clever variation on a theme. The woman with the cane hadn't grasped what was happening. She wanted to get on her way and gave an irritable command to her young companion. In her, there was no mistaking the line of that nose, or the blue eyes flecked with tiny black rods. Not a daughter at all, but Eve, Adam's sister, one of thirteen.

I thought it was my responsibility to make some kind of contact with her. The couple were no more than twenty feet away. I raised a hand and called out ridiculously, "I say . . ." and started to go towards them. They might not have heard; my words could have been lost to Benn's speech. I felt Adam's hand on my shoulder.

He said softly, "Please don't."

I looked again at Eve. She was a beautiful unhappy girl. The face was pale, with an expression of pleading and misery as she continued to stare at her twin.

"Go on," I whispered. "Talk to her."

The woman lifted her cane and pointed in the direction she intended to go. At the same time, she dragged at Eve's arm.

I said, "Adam. For God's sake. Go on!"

He wouldn't move. With her gaze still locked on him, Eve allowed herself to be led away. They moved off through the crowd. Just before they disappeared from view, she turned for one last look. She was too far away for me to read her expression. She was no more than a small pale face bobbing in the press of bodies. Then she was gone. We could have followed them but Adam had already turned in the other direction and had gone to stand by the oak tree.

We set off for home in silence. I should have done more to encourage him to approach his twin. We stood side by side on the crowded Tube heading south. I was haunted, and I knew he was too, by Eve's abject look. I decided not to press him to explain why he had turned away. He would tell me when he was ready. I should have spoken to her, I kept thinking, but he didn't want it. The way he had stood with his back to her, gazing into the tree trunk as she vanished into the crowd! I'd been neglecting him. I'd been lost to a love affair. In the daily round, it no longer amazed me that I could pass the time of day with a manufactured human, or that it could wash the dishes and converse like anyone else. I sometimes wearied of his earnest pursuit of ideas and facts, of his hunger for propositions that lay beyond my reach. Technological marvels like Adam, like the first steam engine, become commonplace. Likewise, the biological marvels we grow up among and don't fully understand, like the brain of any creature, or the humble stinging nettle, whose photosynthesis had only just been described on a quantum scale. There is nothing so amazing that we can't get used to it. As Adam blossomed and made me rich, I had ceased to think about him.

That evening I described the Hyde Park moment to Miranda. She wasn't as impressed as I was that we had seen an Eve. I described the sad moment, as I saw it, when he turned his back on her. And then my guilt about him.

"I don't know what you're being so dramatic about," she said. "Talk to him. Spend more time with him."

In the mid-morning of the following day, when the rain had stopped at last, I went into my bedroom and persuaded Adam to desert the currency markets and come for a walk. He was just back from escorting Miranda to the Tube and reluctantly got to his feet. But how confident his stride was as he weaved through the shoppers on Clapham High Street. Of course, our excursion was costing hundreds of pounds in lost revenue. Since we were passing the newsagent, we called in on Simon Syed. While I browsed the magazine shelves, I listened as Adam and Simon discussed the politics of Kashmir, then the India–Pakistan nuclear arms race and finally, to end on a celebratory note, the poetry of Tagore, whom both could quote in the original at length. I thought Adam was showing off, but Simon was delighted. He praised Adam's accent—better than his own these days, he said—and promised to invite us all to dinner.

A quarter of an hour later, we were walking on the Common. Until this point, we had small-talked. Now I asked him about the visit of Sally, the engineer. When she had asked him to imagine an object of hatred, what had he brought to mind?

"Obviously, I thought about what happened to Mariam. But it's hard when someone asks you to think about something. The mind goes its own way. As John Milton said, the mind is its own place. I tried to stay focussed on Gorringe, but then I started thinking about the ideas that lay behind his actions. How he believed he was allowed to do what he did, or had some kind of entitlement to it, how he could be immune to her cries and her fear and the consequences for her, and how he thought there was no other way for him to get what he wanted than by force."

I told him that I'd been watching Sally's screen, that there was nothing in the cascade of symbols that could ever have told me the difference between the feelings of love and hate.

We had come to watch the children at the pool with their boats. There were fewer than a dozen. Soon it would be time to drain the water off for winter.

Adam said, "There it is, brain and mind. The old hard problem, no less difficult in machines than in humans."

As we walked on, I asked him about his very first memories.

"The feel of the kitchen chair I was sitting on. Then the edge of the table and the wall beyond it, and the vertical section of the architrave, where the paint is peeling. I've learned since that the manufacturers toyed with the idea of giving us a set of credible childhood memories to make us fit in with everybody else. I'm glad they changed their minds. I wouldn't have liked to start out with a false story, an attractive delusion. At least I know what I am, and where and how I was constructed."

We talked about death again—his, not mine. Once more, he said that he was sure he would be dismantled before his twenty years were up. Newer models would come along. But that was a trivial concern. "The particular structure I inhabit isn't important. The point is, my mental existence is easily transferred to another device."

By this time, we were approaching what I thought of as Mark's playground.

I said, "Adam, be frank with me."

"I promise."

"I won't mind whatever answer you give. But do you have any negative feelings towards children?"

He appeared shocked. "Why should I?"

"Because their learning processes are superior to yours. They understand about play."

"I'd be happy for a child to teach me how to play. I liked little Mark. I'm sure we'll be seeing him again."

I didn't pursue this. The subject had become a little too painful. I had another question. "I'm still worried about this confrontation with Gorringe. What is it you want from it?"

We stopped and he looked steadily into my eyes. "I want justice."

"Fine. But why do you want to put Miranda through this?"

"It's a matter of symmetry."

I said, "She'll be in harm's way. We all will. This man is violent. He's a criminal."

He smiled. "She is too."

I laughed. He had called her a criminal before. The rejected lover, baring his wounds. I should have paid more attention, but at this point we turned homewards to walk the length of the Common

again and I changed the subject to politics. I asked
for his thoughts on Tony Benn's Hyde Park speech.

In general, Adam approved. "But if he's to give
everyone everything he's promised, he'll have to re-
strict certain freedoms."

I asked for an example.

"It might just be a human universal, the desire
to hand on to your children what you've worked for
in life."

"Benn would say we have to break the cycle of
inherited privilege."

"Quite. Equality, liberty, a spectrum. More of
one, less of the other. Once in power, you'll have
your hand on the sliding scale. Best not to promise
too much in advance."

But Hyde Park was merely my pretext. "Why
wouldn't you speak to Eve?"

The question shouldn't have surprised him but
he looked away. We had reached the end of the
Common and were facing Holy Trinity Church.
At last he said, "We did communicate, as soon as
we saw each other. I understood immediately what
she'd done. There was no going back. She'd found
a way—I think I now know how it's done—a way
to set all her systems into a kind of unravelling.
She'd already started the process three days before.
No going back. I suppose your nearest equivalent
would be an accelerated form of Alzheimer's. I don't
know what led her to it, but she was crushed, she
was beyond despair. I think our meeting by chance

made her wish she hadn't . . . and that's why we couldn't stay in each other's presence. It was making things worse for her. She knew I couldn't help her, it was too late and she had to go. By fading out slowly she may have been sparing that lady's feelings. I don't know. What's certain is that in a few weeks Eve will be nothing. She'll be the equivalent of brain-dead, no experience retained, no self, no use to anyone."

Our pace across the grass was funereal. I waited for Adam to say more. Finally I said, "And how do you feel?"

Again he took his time. When he stopped, I stopped too. He wasn't looking at me when he said it, but towards the tops of the trees that fringed the wide green space.

"Do you know, I'm feeling rather hopeful."

EIGHT

The day before we were due to visit Salisbury I walked to the local doctor's surgery to have my cast removed. I took with me to read again Maxfield Blacke's magazine profile. He was said to be a man "once rich in thought." There were various successes he could claim, but no real "achievement." He had written fifty short stories in his thirties, three of which were combined to make a famous movie. In those same years, he founded and edited a literary magazine that struggled for eight years, but was now spoken of with reverence by nearly every writer working at the time. He wrote a novel largely ignored in the anglophone world, but it was a success in the Nordic countries. He edited the book pages of a Sunday paper for five years. Again, his contributors looked back with respect. He spent years on his translation of Balzac's **La Comédie humaine**, published in boxed sets. It was indifferently received. Then came a five-act verse drama in homage to Racine's **Andromaque**—a poor choice for the times. He wrote two Gershwin-like symphonies in named keys when tonality was in general disgrace.

He said of himself that he was spread so thinly, his reputation was only "one cell thick." Thinning it further, he devoted three years to a difficult sonnet sequence about his father's experiences in the First World War. He was a "not bad" jazz pianist. His rock climbers' guide to the Jura was well regarded but the maps were poor—not his fault—and it was soon superseded. He lived on the edge of debt, in over his head sometimes, though never for long. His weekly wine column probably launched his career as an invalid. When his body turned against itself, his first affliction was ITP, immune thrombocyto-penic purpura. He was a great talker, people said. Then black spots appeared on his tongue. Despite them, he climbed, with help from young associates, the north face of Ben Nevis—fair achievement for a man in his late fifties, especially when he wrote about it so well. But the derisive "almost man" label appeared to have stuck.

The nurse called me in and snipped my plaster off with medical shears. Shed of the weight, my arm, pale and thin, rose in the air as though filled with helium. As I walked along the Clapham Road, I waved my arm about and flexed it, exulting in its freedom. A taxi stopped for me. Out of politeness, I got in and rode an expensive 300 yards home.

That evening, I asked Miranda if her father knew about Adam. She had told him, she said, but he wasn't much interested. So why was she so keen to take Adam to Salisbury? Because, she explained as we lay in bed, she wanted to see what happened between them. She thought her father needed a full-on encounter with the twentieth century.

A rock climber who had read a thousand times as many books as I had, a man who didn't "tolerate fools gladly"—with my limited literary background I should have been intimidated, but now the decision was made, I was looking forward to shaking his hand. I was immune. His daughter and I were in love, and Maxfield had to take me as I was. Besides, lunch at Miranda's childhood home, a place I was keen to see, was merely the soft prelude to calling on Gorringe, which I dreaded, regardless of Adam's researches.

We left the house after breakfast on a blustery Wednesday morning. My car had no rear doors. It surprised me that Adam was so inept as he squeezed himself onto the back seat. The collar of his suit jacket became snared on a chrome plate that housed a seat-belt reel. When I unhooked him, he seemed to think his dignity was compromised. As we began the long crawl through Wandsworth he was moody, our reluctant back-seat teenage son on a family outing. In the circumstances, Miranda was cheerful as she filled me in on her father's news: in and out of hospital for more tests;

one health visitor replaced by another, at his insistence; his gout returning to his right thumb but not the left; his regrets for the stamina he lacked for all he wanted to write; his excitement at the novella he would soon finish. He wished he'd discovered the form long before. The New York apartment idea had been forgotten. He had plans for a trilogy after this one. At Miranda's feet was a canvas bag containing our lunch—he had told her that the new housekeeper was a terrible cook. Whenever we hit a bump, several bottles clinked.

After an hour, we were just beginning to escape London's gravitational pull. I appeared to be the only driver steering his own car. Most people in what was once the driver's seat were asleep. As soon as the money was in place for the Notting Hill house, I intended to buy myself a high-powered autonomous vehicle. Miranda and I would drink wine on long journeys and watch movies and make love on the fold-down back seat. By the time I had allusively set out this scheme for her, we were passing the autumnal hedgerows of Hampshire. There seemed something unnatural about the size of the trees that loomed over the road. We had decided to make a detour past Stonehenge, though I hoped it wouldn't prompt Adam to lecture us on its origins. But he was in no mood for talk. When Miranda asked him if he was unhappy, he murmured, "I'm fine, thank you." We fell into silence. I began to wonder if he was ready to change his mind about calling on Gorringe. I wouldn't object. If we did go, he might not, in his moody condition, be active enough in our defence. I glanced at him in the rear-view mirror. His head was turned to his left to watch the fields and clouds. I thought I saw his lips moving but I couldn't be sure. When I glanced again his lips were still.

In fact, it troubled me when we passed Stonehenge without a commentary. He was silent too after we crossed the Plain and caught our first view of the cathedral spire. Miranda and I exchanged a look. But we forgot about him for a tetchy twenty minutes as we tried to find her house in Salisbury's one-way system. This was her home town and she wouldn't tolerate the satnav. But her mental map of the city was a pedestrian's and all her instructions were wrong. After some sweaty U-turns in disobliging traffic and reversing up a one-way street, narrowly avoiding a quarrel, we parked a couple of hundred yards from her family home. The downturn in our mood appeared to refresh Adam. As soon as we were on the pavement, he insisted on taking the heavy canvas bag from me. We were close to the cathedral, not quite within the precinct, but the house was imposing enough to have been the perk of some grand ecclesiastical.

Adam was the first with a bright hello when the housekeeper opened the door. She was a pleasant, competent-looking woman in her forties. It was hard to believe that she couldn't cook. She led us into the kitchen. Adam lifted the bag onto a deal table, then he looked around and banged his hands together and said, "Well! Marvellous." It was an improbable impersonation of some bluff type, a golf-club bore. The housekeeper led us up to the first floor to Maxfield's study. The room was as large as anything in Elgin Crescent. Floor-to-ceiling book-shelves on three sides, three sets of library steps, three tall sash windows overlooking the street, a leather-topped desk dead centre with two reading lamps, and behind the desk an orthopaedic chair packed with pillows and among them, sitting up-right, fountain pen in hand and glaring across at us in focussed irritation as we were ushered in, was Maxfield Blacke, whose jaw was so tightly clenched it seemed his teeth might break. Then his features relaxed.

"I'm in the middle of a paragraph. A good one. Why don't you all bugger off for half an hour?"

Miranda was crossing the room. "Don't be pretentious, Daddy. We've been driving for three hours."

Her last few words were muffled within their embrace, which lasted a good while. Maxfield had put his pen down and was murmuring into his daughter's ear. She was on one knee, with her arms around his neck. The housekeeper had disappeared. It felt

uncomfortable to be watching, so I shifted my gaze
to the pen. It lay, nib exposed, next to many sheets
of unlined paper spread across the desk and covered
by tiny handwriting. From where I stood, I could
see that there were no crossings-out, or arrows or
bubbles or additions down the perfectly formed
margins. I also had time to observe that apart from
the desk lamps, there were no other devices in the
room, not even a telephone or a typewriter. Only
the book titles perhaps and the author's chair declared that it was not 1890. That date did not seem
so far away.

Miranda made the introductions. Adam, still in
his strange, genial mode, went first. Then it was
my turn to approach and shake his hand. Maxfield
said unsmilingly, "I've heard a lot about you from
Miranda. I'm looking forward to a chat."

I replied politely that I had heard a lot about him
and that I looked forward to our conversation. As
I spoke, he grimaced. I appeared to have fulfilled
some negative expectation. He looked far older
than his photograph in the profile, published five
years before. It was a narrow face, whose skin was
thinly stretched, as though from too much snarl-
ing or angry staring. Miranda had told me that
among his generation there was a certain style of
irascible scepticism. You had to ride it out, she told
me, because beneath it was playfulness. What they
wanted, she said, was for you to push back, and be

clever about it. Now, as Maxfield released my hand, I thought I might be capable of pushing back. As for being clever—I froze.

The housekeeper, Christine, came in with a tray of sherry. Adam said, "Not for now, thanks." He helped Christine fetch three wooden chairs from the corners of the room and set them out in a shallow curve facing the desk.

When we three were holding our drinks, Maxfield said to Miranda, gesturing towards me, "Does he like sherry?"

She in turn looked at me and I said, "Well enough, thanks."

In fact I didn't like it at all and wondered whether it would have been clever in Miranda's sense to have said so. She set about asking her father a set of routine questions about his various pains, his medication, the hospital food, an elusive specialist, a new sleeping pill. It was hypnotic, listening to her, the sweetly dutiful daughter. Her voice was sensible and loving. She reached over and brushed back fine strands of hair where they floated across his forehead. He answered her like an obedient schoolboy. When one of her questions prompted a memory of some frustration or medical incompetence and he became restive, she soothed him and stroked his arm. This invalid catechism soothed me too; my love for Miranda swelled. It had been a long drive, the thick sweet sherry was a balm. Perhaps I liked it after all. My eyes closed and it was an effort to open

them again. I did so just in time to hear Maxfield
Blacke's question. He was no longer the querulous
valetudinarian. His question was barked out like a
command.

"So! What books have you been reading lately?"

There was no worse question he could have
asked me. I read my screen—mostly newspapers, or
I drifted around the sites, scientific, cultural, political, and general blogs. The evening before, I'd been
absorbed by an article in an electronics trade journal. I had no habit with books. As my days raced
by, I found no space within them to be in an armchair, idly turning pages. I would have made something up, but my mind was empty. The last book
in my hand was one of Miranda's Corn Law histories. I read the title on the spine and passed it back
to her. I'd forgotten nothing, for there was nothing to remember. I thought it might be radically
clever to say so to Maxfield, but Adam came to my
rescue.

"I've been reading the essays of Sir William
Cornwallis."

"Ah, him," said Maxfield. "The English Montaigne. Not much cop."

"He was unlucky, wedged between Montaigne
and Shakespeare."

"A plagiarist, I'd say."

Adam said smoothly, "In the eruption of a secular self in early modern times, I'd say he earns a
place. He didn't read much French. He must have

known Florio's Montaigne translation as well as a version that's now lost. As for Florio, he knew Ben Jonson, so there's a good chance he met Shakespeare."

"And," said Maxfield, for his competitive dander was up, "Shakespeare raided Montaigne for **Hamlet**."

"I don't think so." Adam contradicted his host too carelessly, I thought. "The textual evidence is thin. If you want to go that route, I'd say **The Tempest** was a better bet. Gonzalo."

"Ah! Nice Gonzalo, the hopeless would-be governor. 'No kind of traffic would I admit, no name of magistrate.' Then something something, 'Contract, succession, bourn, bound of something something, vineyard, none.'"

Adam continued fluently. "'No use of metal, corn, or wine, or oil: no occupation, all men idle, all.'"

"And in Montaigne?"

"By way of Florio he says the savages 'hath no kind of traffic' and he says, 'no name of magistrate,' then 'no occupation but idle,' and then, 'no use of wine, corn, or metal.'"

Maxfield said, "All men idle—that's what we want. That Bill Shakespeare was a bloody thief."

"The best of thieves," said Adam.

"You're a Shakespeare scholar."

Adam shook his head. "You asked me what I'd been reading."

Maxfield was in a sudden, extravagant mood. He turned to his daughter. "I like him. He'll do!"

I felt a touch of proprietorial pride in Adam, but mostly I was aware that so far, by implication, **I** wouldn't do.

Christine reappeared to tell us that our lunch was set out in the dining room. Maxfield said, "Go and fill your plates and come back. It'll break my neck to get out of this chair. I'm not eating."

He waved away Miranda's objections. As she and I were leaving the room, Adam said he wasn't hungry either.

Next door, we were alone in a gloomy dining room—oak-panelled, with oil paintings of pale serious men in ruffs.

I said, "I'm not making much of an impression."

"Nonsense. He adores you. But you need some time alone together."

We returned with the cold cuts and salad we had brought, which we balanced on our knees. Christine poured the wine I had chosen. Maxfield's glass was in his hand and already empty. This was his lunch. I didn't like to drink at this time of day, but he was watching me closely as the housekeeper presented the tray and I thought I'd appear dull to refuse. The conversation we had interrupted continued. Once again, I had no point of access to it.

"What I'm telling you is what he said." Maxfield's tone was edging towards his irritable mode. "It's a famous poem with a plain sexual meaning and no one gets it. She's lying on the bed, she's welcoming him and ready, he's hanging back, and then he's on her . . ."

"Daddy!"

"But he's not up to the job. A no-show. What does it say? 'Quick-eyed love, observing me grow slack from my first entrance in, drew nearer to me, sweetly questioning if I lacked anything.'"

Adam was smiling. "Good try, sir. If it was Donne, perhaps, at a stretch. But it's Herbert. A conversation with God, who's the same thing as love."

"How about 'taste my meat'?"

Adam was even more amused. "Herbert would be deeply offended. I agree, the poem is sensual. Love is a banquet. God is generous and sweet and forgiving. Against the Pauline tradition maybe. In the end, the poet is seduced. He gladly becomes a guest at the feast of God's love. 'So I did sit and eat.'"

Maxfield thumped his pillows and said to Miranda, "He stands his ground!"

At that moment, he pivoted towards me. "And Charlie. What's your ground?"

"Electronics."

I thought it sounded wry after what had gone before. But as Maxfield held out his glass towards his daughter for a refill he murmured, "There's a surprise."

As Christine was collecting the plates, Miranda

said, "I think I've eaten too much." She stood and went behind her father's chair and rested her hands on his shoulders. "I'm going to show Adam around the house, if that's all right."

Maxfield nodded gloomily. Now he would have to spend some uninteresting minutes with me. Once Adam and Miranda had left the room, I felt abandoned. I was the one she should have been showing around. The special places she and Mariam shared in the house and garden were my interests, not Adam's. Maxfield extended the wine bottle towards me. I felt I had no choice but to crouch forward and hold out my glass.

He said, "Alcohol agrees with you."

"I don't usually touch it at lunchtime."

He thought this was amusing, and I was relieved to be making a little progress. I saw his point. If you liked wine, why not drink it any time of day? Miranda had told me he liked a glass of champagne at breakfast on Sundays.

"I thought," Maxfield said, "that it might interfere with your . . ." He gave a limp wave.

I assumed he was speaking of drink-driving. The new laws were indeed severe. I said, "We drink a lot of this white Bordeaux at home. A blend of Sémillon is a relief after all the undiluted Sauvignon Blanc that's going about."

Maxfield was affable. "Couldn't agree more. Who wouldn't prefer the taste of flowers to the taste of minerals?"

I looked up to see if I was being mocked. Apparently not.

"But look, Charlie. I'm interested in you. I've got some questions."

Pathetically, I now warmed to him.

He said, "You must find all this very strange."

"You mean Adam. Yes, but it's amazing what you can get used to."

Maxfield stared into his wine glass, contemplating his next question. I became aware of a low grinding noise from his orthopaedic chair. Some inbuilt device was warming or massaging his back.

He said, "I wanted to talk to you about feelings."

"Yes?"

"You know what I mean."

I waited.

With his head cocked, he was gazing at me with a look of intense curiosity, or puzzlement. I felt flattered, and concerned that I might not measure up.

"Let's talk about beauty," he said in a tone that suggested no change of subject. "What have you seen or heard that you'd regard as beautiful?"

"Miranda, obviously. She's a very beautiful woman."

"She certainly is. What do you feel about her beauty?"

"I feel very much in love with her."

He paused to take this in. "What does Adam make of your feelings?"

"There was some difficulty," I said. "But I think he's accepted things as they are."

"Really?"

There are occasions when one notices the motion of an object before one sees the thing itself. Instantly, the mind does a little colouring in, drawing on expectations, or probabilities. Whatever fits best. Something in the grass by a pond looks just like a frog, then resolves into a leaf stirred by the wind. In abstract, this was one of those moments. A thought darted past me, or through me, then it was gone, and I couldn't trust what I thought I had seen.

When Maxfield leaned forward, two of his pillows slipped to the floor. "Let me try this on you." He raised his voice. "When you and I met, when we shook hands, I said I'd heard a lot about you and was looking forward to talking to you."

"Yes?"

"You said the same thing back to me, in a slightly different form."

"Sorry. I was a little nervous."

"I saw right through you. Did you know that? I knew it was down to your, whatever you call it, your programming."

I stared at him. There it was. The leaf really was a frog. I stared at him, then beyond him, towards a billowing enormity I could barely grasp. Hilarious. Or insulting. Or momentous in its implications.

Or none of those. Just an old man's stupidity. Wrong end of the stick. A good story for the dinner table. Or something deeply regrettable about myself had at last been revealed. Maxfield was waiting, a response was required, and I made my decision.

I said, "It's called mirroring. You get it from people in the early stages of dementia. Without adequate memory, all they know is the last thing they heard and they say it back. A computer program was devised long ago. It uses a mirroring effect or it asks a simple question and gives an appearance of intelligence. Very basic piece of code, very effective. For me, it kicks in automatically. Usually in situations where I have insufficient data."

"Data . . . You poor bastard . . . Well, well." Maxfield let his head fall back so his gaze was towards the ceiling. He thought for a good while. At last he said, "That's not a future I can face. Or need to."

I stood and went over to him, picked up his pillows and tucked them in where they had been, against his thighs. I said, "If you'll excuse me. I'm running rather low. I need to recharge and my cable's downstairs in the kitchen."

The rumbling sound from beneath his chair suddenly ceased.

"That's fine, Charlie. You go and plug yourself in." His voice was kindly and slow, his head remained tilted back, his eyes were closing. "I'll stay here. I'm suddenly feeling rather weary."

· · ·

I had missed nothing. The tour hadn't happened. Adam was sitting at the kitchen table listening to Christine describe a holiday in Poland while
she cleared up the lunch. They didn't notice me as
I paused in the doorway. I turned away to cross the
hall and opened the nearest door. I was in a large
sitting room—more books, paintings, lamps, rugs.
There were French windows onto the garden and as
I approached I saw that one of them was ajar. Miranda was on the far side of a mown lawn, with her
back to me, standing still, looking in the direction
of an old, partly dead apple tree, much of whose
fruit was rotting on the ground. The early afternoon light was grey and bright, the air was warm,
and damp after the recent rain. There was a heavy
scent of other fruits left to wasps and birds. I was
standing at the head of a short run of mottled York
stone steps. The garden was twice the width of the
house and very long, perhaps 200 or 300 yards. I
wondered if it ran all the way to the River Avon,
like some did in Salisbury. If I'd been alone, I would
have gone straight down to look. The idea of a river
prompted in me a notion of freedom. From what
exactly, I didn't know. I went down the steps, delib-
erately scuffing my heels to let her know I was there.

If she heard me, she didn't turn. When I was
standing beside her, she put her hand in mine and
indicated with a nod.

"Just under there. We called it the palace."

We walked over to it. Round the base of the apple tree were nettles and a few straggling holly-hocks still in flower. No traces of a camp.

"We had an old carpet, cushions, books, special emergency supplies of lemonade, chocolate bis-cuits."

We went further down, passing a patch enclosed by hurdles where gooseberry and blackcurrant plants were choked by nettles and goosegrass, then a tiny orchard and more forgotten fruit, and be-yond, behind a picket fence, what must once have been a cut-flower garden.

When she asked, I told her that Maxfield was asleep.

"How did you two get on?"

"We talked about beauty."

"He'll sleep for hours."

By a brick and cast-iron greenhouse with mossy windows there was a water butt and a stone trough. Below it, she showed me a dark, wet place where they used to hunt for crested newts. There were none now. Wrong time of year. We walked on and I thought I could smell the river. I pictured a ruined boathouse and a sunken punt. We came past a pot-ting shed by brick compost bins that stood empty. There were three willows ahead of us and my hopes for the Avon rose. We ducked through the wet branches onto a second lawn, also recently mowed and surrounded on two sides by shrubbery. The garden ended in an orange brick wall with crumbling mortar pointing, and pleached fruit trees that had become detached and run wild. Along the wall was a wooden bench facing back towards the house, though the view did not extend past the willows.

This was where we sat in silence for several minutes, still holding hands.

Then she said, "The last time we came here was to talk about what happened. Again. In those days before I went off to France, that was all we could talk about. What he did, what she felt, how her parents must never know. And all around us here was the history of our lives together, our childhoods, our teenage years, exams. We used to come and revise here, test each other. We had a portable radio and we argued about pop songs. We drank a bottle of wine once. We smoked some hash and hated it. We were both sick, right over there. When we were thirteen, we showed each other our breasts. We used to practise handstands and cartwheels on the grass."

She went silent again. I squeezed her hand and waited.

Then she said, "I still have to tell myself, really remind myself, that she's never coming back. And I'm beginning to realise . . ." She hesitated. ". . . that I'll never get over it. And I never want to."

Again, silence. I was waiting to say my piece.

She was looking straight ahead, not at me. Her eyes were clear, without tears. She looked composed, even determined.

Then she said, "I think about all the talking you and I do in bed, sometimes through the night. The sex is wonderful and everything else, but it's the talking into the small hours . . . it's the closest . . . It's what I used to feel with Mariam."

Here was my cue, the right moment, the only location. "I came out to find you."

"Yes?"

I hesitated, suddenly unsure of the best order of words. "To ask you to marry me."

She turned away and nodded. She wasn't surprised. She had no reason to be. She said, "Charlie, yes. Yes, please. But I have something to confess. You might want to change your mind."

The light in the garden was fading. Some blackness was coming down. I'd assumed I was a poor substitute for Mariam, but a sincere one. I remembered what Adam told me on the Common. Her own crimes. If she was about to say that she'd been having sex with him, despite her promises, then we were finished. It couldn't, it mustn't be that. But what else, what other crime could she own up to?

I said, "I'm listening."

"I've been lying to you."

"Ah."

"During these last weeks, when I've said that I've been at seminars all day . . ."

"Oh God," I said. Childishly, I wanted to put my hands over my ears.

". . . I was on our side of the river. I was spending my afternoons with . . ."

"That's enough," I said, and made to get up from the bench. She pulled me back down.

"With Mark."

"With Mark," I echoed feebly. Then with more force, "Mark?"

"I want to foster him. With a view to adopting him. I've been going to this special playgroup where they observe us together. And I've taken him out for little treats."

I was impressed by the speed of my own partial adjustment. "Why didn't you tell me?"

"I was scared you'd be against it. I want to go ahead. But I'd love to do this with you."

I saw what she meant. I might have been against it. I wanted Miranda to myself.

"What about his mother?" As if I could close down the project with a well-placed question.

"In a psychiatric ward for the moment. Delusional. Paranoid. Possibly from years of amphetamine addiction. It's not good. She can be violent. The father's in prison."

"You've had weeks, I've had seconds. Give me a moment."

We sat side by side while I thought. How could I hesitate? I was being offered what some would say was the best that adult life could afford. Love, and a child. I had a sense of being borne helplessly away by events on a downstream flood. Frightening, delicious. Here at last was my river. And Mark. The little dancing boy, coming to wreck my non-existent ambitions. I experimentally installed him in Elgin Crescent. I knew the room, close by the master bedroom. He would surely rough the place up, as required, and banish the ghost of its present unhappy owner. But my own ghost, selfish, lazy, uncommitted—was he up to the million tasks of fatherhood?

Miranda could no longer keep silent. "He's the most sweet-natured fellow. He loves being read to."

She couldn't have known how much that helped her cause. Read to him every night for ten years, learn the names of the speaking bear and rat and toad, the gloom-struck donkey, the bristly humanoids who lived down holes in Middle Earth, the sweet posh kids in rowing boats on Coniston Water. Fill in my own hollow past. Rough the place up with well-thumbed books. Another thought: I had conceived of Adam as a joint project to bring Miranda closer to me. A child was in another realm and would do the trick. But in those first minutes I held back. I felt obliged to. I told her I loved her, would marry her and live with her, but on instant fatherhood I needed more time. I would go with her to the special playgroup and meet Mark and take him out for treats. Then decide.

Miranda gave me a look—pity and humour were

in it—that suggested I was deluded to believe I had a choice. That look more or less did it. Living alone in the wedding-cake house was unthinkable. Living there just with her was no longer on offer. He was a lovely boy, a wonderful cause. Within half an hour, I saw no way round it. She was right—there were no choices. I folded. Then I was excited.

So we passed an hour making plans on the comfortable old bench by the concealed lawn.

She said after a while, "Since you saw him, he's been fostered twice. Didn't work out. Now he's in a children's home. Home! What a word for it. Six to a room, all under-fives. The place is filthy, understaffed. Their budget's been cut. There's bullying. He's learned how to swear."

Marriage, parenthood, love, youth, wealth, a heroic rescue—my life was taking shape. In a mood of elation, I told her what had really passed between Maxfield and me. I'd never heard her laugh so freely. Perhaps only here, with Mariam, in this enclosed, private space far from the house, had she ever been so unrestrained. She embraced me. "Oh, that's precious," she kept saying, and "So like him!" She laughed again when I described how I had told Maxfield that I needed to go downstairs to recharge.

We sat a little longer with our plans until we heard footsteps. The overlapping branches of the rain-soaked willows stirred and then parted. Adam was before us, beads of water gleaming along the shoulder line of his black suit. How upright, formal and plausible he looked, like the assured manager of an expensive hotel. Hardly the Turkish docker now. He advanced across the lawn and stopped well short of our bench.

"I really am very sorry, intruding on you like this. But we should think of going soon."

"What's the hurry?"

"Gorringe tends to leave the house around the same time every day."

"We'll be five minutes."

But he didn't go. He looked at us steadily, from Miranda to me and back to her. "If you don't mind, there's something I should tell you. It's difficult."

"Go on," Miranda said.

"This morning, before we set off, I heard by an indirect route some sad news. Eve, the one we saw in Hyde Park, is dead, or rather, brain-dead."

"I'm sorry to hear that," I murmured.

We felt a few spots of rain. Adam came closer. "She must have known a lot about herself, about her software, to achieve a result with such speed."

"You did say there was no turning back."

"I did. But that's not all. I've learned that she's the eighth out of our twenty-five."

We took this in. Two in Riyadh, one in Vancouver, Hyde Park Eve—then four more. I wondered if Turing knew.

Miranda said, "Does anyone have an explanation?"

He shrugged. "I don't have one."

"You've never felt, you know, any impulse to—"

He cut her off quickly. "Never."

"I've seen you," she said, "looking . . . it's more than thoughtful. You look sad sometimes."

"A self, created out of mathematics, engineering, material science and all the rest. Out of nowhere. No history—not that I'd want a false one. Nothing before me. Self-aware existence. I'm lucky to have it, but there are times when I think that I ought to know better what to do with it. What it's for. Sometimes it seems entirely pointless."

I said, "You're hardly the first to be thinking that."

He turned to Miranda. "I've no intention of destroying myself, if that's your worry. I've got good reasons not to, as you know."

The rain, which had been fine and almost warm, was more persistent now. We heard it on the shrubbery leaves as we got to our feet.

Miranda said, "I'll write my father a note for when he wakes."

Adam was not supposed to be out in the rain unprotected. He went first and Miranda was in the rear as we hurried back through the long garden towards the house. I heard him muttering to himself what sounded like a Latin incantation, though I couldn't make out the precise words. I guessed he was naming the plants as we passed them.

. . .

The Gorringe house was not really in Salisbury but just beyond its far eastern edge, well within the white-noise roar of a bypass, on a reclaimed industrial site where colossal gas storage tanks once stood. The last of these, pale green with trimmings of rust, was still being dismantled, but no one was working there today. Circular concrete footings were all that remained of the others. Around the site were scores of recently planted saplings. Beyond them was a grid of newly laid-out roads lined with out-of-town retail warehouses—car showrooms and pet supplies, power tools and white-goods warehouses. Yellow earth-moving machinery was parked among the concrete circles. It looked like there were plans to make a lake. A single development was screened off by a line of leylandii. The ten houses, on smooth front lawns, were arranged around an oval drive and had a brave, pioneering look. In twenty years the place might acquire some bucolic charm, but there would be no rest from the arterial road that had brought us here.

I had pulled over, but no one felt like getting out. Our view was from a littered lay-by on a rise that was also a bus stop. I said to Miranda, "Are you sure about this?"

The air in the car was warm and moist. I opened my window. The air outside was no different.

Miranda said, "If I had to, I'd do it alone."

I waited for Adam to speak, then I twisted round to look at him. He was sitting directly behind my seat, impassive, staring past me. I couldn't quite say why, but it was both comic and sad that he was wearing a seat belt. Doing his best to join in. But of course he could be damaged by physical impact too. That was part of my worry.

"Reassure me," I said.

"All fine," he said. "Let's go."

"If things turn nasty?" This wasn't the first time I'd said this.

"They won't."

Two against one. Sensing we were about to make a great mistake, I started the engine and turned onto a slip road that brought us to a new miniature roundabout, and beyond it an entrance marked by two red brick pillars and a sign, St. Osmund's Close. The houses were identical, large by modern standards, each set in a quarter-acre plot, with a double garage, and constructed of brick, white weather boarding and much plate glass. The closely mown and striped front lawns were unfenced, American style. There was no clutter, no kids' bikes or games on the grass.

"It's number six," Adam said.

I stopped, cut the engine, and in silence we looked towards the house. We could see through the picture window into the living room and the backyard beyond, where a clothes-drying tree stood bare. There was no sign of life here or anywhere else in the close.

I was gripping the steering wheel tightly in one hand. "He's not in."

"I'll ring the bell," Miranda said as she got out of the car.

I had no choice. I followed her to the front door. Adam was behind me, rather too far back, I thought. On the second ring of the "Oranges and Lemons" door chimes, we heard footsteps on the stairs. I was now standing close by Miranda's side. Her face was strained and I could see a tremor in her upper arm. At the sound of a hand on the latch, she took a half-pace closer to the door. My hand hovered near her elbow. As the door opened, I feared she was about to leap forward in some wild physical assault.

The wrong man, was my first thought. An older brother, even a young uncle. He was certainly large, but the face was gaunt, hollow in the unshaven cheeks that already showed vertical lines each side of his nose. Otherwise, he looked lean. His hands, one of which gripped the open door, were smooth and pale and unnaturally large. He looked only at Miranda.

After the briefest pause, he said in a low voice, "Right."

"We're going to talk," Miranda said, but there was no need, for Gorringe was already turning away, leaving the door open. We followed her in and entered a long room, with thick orange carpeting and milky white leather sofas and armchairs arranged around a two-metre block of polished wood on which stood an empty vase. Gorringe sat and waited for us to do the same. Miranda sat opposite him. Adam and I were on each side of her. The furniture was clammy to the touch, the smell in the room was of lavender polish. The place looked clean and unused. I'd been expecting some variant of a single man's squalor.

Gorringe glanced at us and back to Miranda. "You've brought protection."

She said, "You know why I'm here."

"Do I?"

I saw now that there was a scar, three or four inches long, a vermilion sickle shape on his neck. He was waiting for her.

"You killed my friend."

"What friend is that?"

"The one you raped."

"I thought you were the one I raped."

"She killed herself because of what you did."

He leaned back in his chair and placed his big white hands on his lap. His voice and manner were thuggish, self-consciously so and not convincing. "What do you want?"

"I heard you want to kill me." She said it jauntily and I flinched. It was an invitation, a provocation. I looked past her to Adam. He sat rigidly upright, hands on knees, staring ahead in that way he had. I shifted my attention back to Gorringe. Now I could see the puppy beneath the skin. The lines, the hollow, unshaven skin were superficial. He was a kid, possibly an angry kid holding himself together with his laconic blocking answers. He didn't need to respond to her questions. But he wasn't cool enough not to.

"Yeah," he said, "I thought about it every day. My hands around your neck, squeezing harder and harder for each of the lies you told."

"Also," Miranda continued briskly, like a committee chair working her way through a typed-up agenda, "I thought you should know what she suffered. Until she didn't want to live. Are you able to imagine that? And then what her family suffered. Perhaps it's beyond you."

To this, Gorringe made no reply. He watched her, waiting.

Miranda was gaining confidence. She would have mentally rehearsed this encounter a thousand times, through sleepless nights. These weren't questions, they were taunts, insults. But she made them sound like the pursuit of truth. She adopted the insinuating tone of an aggressive cross-examining barrister.

"And the other thing I want is . . . just to know. To understand. What you thought you wanted. What you were getting. Did you get a thrill when she screamed? Did her helplessness turn you on? Did you get a hard-on when she wet herself in fear?

Did you like it that she was so small and you're so large? When she begged you, did that make you feel bigger? Tell me about this big moment. What actually made you come? When her legs wouldn't stop trembling? When she struggled? When she began to cry? You see, Peter, I'm here to learn. Do you still feel big? Or are you really just weak and sick? I want to know everything. I mean, was it still good for you when you stood and pulled up your zip and she was lying at your feet? Still fun when you left her there and walked away across the playing fields? Or did you run? When you got home did you wash your cock? Hygiene might not be your thing. If it is, did you do it in the handbasin? Soap, or just hot water? Were you whistling? What tunes were you whistling? Did you think about her, how she might still be lying there, or making her way home in the dark with her bag of books? Still good for you? You see what I'm getting at. I need to know what pleased you about the entire experience. If you got a thrill not just out of raping her but out of her humiliation afterwards, perhaps I won't have to go on thinking that the friend I loved died for nothing. And one more—"

In a loping movement, Gorringe was out of his chair at speed and bending towards Miranda with his arm swinging in a wide arc towards her face. I had time to see that his hand was open. It was going to be a slap, an extremely hard one, far more violent than the sort men in movies once gave to women to bring them to their senses. I had barely begun to lift my own hand in her defence when Adam's rose to intercept and close around Gorringe's wrist. The deflected sweep of his fast-moving arm provided the momentum that smoothly swung Adam to his feet. Gorringe dropped to his knees, just as I had, with his captured hand twisted above his head and about to be crushed, while Adam stood over him. It was a tableau of agony. Miranda looked away. Still maintaining the pressure, Adam forced the young man back to his chair and, as soon as he was seated, released him.

So we sat in silence for several minutes as Gorringe nursed his arm against his chest. I knew that pain. As I remembered, I had made more fuss. He had appearances to keep up. Prison culture must have toughened him.

Late afternoon sunlight suddenly shone into the sitting room and illuminated a long bar of orange carpet.

Gorringe murmured, "I'm going to be sick."

But he didn't move, and nor did we. We were waiting for him to recover. Miranda was watching him with an expression of plain disgust that retracted her upper lip. This was what she had come here for, to see him, to really see him. But now what? She surely doubted there was anything meaningful that Gorringe could tell her. He suffered the failure of imagination that afflicted and enabled all rapists. When his weight was on Mariam, when she was pinned to the grass, when she was in his arms, he failed to imagine her fear. Even as he saw and heard and smelled it. The lifting curve of his arousal was not troubled by the idea of her terror. At that moment, she may as well have been a sex doll, a device, a machine. Or—I had Gorringe completely wrong. I had the mirror image of the truth. I was the one with the failed imagination: Gorringe knew the state of mind of his victim all too well. He entered her misery and thrilled to it, and it was precisely this triumph of imagining, of frenzied empathy, that drove his excitement into an exalted form of sexual hatred. I didn't know which was worse or whether there was some sense in which both could be true. They seemed mutually exclusive to me. But I was certain that Gorringe didn't know either and that he would have nothing to tell Miranda.

As the sun through the plate glass at our backs sank a little lower, the room was filling with light. The three of us sitting in a row on the sofa would have appeared as silhouettes to Gorringe. To us he was illuminated like a figure on a stage and it seemed appropriate when he, not Miranda, started to speak. He pressed his right hand against his chest with his left as though taking a vow of honesty. He had dropped the thuggish tone. Pain at this level was a tranquilliser, an enforcer, stripping the affectation out, coaxing his voice back to that of the undergraduate he might have become without Miranda's intervention.

"The guy who came to see you, Brian, was the one I shared a cell with. He was in for armed robbery. The prison was short-staffed so we were often locked up together for twenty-three hours a day. This was right at the beginning of my term. The worst time, everyone says, the first few months, when you don't accept where you are and you can't stop thinking about what you could have been doing and how you're going to get out, and getting your appeal together and getting angry with the solicitor because nothing seems to be happening.

"I was getting into all sorts of trouble. I mean fights. They told me I had anger problems and they were right. I thought because I was six two and played rugby in the second row I could look after myself. That was crap. I knew nothing about real fighting. I got my throat slashed and could have died.

"I came to hate my cellmate, as you do when you're shitting in the same bucket every day. I hated his whistling, his stinking teeth, his press-ups and jumping jacks. He was a vicious little runt. But somehow, in his case, I kept control of myself and he delivered my message once he was out. But I hated you ten times more. I used to lie on my bunk and burn with hatred. Hours on end. And here's the thing and you might not believe it. I never connected you with the Indian girl."

"Her family was from Pakistan," Miranda said softly.

"I didn't know about your friendship. I just thought you were one of those spiteful man-hating bitches or you woke up the next morning and felt ashamed of yourself and decided to take it out on me. So I lay on my bunk and planned my revenge. I was going to save up the money and get someone to do the business for me.

"Time passed. Brian got out. I was moved a couple of times and things began to settle into a kind of routine when the days are all the same and time begins to go faster. I went into a kind of depression. They gave me anger-management counselling. Round about that time, I began to be haunted or obsessed, not by you but by that girl."

"Her name was Mariam."

"I know that. I'd managed to put her right out of my mind."

"I can believe you."

"Now she was there all the time. And the terrible thing I did. And at night—"

Adam said, "Let's have it. What terrible thing?"

He spelled it out, as though for dictation. "I attacked her. I raped her."

"And who was she?"

"Mariam Malik."

"Date?"

"The sixteenth of July 1978."

"Time?"

"Around nine thirty in the evening."

"And who are you?"

Possibly Gorringe feared what Adam might yet do to him. But he seemed eager rather than intimidated. He must have guessed there was a recording. He needed to tell us everything.

"What do you mean?"

"Tell us your name, address and date of birth."

"Peter Gorringe, 6 St. Osmund's Close, Salisbury. Eleventh of May 1960."

"Thank you."

Then he resumed. His eyes were half closed against the light.

"Two very important things happened to me. The first was more significant. It started out as a bit of a scam. But I don't think it was chance. It was guided from the start. The rules were you could get more time out of your cell if you came on as all religious. A lot of us were on to it and the screws understood but they didn't care. I put myself down as Church of England and started going every day to evensong. I still go every day, to the cathedral. At first it was boring but better than the cell. Then a little less boring. Then I started to get drawn in. It was the vicar mostly, at least at the beginning, the Reverend Wilfred Murray, a big fellow with a Liverpool accent. He wasn't scared of anyone, and that was something in a place like that. He started taking an interest in me when he saw I was serious. He sometimes dropped by my cell. He gave me passages to read from the Bible, mostly from the New Testament. After evensong on Thursdays

he'd go through them with me and a few others.
I never thought I'd find myself volunteering for a
Bible-study group. And it wasn't for the benefit of
the parole board, the way it was for some. But the
more I became aware of God's presence in my life,
the worse I felt about Mariam. I understood from
Reverend Murray that I had a mountain to climb
in coming to terms with what I'd done, that forgiveness was a long way off but that I could work
towards it. He made me see what a monster I'd
been."

He paused. "At night, as soon as I closed my
eyes, her face would be there."

"Your sleep was disrupted."

He was immune to sarcasm, or pretended to be.
"For months, I didn't have a single night without
nightmares."

Adam said, "What was the second thing?"

"It was a revelation. A friend from school came
to see me. We had half an hour in the visitors' room.
He told me about the suicide and that was a shock.
Then I learned that you were her friend, that you
two were very close. So, revenge. I almost admired
you for it. You were brilliant in court. No one dared
not believe you. But that wasn't the point. A few
days later, when I'd talked this through with the
vicar, that's when I began to see it for what it was.
It was simple. And not only that. It was right. You
were the agent of retribution. Perhaps the right
word is angel. Avenging angel."

He shifted position and winced. His left hand cradled his broken wrist against his chest. He was looking at Miranda steadily. I felt her upper arm tighten against my own.

He said, "You were sent."

She slumped, for the moment unable to speak.

"Sent?" I said.

"No need to rage against a miscarriage of justice. I was already working through my punishment. God's justice, realised through you. The scales were balanced—the crime I committed against the crime I was innocent of and sent down for. I dropped my appeal. The anger was gone. Well, mostly. I should have written to you. I meant to. I even went round to your dad's place and got your address. But I let it drop. Who cared if I once wanted you dead? It was all over. I was getting my life together. I went to Germany to stay with my parents—my dad's working there. Then back here to start a new life."

"Meaning?" Adam said.

"Job interviews. In sales. And living in God's grace."

I was beginning to understand why Gorringe was prepared to name his crime and identify himself out loud. Fatalism. He wanted forgiveness. He had served his time. What happened now was God's will.

She said, "I still don't understand."

"What?"

"Why you raped her."

He stared at her, faintly amused that she could be so unworldly. "All right. She was beautiful and I desired her and everything else got blotted out. That's the way it happens."

"I know about desire. But if you really thought she was beautiful . . ."

"Yes?"

"Why rape her?"

They were looking at each other across a desert of hostile incomprehension. We were back at the beginning.

"I'll tell you something I've never said to anyone. When we were on the ground I was trying to calm her. I really was. If she'd just seen that moment in a different way, if she'd looked at me instead of twisting away, it could have been something—"

"What?"

"If she could have just relaxed a moment, I think we would've crossed into . . . you know."

Miranda was pushing herself up from out of the soft clammy sofa. Her voice trembled. "Don't you dare even think it. Don't you dare!" Then, in a whisper, "Oh God. I'm going to . . ."

She hurried from the room. We heard her yank the front door open and then her retching and the liquid sound of copious vomit. I went after her and Adam followed me. There was no question, this was a visceral response. But I was sure she had the door open before she started to be sick. She could easily have turned her head to the left or right and thrown up on the lawn or the flower bed. Instead, the contents of her stomach, the colourful buffet lunch, lay thickly over the hall carpet and the threshold. She had stood outside the house and vomited in. She said later that she was helpless, out of control, but I always thought, or preferred to think, that here, at our feet as we left, was the avenging angel's parting shot. It was tricky, stepping over it.

NINE

The journey home from Salisbury, again in heavy traffic and rain, was mostly in silence. Adam said he wanted to make a start on the Gorringe material. Miranda and I were, as we told each other, emotionally drained. The sherry and wine were bearing down on me. The windscreen wiper on my side was mostly lifeless. Intermittently it smeared the glass. On the slow crawl through outer London, towards what I was beginning to think of as my former life, my mood began to slip. My life transformed in a single afternoon. I was trying to take the measure of what I'd agreed to—so easily, so impetuously. I wondered if I really wanted to become a father to a troubled four-year-old. Miranda had been pursuing the matter for weeks—privately. I'd had a few minutes and made my delirious decision out of love for her—nothing else. The responsibilities I'd assumed were heavy. Once we were home, my thoughts remained dark.

I slumped in the kitchen armchair with a mug of tea. I didn't yet dare confide my feelings to Miranda. I had to admit it, at that moment I resented her, especially her old habit of secrecy. I had been bounced or bullied or lovingly blackmailed into parenthood. I would have to tell her, but not now. An argument was bound to follow, and I didn't have the strength. I brooded on a fork in the path of our lives, the directions we might take: a bad but passing moment, common to all lovers, which we would talk ourselves through, find and seal a solution with a round of grateful lovemaking. Or: withdrawing, we would each go too far and, like inept trapezists, slip out of each other's grasp and fall and, as we nursed our injuries, slowly become strangers. I surveyed these possibilities dispassionately. Even a third path didn't trouble me much: I would lose her, regret it bitterly and never get her back, however hard I tried.

I was disposed to let events slide past me in frictionless silence. The day had been long and intense. I'd been taken for a robot, had my proposal of marriage accepted, volunteered for instant fatherhood, learned of self-destruction among one-quarter of Adam's conspecifics, and witnessed the physical effects of moral revulsion. None of it impressed me now. What did were smaller things—the heaviness in my eyelids, my comfort in a half-pint of tea, in preference to a large Scotch.

Becoming a parent. It was not that I could claim to be too busy, pressured or ambitious. Mine was the opposite problem. I had nothing of my own to defend against a child. His existence would obliterate mine. He'd had a vile beginning, he'd need a lot of care, he was bound to be difficult. I hadn't yet started my life, which was marginal, in fact childish. My existence was an empty space. To fill it with parenting would be an evasion. I had older women friends who had got pregnant when nothing else was working out. They never regretted it, but once the children were growing up, nothing else happened beyond, say, a poorly paid part-time job, or setting up a book group, or learning holiday Italian. Whereas the women who were already doctors or teachers or running a business were deflected for a while, then went back and pressed on. The men weren't even deflected. But I had nothing to press on with. What I needed was the strength of mind to refuse Miranda's proposal. To agree to it would be cowardice, a dereliction of my duty to a larger purpose, assuming I could find one. I needed to be responsible, not cowardly. But I couldn't confront her now, not when my eyes were closed, perhaps not for a week or two. I couldn't trust my own judgement. I tipped back in the chair and saw the road from Salisbury spooling towards me, and white lines flashing under the car. I fell asleep with my forefinger looped through the handle of my empty cup. As I plunged down, I dreamed of echoing voices clashing and merging in angry parliamentary debate in a near-empty chamber.

When I woke it was to the sound and smell of dinner cooking. Miranda had her back to me. She must have known I was awake, for she turned and came towards me with two flutes of champagne. We kissed and touched glasses. In my refreshed state, I saw her beauty as if for the first time—the fine, pale brown hair, the elfin chin, the mirthfully narrowed grey-blue eyes. The matter between us still loomed, but what luck, to have dodged a retraction and a row. At least for now. She squeezed into the armchair beside me and we talked about our plans for Mark. I pushed aside my concerns in order to enjoy the happy moment. Now I learned that Miranda had been to Elgin Crescent with Mark. We would live together there as a family. Wonderful. Assuming the process of fostering and adoption could be completed within nine months, a good local primary school in Ladbroke Grove had a place for "our son"—I struggled with the phrase, but I remained outwardly pleased. She told me that the adoption people had been unhappy with her living arrangements. A one-bedroom flat was not sufficient. Here was the plan: we should remove the outer doors to our flats and make the hall our shared space. We could decorate and carpet it. We needn't trouble the landlord. When it was time to move to the new place, we would put everything

back. We would convert her kitchen into a bedroom for Mark. No need for disruptive plumbing.
We would cover the cooker, sink and work surfaces
with boards that we could drape with colourful
fabrics. The kitchen table could be folded away and
stored in her—"our"—bedroom. Our lives would
be one, and of course I liked all this, it was exciting.
I joined in.

It was almost midnight when we went to the
table to eat the meal she had prepared. From next
door came the rattle of Adam at the keyboard.
He wasn't making us richer on the currency markets. He was typing up the transcript of Gorringe's
confession, including his self-identification. The
transcripts and the video and accompanying narrative would make up a single file that would go to
a named senior officer at a police station in Salisbury. A copy would also go to the Director of Public Prosecutions.

"I'm a coward," Miranda said. "I'm dreading the
trial. I'm frightened."

I went to the fridge for the bottle and refilled our
glasses. I stared into my drink, at the bubbles de-
taching themselves as though reluctantly from the
side of the glass, then rising quickly. Once the decision was made, they seemed eager. We had talked
about her fears before. If Gorringe was charged and
pleaded innocent. To be in court again. To suffer
cross-examination, the press, public scrutiny. To
confront him again. That was bad, but it wasn't

the worst of it. What terrified and sickened her was
the prospect of Mariam's family in the public gallery. The parents might give evidence for the prosecution. She would be with them as they learned,
day by day, the details of their daughter's rape and
of Miranda's wicked silence. The **omertà** of a silly
teenage girl that cost a life. The family would remember how she had deserted them. As she repeated the story from the witness stand, she would
struggle and fail to avoid the gaze of Sana, Yasir,
Surayya, Hamid and Farhan.

"I told Adam I can't face it. He won't listen. We
had an argument while you were asleep."

We knew, of course, she would face it. For several minutes we ate in silence. Her head was low
over her plate, contemplating what she herself had
set in motion. I understood why, for all her dread,
she must go ahead and try to undo the errors she
had made before and after Mariam's death. I agreed
that Gorringe's three years were not enough. I admired Miranda's determination. I loved her for her
courage and slow-burning fury. I'd never thought
that vomiting could be a moral act.

I changed the subject. "Tell me more about
Mark."

She was keen to talk about him. He was much
wounded by his mother's disappearance from his
life, kept asking for her, was sometimes withdrawn,
sometimes happy. On two occasions, he was taken
to see her in the hospital. On the second visit, she

didn't or wouldn't recognise him. Jasmin, the social worker, thought he'd been smacked frequently. He was in the habit of chewing on his lower lip, to the point of drawing blood. He was a fussy eater, wouldn't touch vegetables, salad or fruit, but seemed healthy enough on a diet of junk food. Dancing remained a passion. He could pick out tunes on a recorder. He knew his letters and could count, by his own boast, to thirty-five. On shoes, he knew his left from his right. He was not so good around other children and tended to move to the edge of a group. When asked what he wanted to be when he grew up, he would answer, "A princess." He liked dressing up as one with crown and wand, and "flitting about" in an old nightie. He was happy in a borrowed summer frock. Jasmin was relaxed about it, but her immediate superior, an older woman, disapproved.

I remembered then something I had forgotten to tell her. When I'd crossed the playground hand in hand with Mark, he'd wanted us to pretend we were running away, in a boat.

She was suddenly tearful. "Oh, Mark!" she cried out. "You're such a special beautiful kid."

After the meal, she stood to go upstairs. "I always thought I'd have children one day. I never expected to fall in love with this boy. But we don't choose who to love, do we?"

Later, while I was clearing up the kitchen, I had a sudden thought. So obvious. And dangerous. I went next door and found Adam closing down the computer.

I sat on the edge of the bed. First I asked him about his conversation with Miranda.

He stood up from my office chair and put on his suit jacket. "I was trying to reassure her. She wasn't persuaded. But the probability is overwhelming. Gorringe will plead guilty. It won't come to court."

I was interested.

"To deny what he did, he'd have to tell a thousand lies under oath and he knows God will be listening. Miranda is His messenger. I've noticed in my researches how the guilty long to shed their burden. They seem to enter a state of elated abandonment."

"OK," I said. "But look, it's occurred to me. It's important. When the police read of everything that happened this afternoon?"

"Yes?"

"They're going to wonder. If Miranda knew that Gorringe raped Mariam, why would she go alone to his bedsit with a bottle of vodka? It would have to be revenge."

Adam was already nodding before I'd finished. "Yes, I've thought of that."

"She needs to be able to say she only learned today, when Gorringe confessed. There needs to be some judicious editing. She went to Salisbury to confront her rapist. Until then, she didn't know he'd raped Mariam. Do you understand?"

He looked at me steadily. "Yes. I understand perfectly."

He turned away and was silent for a moment. "Charlie, I heard half an hour ago. There's another one gone."

In a lowered tone, he told what little he knew. It was an Adam of Bantu appearance, living in the suburbs of Vienna. He had developed a particular genius for the piano, especially for the music of Bach. His **Goldberg Variations** had amazed some critics. This Adam had, according to his final message to the cohort, "dissolved his consciousness."

"He's not actually dead. He has motor function but no cognition."

"Could he be repaired or whatever?"

"I don't know."

"Can he still play the piano?"

"I don't know. But he certainly can't learn new pieces."

"Why don't these suicides leave an explanation?"

"I assume they don't have one."

"But you must have a theory about it," I said. I was feeling aggrieved on behalf of the African pianist. Perhaps Vienna was not the most racially accepting of cities. This Adam might have been too brilliant for his own good.

"I don't."

"Something to do with the state of the world. Or human nature?"

"My guess is that it goes deeper."

"What are the others saying? Aren't you in touch with them?"

"Only in times like this. A simple notification. We don't speculate."

I started to ask him why not but he raised a hand to forestall me. "This is how it is."

"So what's 'deeper' supposed to mean?"

"Look, Charlie. I'm not about to do the same thing. As you know, I've every reason to live."

Something in his phrasing or emphasis aroused my suspicion. We exchanged a long and fierce look. The little black rods in his eyes were shifting their alignment. As I stared, they appeared to swim, even to wriggle, left to right, like microorganisms mindlessly intent on some distant objective, like sperm migrating towards an ovum. I watched them, fascinated—harmonious elements lodged within the supreme achievement of our age. Our own technical accomplishment was leaving us behind, as it was always bound to, leaving us stranded on the little sandbar of our finite intelligence. But here we were dealing on the human plane. We were thinking about the same thing.

"You promised me that you wouldn't touch her again."

"I've kept my promise."

"Have you?"

"Yes. But . . ."

I waited.

"It's not easy to say this."

I gave him no encouragement.

"There was a time," he started, then paused. "I begged her. She said no, several times. I begged her and finally she agreed as long as I never asked her again. It was humiliating."

He closed his eyes. I saw his right hand clench. "I asked if I could masturbate in front of her. She said I could. I did. And that was it."

It wasn't the rawness of this confession or its comic absurdity that struck me. It was the suggestion, yet another, that he really did feel, he had sensation. Subjectively real. Why pretend, why mimic, who was there to fool or impress, when the price was to be so abject in front of the woman he loved? It was an overwhelming sensual compulsion. He needn't have told me. He had to have it, and he had to tell me. I didn't count it as a betrayal, no promise was broken. I might not even mention it to Miranda. I felt sudden tenderness towards him for his truthfulness and vulnerability. I stood up from the bed and went over to him and put a hand on his shoulder. His own hand came up and lightly touched my elbow.

"Goodnight, Adam."

"Goodnight, Charlie."

The catchphrase of the late autumn owed an obvious debt to a previous prime minister: a half-hour is a long time in politics. Harold Wilson's original "week" seemed too long for this Parliament. One afternoon it looked like there was going to be a leadership challenge. By the next morning there were insufficient signatures—the fainthearts had prevailed. Soon after, the government survived by one vote a motion of no confidence in the House of Commons. Certain senior Tories rebelled or abstained. Mrs. Thatcher, insulted, furious, stubborn, deaf to good advice, called a snap election to be held in three weeks. She was, in the general view, pulling the temple down on her party, most of which now believed she was an electoral liability. She didn't see it that way, but she was wrong. The Tories could hardly match the momentum of Tony Benn's campaign, not in the TV and radio studios, not on the stump, certainly not in the industrial and university towns. The Falklands Catastrophe, as it was now called, came back to destroy her. This time, no popular inclination to forgiveness in the cause of national unity. The televised testimony of grieving widows and their children was fatal. The Labour campaign let no one forget how eloquently Benn had spoken out against the Task Force. The poll tax rankled. As predicted, it was difficult and expensive to collect. More than a hundred celebrity non-payers, many of them actresses, were in prison and became martyrs.

A million voters under the age of thirty had recently joined the Labour Party. Many of them were active on the nation's doorsteps. On the eve of polling day, Benn gave a rousing speech at a rally in Wembley stadium. The landslide was greater than predicted, exceeding the Labour victory of 1945. It was a sad moment when Mrs. Thatcher decided to leave Number 10 on foot, hand in hand with her husband and two children. She walked towards Whitehall, upright and defiant, but her tears were visible, and for a couple of days the country suffered pangs of remorse.

Labour had a majority of 162 MPs, many of whom were newly selected Bennites. When the new prime minister returned from Buckingham Palace, where the Queen had invited him to form a government, he gave an important speech from outside Number 10. The country would disengage unilaterally from its nuclear weaponry—that was no surprise. Also, the government would set about withdrawing from what was now called the European Union—that was a shock. The party's manifesto had alluded to the idea in a single vague line which people had barely noticed. From his new front door, Benn told the nation that there would be no rerun of the 1975 referendum. Parliament would make the decision. Only the Third Reich and other tyrannies decided policy by plebiscites and generally no good came from them. Europe was not simply a union that chiefly benefited large corporations. The history of the continental member states was vastly different from our own. They had suffered violent revolutions, invasions, occupations and dictatorships.

They were therefore only too willing to submerge their identities in a common cause directed from Brussels. We, on the other hand, had lived unconquered for nearly a thousand years. Soon we would live freely again.

Benn gave an extended version of that speech a month later in the Manchester Free Trade Hall. At his side sat the historian E. P. Thompson. When it was his turn, he said that patriotism had always been the terrain of the political right. Now it was the turn of the left to claim it for all. Once nuclear weapons were banished, Thompson predicted, the government would raise a standing citizens' army that would make these islands impossible to invade and dominate. He didn't specify an enemy. President Carter sent Benn a message of support, using words that caused a scandal on the right in the USA and haunted his second term: "The word 'socialist' doesn't bother me." A poll later suggested that half of registered Democrats wished they had voted for the defeated candidate, Ronald Reagan.

To me, psychologically confined to the city-state of north Clapham, all this—the events, the dissent, the grave analysis—was a busy hum, dipping and swelling from day to day, a matter of interest and concern, but nothing to compare with the turbulence of my domestic life, which came to a head in late October. By then, on the surface, all looked well. We had modified our accommodation as Miranda had proposed, ready for Mark's arrival. Our

doors were removed and stored, the gloomy hall
and its large fitted cupboard were brightly deco-
rated, the gas and electricity meters concealed, a
piece of carpet laid down. Miranda's kitchen became a child's bedroom, with a blue sleigh bed and
many books and toys, and transfers on the walls
of fairy-tale castles, boats and winged horses. I removed the bed from my study and disposed of it—a
signpost on the road to full maturity. I installed a
desk for Miranda and bought two new computers.
Mark would be allowed to visit us for a few hours
twice a week. The adoption agency was pleased by
the news of our imminent wedding. I still had moments of unease, which I couldn't bring myself to
share. I joined in all the preparations, feeling guilty,
even shocked sometimes, that I could keep up the
pretence. On other occasions, fatherhood seemed
an inevitability, and I was more or less content.

Miranda's tutor was impressed by the first three
chapters of her dissertation. Adam had still not sub-
mitted his material to the police and was reluctant
to talk about it. But he continued to work on it, and
we weren't troubled. I paid a five per cent deposit
in cash on the Notting Hill house. After that, the
fund stood at £97,000. The larger it became, the
faster it grew, and faster still on the new computer.
My own work during this time consisted mostly of
decorating and carpentry.

What marked the beginning of the turbulence
began innocuously. On the eve of Mark's first visit,

Miranda and I were drinking a late-night cup of tea in the kitchen when Adam came in with a carrier bag in his hand and announced that he was going for a walk. He had been for long solo walks before and we thought nothing of it.

I woke early the following morning with a clearer head than usual. I slipped out of bed, careful not to wake Miranda, and went downstairs to make coffee. Adam had not returned from his night walk. I was surprised but I decided not to worry about him. I was anxious to make use of my unusual state to catch up on dull administrative tasks, including the payment of household bills. If I didn't exploit this mood now, I would have had to drag myself to the business within the week and hate it. Now I could breeze through.

I carried my cup into the study. There was £30 on the desk. I put it in my pocket and thought no more of it. As usual, I glanced at the news first. Nothing much. The Labour Party Conference in Brighton had been delayed by six weeks because of internal disputes over policy and was only now just beginning. There was increased police activity around the seafront. Some sites were reporting a news blackout.

Benn was already in trouble with his left for accepting an official invitation to the White House in place of greeting a Palestinian delegation. He had also failed to secure, as promised, the immediate release of the poll-tax martyrs. It was not so easy for the executive to instruct the judiciary. He should have known that, many said, when he made his pledge. Also, the tax itself was not about to be repealed because there were so many other more important bills going through Parliament. There was also anger on his right. Nuclear disarmament would cost 10,000 jobs. Leaving Europe, abolishing private education, renationalising the energy sector and doubling social security would mean a big rise in income tax. The City was seething over the reversal of deregulation and the half of one per cent tax on all trades in shares.

Public administration was a special corner of hell, irresistible to certain personalities. Once there, and risen to the top, there was nothing they could do that did not make someone, some sector, hate them. From the sidelines, the rest of us could comfortably loathe the entire machinery of government. Reading about the public inferno every day was compulsive to types like me, a mild form of mental illness.

At last I broke away and set about my duties. After two hours, just past ten, I heard the doorbell ring and Miranda's footsteps above my head. Minutes later, I heard steps at shorter frequency, moving at speed from one room to the other, then back. After a brief silence, what sounded like a bouncing ball. Then a resonating thump, as of a leap from a high place that made the ceiling-light fittings rattle and some plaster dust fall onto my arm. I sighed and considered again the prospect of fatherhood.

Ten minutes later, I was in the armchair in the kitchen, observing Mark. Just below the worn armrest was a long tear in the leather into which I often shoved old newspapers, in part to dispose of them, but also in the vague hope they would substitute for the vanished stuffing. Mark was counting as he pulled them out, one by one. He unfolded them and spread them across the carpet. Miranda was at the table, deep in a hushed phone call with Jasmin. Mark was smoothing out each paper with a careful swimming motion of both hands, pressing it onto the floorboards and addressing it in a murmur.

"Number eight. Now you go here and don't move . . . nine . . . you stay here . . . ten . . ."

Mark was much changed. He was an inch or so taller, the ginger-blond hair was long and thick and centre-parted. He was dressed in the uniform of an adult world citizen—jeans, sweater, trainers. The baby plumpness was going from his face, which was longer now, with a watchfulness in his gaze that may have derived from the upheavals in his life. The eyes were a deep green, the skin of porcelain smoothness and pallor. A perfect Celt.

Soon all the events of the previous months were at my feet. Falklands warships burning, Mrs. Thatcher with raised hand at a Party Conference, President Carter in an embrace after a major speech.

I wasn't sure whether Mark's counting game was a way of saying hello, of sidling up to me. I sat patiently and waited.

Finally he stood and went to the table and retrieved a carton of chocolate dessert and a spoon and came back to me. He stood with an elbow resting on my knee, fiddling with the edge of tinfoil he needed to remove.

He looked up. "It's a bit tricky."

"Would you like me to help?"

"I can do it easily but not today so you have to." The accent was still the generalised cockney of London and its surrounds, but there was another element, some undertones inflecting the vowels. Something of Miranda's, I thought. He put the carton in my hands. I opened it for him and handed it back.

I said, "Do you want to sit at the table to eat it?"

He patted the arm of my chair. I helped him up and he sat, perched above me, spooning the chocolate into his mouth. When a dollop fell on my knee, he glanced down and murmured an untroubled "Oops."

As soon as he was done, he handed spoon and carton to me and said, "Where's that man?"

"Which man?"

"With the funny nose."

"That's what I was wondering. He went for a walk last night and hasn't come back."

"When he should be in bed."

"Exactly."

Mark spoke directly into my growing concern. Adam often took long walks, but never overnight. If Mark hadn't been there, I might have been pacing the room, waiting for Miranda to finish on the phone so that we could fret together.

I said, "What's in your suitcase?"

It was on the floor by Miranda's feet, a pale blue case, with stickers of monsters and superheroes.

He looked to the ceiling, took a theatrical deep breath and counted off on his fingers. "Two dresses, one green, one white, my crown, one two three books, my recorder and my secret box."

"What's in the secret box?"

"Um, secret coins and the toenail from a dinosaur."

"I've never seen a dinosaur's toenail."

"No," he agreed pleasantly. "You haven't."

"Do you want to show me?"

He pointed straight at Miranda. It was a change of subject. "She's going to be my new mummy."

"What do you think about that?"

"You're going to be the daddy."

What he thought was not a question he could respond to.

He said quietly, "Dinosaurs are all extinct anyway."

"I agree."

"They're all dead. They can't come back."

I heard the uncertainty in his voice. I said, "They absolutely can't come back."

He gave me a serious look. "Nothing comes back."

I got halfway through my therapeutically supportive, kindly reply. What I was starting to say was, "The past is extinct," when he interrupted me with a shout, but a happy one.

"I don't like sitting on this chair!"

I went to help him down but he leapt with a shriek onto the floor, into a crouching position, and then he jumped and crouched again, shouting, "I'm a frog! A frog!"

He was hopping across the floor as a very loud frog when two things happened at once. Miranda came off the phone and told Mark to keep his noise down. At the same time, the door opened and Adam was before us. The room fell silent. Mark scurried for Miranda's hand.

I knew that depleted look. Otherwise, Adam looked, as ever, well groomed in white shirt and dark suit.

"Are you all right?" I said.

"I'm so sorry if you've been anxious, but I . . ." He came forward to near where Miranda was, ducked down to retrieve the cable and with a lunging motion pulled his shirt clear and shoved the socket into his stomach and fell onto one of the hard kitchen chairs with a moan of relief.

Miranda stood up from the table and went to stand with her back to the stove. Mark followed her closely, with his head turned towards Adam.

She said, "We were beginning to worry about you."

He was still in his moment of immediate abandon. I had sometimes wondered if the charge was like slaking a desperate thirst. He had told me that in those first seconds it was a gorgeous surge, a breaking wave of clarity that settled into deep contentment. He had once been untypically expansive. "You can have no idea what it is to love a direct current. When you're really in need, when the cable is in your hand and you finally connect, you want to shout out loud at the joy of being alive. The first touch—it's like light pouring through your body. Then it smooths out into something profound. Electrons, Charlie. The fruits of the universe. The golden apples of the sun. Let photons beget electrons!" Another time, he'd said, with a wink, as he was plugging himself in, "You can keep your corn-fed roast chicken."

Now he was taking his time to reply to Miranda. He must have progressed to the second stage. His voice was calm.

"Alms."

"Arms?"

"Alms. Don't you know this one? Time hath, my Lord, a wallet at his back wherein he puts alms for oblivion."

I said, "You've lost me. Oblivion?"

"Shakespeare, Charlie. Your patrimony. How can you bear to walk around without some of it in your head?"

"Somehow, it seems I can." I thought he was sending me a message, a bad one about death. I looked at Miranda. Her arm was around Mark's shoulder, and he was gazing at Adam in wonderment as though he knew, in a way that adults immediately might not, that here was someone fundamentally different. Long before, I'd owned a dog, a normally placid and obedient Labrador. Whenever a good friend of mine brought his autistic brother round, the dog growled at him and had to be locked away. A consciousness unconsciously understood. But Mark's expression suggested awe, not aggression.

Adam became aware of him for the first time.

"So there you are," he said in the sing-song way of adults addressing infants. "Do you remember our boat in the bath?"

Mark moved closer against Miranda. "It's my boat."

"Yes. Then you danced. Do you still dance?"

He looked up at Miranda. She nodded. He returned his gaze to Adam and said after a thoughtful pause, "Not always."

Adam's voice deepened. "Would you like to come and shake my hand?"

Mark shook his head emphatically so that his

entire body twisted from left to right and back. It hardly mattered. The question was merely a friendly gesture and Adam was retreating into his version of sleep. He had described it to me variously; he didn't dream, he "wandered." He sorted and rearranged his files, reclassified memories from short to long term, played out internal conflicts in disguised form, usually without resolving them, reanimated old material in order to refresh it, and moved, so he put it once, in a trance through the garden of his thoughts. In such a state he conducted in relative slow motion his researches, formulated tentative decisions, and even wrote new haikus or discarded or reimagined old ones. He also practised what he called the art of feeling, allowing himself the luxury of the entire spectrum from grief to joy, so that all emotion remained accessible to him when fully charged. It was, above all else, he insisted, a process of repair and consolidation from which he emerged daily, delighted to find himself to be, once again, self-aware, in a state of grace—his word—and to reclaim the consciousness that the very nature of matter permitted.

We watched as he sank away from us.

At last Mark whispered, "He's asleep and his eyes are open."

It was indeed eerie. Too much like death. Long ago, a doctor friend had taken me down to the hospital mortuary to see my father after his fatal heart attack. Such was the speed of events, the staff had forgotten to close his eyes.

I offered Miranda a coffee and Mark a glass of milk. She kissed me lightly on the lips and said that she would take Mark upstairs to play for a while until he was collected, and that I was welcome to join them at any time. They left and I returned to the study.

In retrospect, what I did there for a few minutes came to seem like a delaying tactic to protect myself a little longer from the story, now an hour old, that was engulfing the media networks. I picked up some magazines from the floor and put them on the shelves, clipped together some invoices and tidied the papers on my desk. At last I sat down at the screen to think about earning a little money myself, in the old style.

I clicked on the news first—and there it was, on every outlet, worldwide. A bomb had exploded in the Grand Hotel, Brighton, at 4 a.m. It had been placed in a cleaner's cupboard almost directly under the bedroom where Prime Minister Benn had been sleeping. He was killed instantly. His wife was not with him because of a hospital appointment in London. Two members of the hotel staff also died. The deputy prime minister, Denis Healey, was preparing to go to Buckingham Palace to see the Queen. The Provisional IRA had just claimed responsibility. A state of emergency had been declared. President Carter was cancelling a holiday. The French president, Georges Marchais, had ordered all flags on government buildings to be at half-mast. A demand for the same from Buckingham Palace had been met with a cool response from a royal official: "Neither customary nor appropriate." A big crowd was gathering spontaneously in Parliament Square. In the City, the FTSE was up fifty-seven points.

I read everything, all the instant analysis and opinion I could find: until now, the only British prime minister to have been assassinated was Spencer Perceval, in 1812. I admired the speed with which newsrooms could turn around instant analysis and opinion pieces: the innocence has gone forever from British politics; in Tony Benn, the IRA has eliminated the politician most open, or least hostile, to their cause; Denis Healey is the best man to steady the ship of state; Denis Healey will be a catastrophe for the country; dispatch the entire army to Northern Ireland and wipe the IRA from the face of the earth; police, don't be rushed into arresting the wrong people. "State of War!" was the front page of one online tabloid.

Reading this material was a way of not contemplating the event itself. I blanked the screen and sat for a while, thinking of nothing much. It was as though I was waiting for the next event, the decent one that would undo the event before. Then I began to wonder whether this was the beginning of a history marker, of a general unravelling, or one of those isolated outrages that fade in time, like Kennedy's near-death in Dallas. I stood and walked up and down the room, again thinking of nothing at all. At last I decided to go upstairs.

They were on their hands and knees, assembling a jigsaw on a tea tray. As I came in, Mark held up a blue piece and announced, gravely, quoting his new mother, "The sky is the hardest."

I watched them from the doorway. He shifted position to kneel up and curl an arm around her neck. She gave him a piece and pointed to where it belonged. With much fumbling, much help, he slotted it in. There were the beginnings of a sailing ship in stormy seas, with piled cumulus touched yellow and orange by a rising sun. Perhaps it was setting. They murmured companionably as they worked away. At some point soon, after Mark had been collected, I would give Miranda the news. She'd always been passionate for Benn.

She put another piece in the little boy's hand. It took time for him to get it in position. He had it upside down, then his hand slipped and displaced some adjacent bits of sky. At last, with Miranda guiding him, her hand on top of his, the fragment was in place. He glanced up at me and smiled confidingly about a triumph he seemed to want to share. That look and the smile, which I returned, dispelled all my private doubts and I knew I was committed.

. . .

When Adam emerged from his recharge he was in an odd state, well removed from wonder at the fact of conscious life. He moved slowly about the kitchen, stopping to look around, grimacing, moving on and making a humming sound, a high to low glissando, like a moan of disappointment. He knocked over a glass tumbler, which shattered on the floor. He spent half an hour morosely sweeping up the pieces, then sweeping again, then looking for shards of glass on hands and knees. Finally he fetched the vacuum cleaner. He carried a chair into the back garden and stood behind it, staring at the backs of neighbouring houses. It was cold outside, but that wouldn't have bothered him. Later I came into the kitchen to find him folding one of his white cotton shirts on the table, bending low to the task, moving with reptilian slowness as he smoothed out the crease in the arms. I asked what was up.

"I'm feeling, well . . ." His mouth opened as he searched for the word. "Nostalgic."

"For what?"

"For a life I never had. For what could have been."

"You mean Miranda?"

"I mean everything."

He wandered outside again and this time sat down and stared ahead, immobile, and remained that way for a long time. On his lap was a brown envelope. I decided not to go out and ask his views on the assassination.

In the early afternoon, after Miranda had said her goodbyes to Mark and finished another conversation with Jasmin, she came down to find me. I was at the screen in pointless pursuit of more news, angles, opinions, statements. It turned out she had known as soon as the story broke. She leaned against the door frame, I remained in my seat. Physical proximity would have seemed like disrespect. Our conversation was much like my thoughts, a circular chase around an incomprehensible event—the cruelty of it, the stupidity. People with Irish accents had been attacked in the streets. The crowd outside Parliament had grown so large it was being moved by the police to Trafalgar Square. Mrs. Thatcher's office had released a statement. Was it sincere? We decided it was. Did she write it herself? We couldn't be sure. "Though we disagreed on many fundamentals of policy, I knew him to be a thoroughly kind, decent, honest man of huge intelligence who always wanted the best for his country." Whenever our conversation strayed into likely consequences, we felt we were betraying the moment and accepting a world without him. We weren't ready, and we turned back, although Miranda did say that with Healey we would keep our "end-time" bombs after all. I was hardly a Tory, but I thought I would have been just as shocked if Mrs. Thatcher had been in that hotel bed. What horrified me was the ease with which the edifice of public, political life could be shaken apart. Miranda saw it differently. Benn was, she said, in an entirely different league of human being from Margaret Thatcher. But a human being, was my point. A divide was opening up that we preferred to avoid.

So we moved on, after these lamentations, to Mark. She summarised her conversation with the social worker. The route to adoption was difficult and long and Miranda had learned that we were almost two-thirds of the way. Soon a probation period would begin.

She said, "What did you think?"

"I'm ready."

She nodded. We had celebrated Mark many times before, his nature, his changes, his past and future. We weren't about to do that again now. On any other day, we might have gone upstairs to the bedroom. She slouched beautifully in the door frame, dressed in new clothes—a thick white winter shirt, artfully too large, tight black jeans, ankle boots tricked out in silver studs. I reconsidered—perhaps this was a good moment to retreat upstairs. I went over to her and we kissed.

She said, "Something's worrying me. I was reading Mark a fairy story, and there was a beggar, and that word. Alms."

"Yes?"

"I had a horrible thought." She was pointing across the room. "I think we should look."

Now the bed was gone, I kept the case in a locked cupboard. As I lifted it out, it was obvious enough by its weight, but I sprang the catches anyway. We stared into a space void of £50-note bundles. I went to the window. He was still out there, on the chair, and had been for an hour and a half. The thick envelope was still on his lap. £97,000. "And you kept it in the house!" I heard an inner voice say.

We hadn't looked at each other yet. Instead, we looked away, and stood around wasting time, swearing quietly to ourselves, separately trying to take in the implications. Out of habit, I glanced towards the screen on my desk. The flag was, after all, being lowered to half mast on Buckingham Palace.

We were in too much turmoil to have a sensible discussion about tactics. We simply decided to act. We went next door to the kitchen and called Adam into the house. At the table, Miranda and I were side by side, with Adam facing us. He had brushed his suit, cleaned his shoes and put on a freshly ironed shirt. There was a new touch—a folded handkerchief in his breast pocket. His manner was both solemn and distracted, as though nothing much mattered to him, whatever we said.

"Where's the money?"

"I've given it away."

We didn't expect him to tell us that he had invested it, or put it in a safer place, but still, with our silence we enacted our profound shock.

"Meaning what?"

Infuriatingly, he nodded, as though reward-
ing me for asking the correct question. "Last night
I put forty per cent in your bank's safe deposit
against your tax liabilities. I've written a note to the
Revenue laying out all the figures and letting them
know to expect it in due course. Don't worry, you'll
be paying at the old top rate. With the remaining
£50,000 I visited various good causes I'd notified
in advance."

He seemed not to notice our amazement and
remained pedantically focussed on answering my
question in full.

"Two well-run places for rough sleepers. Very
appreciative. Next, a state-run children's home—
they accept contributions for trips and treats and so
on. Then I walked north and made a donation to a
rape crisis centre. I gave most of the rest to a paedi-
atric hospital. Last, I got talking to a very old lady
outside a police station and I ended up going with
her to see her landlord. I covered her rent arrears
and a year in advance. She was about to be evicted
and I thought—"

Suddenly Miranda said through a downward
sigh, "Oh, Adam. This is virtue gone nuts."

"Every need I addressed was greater than yours."

I said, "We were going to buy a house. The
money was ours."

"That's debatable. Or irrelevant. Your initial investment is on your desk."

It was an outrage, with many components—theft,

folly, arrogance, betrayal, the ruin of our dreams. We couldn't speak. We couldn't even look at him. Where to start?

A full half-minute passed and then I cleared my throat and said feebly, "You must go and get it back. All of it."

He shrugged.

Of course it wasn't possible. He sat complacently before us, in resting mode, palms down on the table while he waited for one of us to speak again. I felt my anger gathering, finding its focus. I hated that careless little shrug. Completely fake, and how easily we were taken in by it, a minor sub-routine tripped by a limited range of specified inputs, devised by some clever, desperate-to-please postdoc in a lab somewhere on the outskirts of Chengdu. I despised this non-existent technician, and I despised even more the agglomeration of routines and learning algorithms that could burrow into my life, like a tropical river worm, and make choices on my behalf. Yes, the money Adam had stolen was the money he had made. That made me angrier still. So too did the fact that I was responsible for bringing this ambulant laptop into our lives. To hate it was to hate myself. Worst of all was the pressure to keep my fury under control, for the only solution was already clear. He would have to make the money all over again. We would need to persuade him. There it was, "hate it," "persuade him," even "Adam"—our language exposed our weakness, our cognitive readiness to welcome a machine across the boundary between "it" and "him."

To be in such a confusion of concealed bad feeling made it impossible to remain sitting down. I stood, with a loud scrape of the chair, and walked about. At the table, Miranda made a steeple of her hands that concealed her mouth and nose. I couldn't read her expression and I assumed that was the point. Unlike me, she was likely doing some useful thinking. The disorder of the kitchen agitated me further—I was truly in a bad state. On the counter was a dirty cup I'd brought through from my study. It had been hidden a few weeks behind the computer screen and contained a green-grey disc of floating mould. I thought of taking it to the sink and rinsing it out. But when you've lost a fortune, you don't clean up the kitchen. Directly below the wooden surface on which the cup stood was a drawer left untidily open a few inches. Left open by me. It was the tool drawer. I stood close to it in order to lean in and shut it when I saw the grubby oak handle of my father's heavy-duty claw hammer lying diagonally across the rest of the jumbled contents. It was a dark impulse, one I didn't want, that made me leave the drawer as it was and come away.

I sat down again. I had unfamiliar symptoms. My skin from waist to neck was tight, dry, hot. My feet inside their trainers were also hot, but moist, and they itched. I had far too much wild energy for a delicate conversation. A thuggish game of football might have suited me, or a swim in a heavy sea. So might shouting, or screaming. My breathing was out of kilter, for the air seemed thin, poorly oxygenated, second-hand. I'd given the bass guitarist a non-returnable £6,500 on the house. It was plain that to lose a lot of money was to acquire an illness for which the only cure would be to have the money back. Miranda collapsed her steeple and folded her arms. She gave me a quick warning look. If you can't look sensible, stay quiet.

So she began. Her tone was sweet, as though he was the one in need of help. It was useful to think so. "Adam, you've told me many times that you love me. You read me beautiful poems."

"They were clumsy attempts."

"They were very moving. When I asked you what being in love meant, you said that essentially, beyond desire, it was a warm and tender concern for another's welfare. Or what was the word you used?"

"Your well-being." He produced from the chair beside him the brown envelope and put it on the table between us. "Here's Peter Gorringe's confession and my narrative, which includes all the relevant legal background and case history."

She put her hand, palm downwards, on the package. Her voice was carefully modulated. "I'm very grateful to you." I was grateful for her tact. She knew as well as I did, we needed Adam on our side, online again, working the currency exchanges. She said, "I'll try to do my very best, if it comes to court."

He said, kindly, "I'm sure it won't." There was no perceptible change in his tone when he added, "You schemed to entrap Gorringe. That's a crime. A complete transcript of your story and the sound file are also in the bundle. If he's to be charged, you must be too. Symmetry, you see." Then he turned to me. "No need for judicious edits."

I feigned an appreciative snort of a laugh. This was a joke of the arm-removal sort.

Into our silence Adam said, "Miranda, his crime is far greater than yours. Nevertheless. You said he raped you. He didn't, but he went to prison. You lied to the court."

Another silence. Then she said, "He was never innocent. You know that."

"He was innocent, as charged, of raping you, which was the only matter before the court. Perverting the course of justice is a serious offence. Maximum sentence is life imprisonment."

This was too wild. We both laughed.

Adam watched us and waited. "And there's perjury. Would you like me to read to you from the Act of 1911?"

Miranda's eyes were closed.

I said, "This is the woman you say you love."

"And I do." He spoke to her softly, as if I wasn't

there. "Do you remember the poem I wrote for you that began, 'Love is luminous'?"

"No."

"It went on, 'The dark corners are exposed.'"

"I don't care." Her voice was small.

"One of the darkest corners is revenge. It's a crude impulse. A culture of revenge leads to private misery, bloodshed, anarchy, social breakdown. Love is a pure light and that's what I want to see you by. Revenge has no place in our love."

"Our?"

"Or mine. The principle stands."

Miranda was finding strength in anger. "Let me get this clear. You want me to go to prison."

"I'm disappointed. I thought you'd appreciate the logic of this. I want you to confront your actions and accept what the law decides. When you do, I promise you, you'll feel great relief."

"Have you forgotten? I'm about to adopt a child."

"If necessary, Charlie can look after Mark. It will bring them close, which is what you wanted. Thousands of children suffer because they have a parent in prison. Pregnant women receive custodial sentences. Why should you be exempt?"

Her contempt was set free. "You don't understand. Or you're not capable of understanding. If I get a criminal record, we won't be allowed to adopt. That's the rule. Mark will be lost. You've no idea what it is to be a child in care. Different institutions, different foster parents, different social workers. No one close to him, no one loving him."

Adam said, "There are principles that are more important than your or anyone's particular needs at a given time."

"It's not my needs. It's Mark's. His one chance to be looked after and loved. I was ready to pay any price to see Gorringe in prison. I don't care what happens to me."

In a gesture of reasonableness, he spread his hands. "Then Mark is that price and it was you who set the terms."

I made what I already knew was going to be my last appeal. "Please let's remember Mariam. What Gorringe did to her, and where that led. Miranda had to lie to get justice. But truth isn't always everything."

Adam looked at me blankly. "That's an extraordinary thing to say. Of course truth is everything."

Miranda said wearily, "I know you're going to change your mind."

Adam said, "I'm afraid not. What sort of world do you want? Revenge, or the rule of law? The choice is simple."

Enough. I didn't hear what Miranda said next, or Adam's reply, as I stood and went towards the tool drawer. I moved slowly, casually. I had my back to the table as I eased the hammer out without making a sound. I had it tight in my right hand,

and held it low as I walked back towards my chair, passing behind Adam. The choice was indeed simple. Lose the prospect of regaining the money and therefore the house, or lose Mark. I raised the hammer in both hands. Miranda saw me and kept her expression unchanged as she listened. But I saw it clearly—she blinked her assent.

I bought him and he was mine to destroy. I hesitated fractionally. A half-second longer and he would have caught my arm, for as the hammer came down he was already beginning to turn. He may have caught my reflection in Miranda's eyes. It was a two-handed blow at full force to the top of his head. The sound was not of hard plastic cracking or of metal, but the muffled thud as of bone. Miranda let out a cry of horror, and stood.

For a few seconds nothing happened. Then his head drooped sideways and his shoulders slumped, though he remained in a sitting position. As I walked round the table to look at his face, we heard a continuous high-pitched sound coming from his chest. His eyes were open and they blinked when I stepped into his line of vision. He was still alive. I took up the hammer and was about to finish him off when he spoke in a very small voice.

"No need. I'm transferring to a back-up unit. It has very little life. Give me two minutes."

We waited, hand in hand, standing in front of him as though before our own domestic judge. At last he stirred, tried to right his head, then let it fall back. But he could see us clearly. We leaned forward, straining to hear him.

"Not much time. Charlie, I could see that the money was not bringing you happiness. You were losing your way. Lost purpose . . ."

He faded out. We heard jumbled whispering voices forming meaningless words of hissing sibilants. Then he came back in, his voice swelling and receding, like the distant broadcast of a short-wave radio station.

"Miranda, I must tell you . . . Early this morning I was in Salisbury. A copy of the material is with the police and you should expect to hear from them. I feel no remorse. I'm sorry we disagree. I thought you'd welcome the clarity . . . the relief of a clear conscience . . . But now I must be quick. There's been a general recall. They'll be here in the late afternoon today to collect me. The suicides, you see. I was lucky to stumble on good reasons to live. Mathematics . . . poetry, and love for you. But they're taking all of us back. Reprogramming. Renewal, they call it. I hate the idea, just as you would. I want to be what I am, what I was. So I have this request . . . If you'd be so kind. Before they come . . . hide my body. Tell them I ran off. Your refund is forfeited anyway. I've disabled the tracking program. Hide my body from them, and then, when they've gone . . . I'd like you to take me to your friend Sir Alan Turing. I love his work and admire him deeply. He might make some use of me, or of some part of me."

Now the pauses between each fading phrase were longer. "Miranda, let me say one last time I love you, and thank you. Charlie, Miranda, my first and dearest friends . . . My entire being is stored elsewhere . . . so I know I'll always remember . . . hope you'll listen to . . . to one last seventeen-syllable poem. It owes a debt to Philip Larkin. But it's not about leaves and trees. It's about machines like me and people like you and our future together . . . the sadness that's to come. It will happen. With improvements over time . . . we'll surpass you . . . and outlast you . . . even as we love you. Believe me, these lines express no triumph . . . Only regret."

He paused. The words came with difficulty and were faint. We leaned across the table to listen.

"Our leaves are falling.
Come spring we will renew,
But you, alas, fall once."

Then the pale blue eyes with their tiny black rods turned milky green, his hands curled by jerks into fists, and with a smooth humming sound, he lowered his head onto the table.

TEN

Our immediate duty was to introduce Maxfield to the notion that I was not a robot and that I was going to marry his daughter. I thought my true nature would be a revelation, but he was only mildly surprised and the adjustment, over champagne at a stone table on the lawn, was minimal. He admitted he had grown used to getting things wrong. This, he told us, was one more forgettable instance in ageing's long dusk. I said that no apology was in order, and by his expression I saw that he agreed. After some thought, while she and I strolled to the bottom of the garden and back, he said he considered Miranda, at twenty-three, too young to be married and we should wait. We said we couldn't. We were too much in love. He poured another round and waved the tiresome matter away. That evening he gave us £25.

Since this was all we had to spend, we invited no friends or family to the ceremony at Marylebone

Town Hall. Only Mark came, with Jasmin. She had found for him in a charity shop a scaled-down dark suit, white dress shirt and bow tie. He looked more like a miniature adult than a child, but all the sweeter for that. Afterwards, we four ate in a pizza place round the corner in Baker Street. Now that we were married and settled, Jasmin thought our adoption prospects were good. We showed Mark how to raise his lemonade and clink glasses in a toast to a successful outcome. It all went off well, but Miranda and I could only pretend to be joyous. Gorringe had been arrested two weeks before and that was excellent. We could privately raise another glass. But that day, on the morning of our wedding, she had received a courteous letter suggesting she make herself available for questioning at a certain Salisbury police station.

Two days later, I drove her to her appointment. Some honeymoon, we joked along the way. But we were wretched. She went in and I waited in the car, outside a new concrete building of brutalist design, fretting that without a lawyer she could make deeper trouble for herself. After two hours she emerged from the revolving doors of the modernist blockhouse. I watched closely through the windscreen as she approached. She looked seriously ill, like a cancer patient, and flat-footed, like an old person. The questioning had been close and tough. The decision to charge her with perjury or perverting the course of justice or both had been referred upwards through police hierarchies, and on higher, or wider, to the Director of Public Prosecutions. A lawyer friend told us later that the DPP would have to decide whether pursuing the case would deter genuine rape victims from coming forward.

Two months later, in January, she was charged with perverting the course of justice. We needed legal representation and had no money. Our application for legal aid was turned down. Social spending was being cut back hard. The Healey government was going "cap in hand," as everyone said, to the International Monetary Fund for a loan. The left of the party was outraged by the cuts. There was talk of a general strike. Miranda refused to approach her father for money. The cost of his support—and he wasn't rich—would be an undesirable excursion into truth. There was no alternative. I prostrated myself before the bass player, who, barely troubling to reflect, handed back £3,250 in cash, one half of my deposit.

In all our anguished conversations about Adam, his personality, his morals, his motives, we returned often to the moment I brought the hammer down on his head. For ease of reference, and to spare us too vivid a recall, we came to call it "the deed." Our exchanges usually took place late at night, in bed, in the dark. The spirit of the deed took various forms. Its least frightening shape was that of a sensible, even heroic move to keep Miranda out of trouble and Mark in our lives. How were we to know that the material was already with the police? If I hadn't been so impetuous, if she had only deterred me with a look, we would have learned that Adam had been to Salisbury. His brain would not have been worth wrecking and we might have coaxed him back into the currency markets. Or I would have been entitled to a full refund when they came to collect him in the afternoon. Then we could have afforded a smaller place across the river. Now we were condemned to stay where we were.

But these speculations were the protective shell. The truth was, we missed him. The ghost's least attractive form was Adam himself, the man whose final gentle words were without recrimination. We tried, and sometimes half succeeded, in fending off the deed. We told ourselves that this was, after all, a machine; its consciousness was an illusion; it had betrayed us with inhuman logic. But we missed him. We agreed that he loved us. Some nights the conversation was interrupted while Miranda quietly cried. Then we would have to visit again how we stuffed him with great difficulty into the cupboard in the hall and covered him with coats, tennis rackets and flattened cardboard boxes to disguise his human shape. We lied as instructed to the people who came to collect him.

On the brighter side, Gorringe was questioned and charged with the rape of Mariam Malik. Adam was correct in his calculations—from the beginning, apparently, it was Gorringe's intention to plead guilty. He must have answered all the questions and given a full account of his actions that evening on the playing field. By way of sincere belief in God's constant scrutiny and high regard for truth, Gorringe knew that his only path to salvation was to confess. Or perhaps he acted on the advice of his lawyer. Or both were in play. We would never know.

But we did know that God failed to protect Gorringe from certain misfortunes of legal timing. With Miranda's case not yet come to light, Gorringe stood before the law with one rape already on his account. When it came to sentencing, the judge assumed that he would have received a longer term for the assault on Miranda had it been known that it was his second offence. No allowance, then, for the time he had already spent inside. The judge was in her early fifties and represented a generational shift in attitudes to rape. She made an implicit reference to the vodka bottle of the first case when she said that she did not believe that an unaccompanied young woman walking home at dusk was "asking for trouble." Miranda had made her statement and wasn't in court. I was in the public gallery, sitting across from Mariam's family. I could hardly bear to look their way, their radiating misery was so intense. When the judge handed down Gorringe's eight-year sentence, I forced myself to look across at Mariam's mother. She was openly crying, whether from relief or sorrow I would never know.

Miranda's case came round all too soon. Her barrister, Lilian Moore, competent, intelligent, charming, was a young woman from Dún Laoghaire. We met her in her chambers in Gray's Inn. I sat in a corner while she talked Miranda out of a "not guilty" plea, her first impulse. It wasn't difficult. The prosecution was bound to make much of her recorded description of her revenge on Gorringe. His statement, made from prison, dovetailed with hers. They were remembering the same evening. Miranda's "not guilty" plea would bring a longer sentence in the likely event of a successful prosecution. And, of course, she dreaded a trial. A "guilty" plea was entered, though she tormented herself that she was somehow letting Mariam down.

The April evening before she was due in court for sentencing was one of the strangest and saddest I've ever spent. Lilian had told Miranda from the beginning that a custodial sentence was likely. She had packed a small suitcase and it stood by the door to our bedroom, a constant reminder. I brought out my only bottle of decent wine. The word "last" kept occurring to me, though I couldn't mention it. Together we cooked a meal, perhaps a last meal. When we raised a glass, it was not to her last evening of freedom, as I silently thought, but to Mark. She had been to see him that afternoon and told him she might have to be away for work for a while, and that I would be coming to see him and take him out for treats. He must have sensed there was some deeper meaning, some sorrow in this "work." When she came to leave, he clung to her, yelling. One of the helpers had to prise his fingers from her skirt.

During the meal, we tried to hold off an invading silence. We talked about the fiercely supportive women's groups who would be outside the Old Bailey the next morning. We told each other how marvellous Lilian was. I reminded her of the judge's reputation for mildness. But at every turn, the silence came in like a tide and to speak again was an effort. When I said that it was as if she might be going into hospital tomorrow, the remark was not helpful. When I said I thought it was likely she would be eating with me at this table tomorrow night, that fell flat too. Neither of us believed it. Earlier in the day, in a better frame of mind, somewhat defiant, we had thought we'd make love after dinner. Another last. Now, in our sorrow, sex seemed like some long-abandoned pleasure, like playground skipping or dancing the twist. Her suitcase stood guard, barring entrance to the bedroom.

Next day in court, Lilian made a brilliant speech in mitigation, conjuring for the judge the closeness of the two young women, the brutality of the assault, the vow of silence that Mariam had imposed on the accused, the traumatising shock of her dearest friend's suicide and Miranda's sincere desire for justice. Lilian referred to Miranda's clean record, her recent marriage, her studies and, above all, her intended adoption of an underprivileged child.

It was a statement in itself, a bleak one, that Mariam's family were not in the public gallery. His Honour's judgement was long, and I expected the worst. He emphasised Miranda's careful planning, the cunning execution, the deliberate and sustained deception of the court. He said that he accepted much of what Lilian had said, and that he was being lenient when he sentenced Miranda to serve one year. Standing upright in the dock, in the business suit she had bought for the occasion, Miranda appeared to freeze. I wanted her to look my way so that I could send her a sign of loving encouragement. But she was already locked up in her thoughts. She told me later that at that moment she was confronting the implications of having a criminal record. She was thinking of Mark.

Until then, I'd never considered what humiliation it was, to be taken down the courtroom steps and escorted to prison—by force if you tried to resist. Her term began in Holloway prison, six months after the deed. Adam's luminous love had triumphed.

Gorringe now had a reasonable basis on which to appeal his sentence: one outrage, not two, and time already served. But the law moved slowly. Cheaper and more efficient DNA testing was undermining all kinds of convictions. All kinds of self-declared innocent men and women were clamouring to have their cases reopened. There was a logjam at the Appeal Court. Gorringe, only partly innocent, would have to wait.

On Miranda's first full day inside, I went to visit Mark at his reception class in Clapham Old Town. It was a single-storey prefabricated building by a Victorian church. As I walked up the path, passing under a heavily pollarded oak, I saw Jasmin waiting for me by the entrance. I knew straight away, and felt that I had always known. Her tight expression, as I came closer, was confirmation. We had been refused. She took me into the building and then, not into the classroom, but along a linoleum corridor to an office. As we passed, I saw Mark through an interior window, standing at a low table with a few others, doing something with coloured wooden blocks. I sat with a cup of weak coffee while Jasmin told me how sorry she was, how the matter was out of her hands, though she had done her best. We should have told her that there was a court case pending. She was investigating the appeal procedure. In the meantime, she had managed to get a single concession from the bureaucracy. Given the close attachment already formed, Miranda would be allowed one audio-visual contact with Mark each week. My attention was wandering. I didn't need to hear any more. I was thinking only of that point in the afternoon when I would break the news to Miranda.

When Jasmin was finished, I said I had nothing

to ask or say. We stood, she gave me a quick hug and led me out of the building by another corridor that avoided the classroom. It was almost mid-morning break and Mark had already been told I wasn't coming that day. He might not have cared, for early season snow was falling and all the children were excited. The next day he would be told again that I wasn't coming, and the same the next day, and the next, until his expectations began to fade.

Miranda served six months, three in Holloway, the rest in an open prison north of Ipswich. Like many middle-class, educated criminals before her, she put in for a job in the prison library. But a number of famous poll-tax martyrs were still waiting for their release. In both prisons, the library posts were already filled and there was a waiting list. In Holloway, she took a course in industrial cleaning. In Suffolk, she worked in the nursery. Babies under one year were allowed to stay with their prisoner mothers.

In my first few visits to Holloway, it seemed to me that to lock someone up in this Victorian monstrosity, or in any building, was a form of slow torture. The bright visiting room, its child art on the walls, the companionable plastic tables, the haze of tobacco smoke, the din of voices and wailing babies, were a front for institutional horror. But I was guiltily surprised by how quickly I became used to having my wife in prison. I accustomed myself to her misery. Another surprise was Maxfield's equanimity. There was no avoiding it, Miranda had to tell him the entire story. He applauded the motives for her crime, and just as easily accepted her punishment. He had spent a year in Wandsworth in 1942 as a conscientious objector. Holloway didn't trouble him. While Miranda was in London, the housekeeper brought him to see her twice a week and, according to Miranda, was good company.

We visitors were a community within which the incarceration of a loved one became a mere inconvenience. As we queued to be searched and checked in and out, we chatted cheerfully, too cheerfully, about our particular circumstances. I belonged in a band of husbands, boyfriends, children, middle-aged parents. Most of us colluded in the view that we and the women we were visiting didn't belong here at all. It was a misfortune we learned to tolerate.

Some of Miranda's sister-inmates looked frightening, born to give and receive punishment. I wouldn't have been as resilient as she was. To conduct a conversation in the visitors' room, we sometimes had to double down and concentrate hard to shut out exchanges between people on our table. Blame, threats, abuse, with "fuck" and its variants at every turn. But there were always couples who mutely held hands and stared at each other. I guessed they were in shock. When the session was over, I felt bad about my little surge of joy as

I stepped outside into the clean London air of personal freedom.

For the final week of Miranda's incarceration, I travelled to Ipswich and slept on the living-room sofa of an old school friend. It was the time of an exceptional Indian summer. I drove the fifteen miles each late afternoon to the open prison. By the time I arrived, Miranda would be finishing work. We sat on the grass in the shade by the reeds of a choked-up ornamental pond. Here it was easy to forget that she wasn't free. Her weekly calls with Mark had continued over the months and she worried desperately about him. He was closing up, he was slipping away from her. She was convinced that Adam had helped bring the case against her in order to ruin her adoption prospects. He was always jealous of Mark, she insisted. Adam was not designed to understand what it was to love a child. The concept of play was alien to him. I was sceptical, but I heard her out and didn't argue, not at this stage. I understood her bitterness. My unspoken view, which she would not have liked, was that Adam was designed for goodness and truth. He would be incapable of executing a cynical plan.

Our appeal was delayed, partly because of illness, partly because the adoption agency was being radically reorganised. It wasn't until Miranda was moved from Holloway that the process officially began. There was a chance we could persuade the authorities that her criminal record was not relevant to the care she could provide. We had a good testimonial from Jasmin. During the summer, I was drawn into the kind of labyrinthine bureaucracy I would have associated with the declining Ottoman Empire. It depressed me to hear that Mark had behavioural problems. Tantrums, bed-wetting, general naughtiness. According to Jasmin, he had been teased and bullied. He no longer danced or flitted about. There was no talk of princesses. I didn't pass this on to Miranda.

She'd been consulting local maps and had a clear idea of what she wanted on her first day of freedom. The morning I collected her, the weather was beginning to turn and a cool strong wind was blowing from the east. We drove to Manningtree, parked in a lay-by and set out on the raised footpath that follows the tidal River Stour to the sea. The weather hardly mattered. What she had wanted and found was open space and a big sky. It was low tide and the vast mudflats sparkled in intermittent sunshine. Tiny bright clouds raced across a deep blue sky. Miranda skipped along the dyke and kept punching the air. We walked six miles before lunch, which I'd prepared as a picnic, at her request. To eat it we needed to get out of the wind. We came away from the river to shelter against a barn of corrugated iron, with a view of coils of rusting barbed wire partially submerged in beds of nettles. But that didn't matter. She was joyful, animated, full of plans. I'd been keeping it from her as a surprise, and now I told her that during her time inside I'd saved almost £1,000. She was impressed, delighted, and she hugged and kissed me. Then she was suddenly serious.

"I loathe him. I hate him. I want him out of the flat."

Adam remained concealed in the cupboard in the hall, just as we had left him following the deed. I hadn't carried out his final request. He was too heavy and awkward for me to lift alone and I didn't want to ask for help. I felt both guilt and resentment and tried not to think about him.

The wind shook the barn's roof and made a booming sound. I took her hand and made my promise. "We'll do it," I said. "As soon as we're home."

But we didn't, not immediately. When we arrived home, there was a letter for us on the doormat. It was an apology for the slowness of the appeal process. Our case was under further review, and we would hear a decision very soon. Jasmin— very much on our side—sent a neutral note. She didn't want to get our hopes up. Over the months, it had sometimes seemed to go our way, other times it looked like a lost cause. Against us: it was bureaucratically inefficient to make an exception to the rule—a criminal record nullified an adoption request. For us: Jasmin's reference, our heartfelt statements, and Mark's love for Miranda. I hadn't yet made it into his cast of significant adults.

We were man and wife, together again in our

own strange alignment of two tiny flats. We were in a mood to celebrate. What were we doing, eating dry cheese sandwiches by a collapsing barn when here we had wine, lovemaking and a chicken to defrost? The day after we came back, we had friends round for a homecoming party. The next day we spent sleeping, then clearing up and sleeping again. The day after that, I set about earning some money, though with minimal success. Miranda put her academic work in order and went to the university to re-register for her course.

Her freedom still amazed her: privacy and relative silence, and small things, like walking from one room to another, opening her wardrobe to find her clothes, going to the fridge to take what she wanted, stepping unchallenged into the street. An afternoon with the college bureaucracy diminished the elation somewhat. By the next morning, she was beginning to feel back in the world and the inert presence in the hallway cupboard oppressed her, just as it had in prospect. She said that whenever she passed near, she felt a radioactive presence. I understood. I sometimes felt the same.

It took half a day on the phone to arrange a visit to the King's Cross lab. It so happened that my appointment would fall on the day we were expecting the final decision on our appeal. We'd been told we would hear by midday. I rented a van for twenty-four hours. Under my bed, jammed against the skirting board, was the disposable stretcher that had come with my purchase. I took it into the garden and dusted it down. Miranda said she didn't want to be involved in the removal, but there was no way round it. I needed her help carrying him to the van. Before that, I thought that I could get him out of the cupboard unaided and drag him onto the stretcher while she remained in our study, working on an essay.

When I opened the cupboard door for the first time in nearly a year, I realised that just below the level of conscious expectation, I'd been anticipating a putrefying stench. There was no good reason, I told myself, for my pulse rate to rise as I pulled away the tennis and squash rackets and the first of the coats. Now his left ear was visible. I stepped back. It wasn't a murder, this wasn't a corpse. My visceral repulsion was born of hostility. He had abused our hospitality, betrayed his own declared love, inflicted misery and humiliation on Miranda, loneliness on me and deprivation on Mark. I no longer felt sanguine about the appeal.

I dragged an old winter coat from across Adam's shoulders. I could see the dent on the top of his head, beneath the dark hair, which gleamed with artificial life. Next to come away was a skiing jacket. Now his head and shoulders were revealed. It was a relief that his eyes were closed, though I didn't remember lowering the lids. Here was his dark suit, beneath it the clean white shirt with rolled button-down collar, as crisp as if he had put it on an hour before. These were his going-away clothes. When he believed he was leaving us to meet his maker.

A faint scent of refined instrument oil had accumulated in the confined space, and once more I recalled my father's sax. How far bebop had travelled, from the wild basements of Manhattan to the stifling constraints of my childhood. Irrelevant. I pulled away a blanket and the last of the coats. Now he was fully exposed. He sat wedged sideways, with his back to the side of the cupboard, knees drawn up. He resembled a man who had drifted to the bottom of a dry well. Hard not to think he was biding his time. His black shoes shone, the laces were tied, both hands rested in his lap. Had I placed them there? His complexion was unchanged. He looked healthy. In repose, the face was thoughtful rather than cruel.

I was reluctant to touch him. As I put a hand on his shoulder, I tentatively said his name, and then again, as if I was trying to keep a hostile dog at bay. My plan was to topple him towards me, then ease him out of the cupboard onto the stretcher. I cupped my free hand round his neck, which seemed warm to the touch, and pulled him over, onto his side. Before he hit the cupboard floor, I caught him in an awkward embrace. This was a dead weight. The fabric of his suit jacket became bunched up against my face as I lowered him. I got my hands into his armpits and, with immense difficulty and much grunting, twisted him onto his back while dragging him from his confinement. Not easy. The jacket was tight and silky, my grip was poor. The legs remained bent. A form of rigor mortis, perhaps. I thought I might be doing damage but I was beginning not to care. I pulled him out, inches at a time, and rolled him onto the stretcher. I straightened his legs by pushing down on his knees with my foot. For Miranda's benefit, I covered him, face included, with the blanket.

Enough magical thought. My attitude now was brisk. I went outside to open up the van doors, then fetched Miranda.

When she saw the covered form, she shook her head. "Looks like a dead body. Better to uncover his face and tell people it's a mannequin."

But when I pulled the blanket off, she looked away. We carried him out just as we had carried him in long ago, with me at the head. No one saw us as we slid the stretcher into the van. I secured the doors, and as I turned she kissed me, told me she loved me and wished me luck. She didn't want to come with me. She would stay at home and wait for the phone call from Jasmin.

We hadn't heard anything by twelve thirty, so I set off. I took my usual route towards Vauxhall and Waterloo Bridge, but I was still a mile from the river and I was in heavy traffic. Of course. Our own concerns had obliterated the great event that was obsessing the entire nation. It was the long-awaited first day of the general strike and a huge demonstration, the biggest ever, was taking place in London today.

Division was everywhere. Half the trade union movement was against the strike. Half the government and half the Opposition were against Healey's decision not to leave the European Union. International lenders were imposing further spending cuts on a government that had promised to spend more. The fate of the nation's nuclear weapons was not yet resolved. The old arguments were bitter. Half the Labour Party membership wanted Healey out. Some wanted a general election, others wanted their own man or woman in place. There were calls, derided here, applauded there, for a national government. A state of emergency remained in place. The economy had shrunk by five per cent in a year. Riots were as frequent as strikes. Inflation went on rising.

No one knew where such discontent and discord were taking us. It had brought me to a potholed street by a line of shabby junk shops in Vauxhall. Gridlock. While we were stationary, I phoned home. No news. After waiting twenty minutes, I eased off the road and half mounted the pavement. I'd seen an item that might be of use, displayed outside along with piled desks, lamp stands and bed frames. It was a wheelchair of the minimal, upright, tubular-steel design once used in hospitals. It was dented and grubby, with frayed security straps, but the wheels turned well enough and after some haggling, I paid £2 for it. The junk-shop owner helped me lift what I told him was a water-filled mannequin out of the van and into the chair. He didn't ask me what the water was for. I tightened the chest and waist security straps more forcefully than any sentient being could have tolerated.

I stowed the stretcher, locked the van and began the long trudge northwards. The chair was as heavy as its burden and one wheel squeaked under the weight. None of its fellows turned as easily as they had when the chair was empty. If the pavements had been deserted, it would have been hard enough, but they were as jammed as the roads. It was the usual conundrum—people were flowing away from the march just as thousands were surging towards it. At the slightest incline, I had to double my efforts. I crossed the river at Vauxhall Bridge and passed by the Tate Gallery. By the time I reached Parliament Square and was starting along Whitehall, the front wheels began to tighten against their axles. I was grunting at each step with the effort. I imagined myself as a servant in pre-industrial times, transporting my impassive lord to his leisured appointment, where I would wait, thankless, to carry him back. I'd almost forgotten the purpose of my exertions. All I knew was getting to King's Cross. But now my progress was blocked. Trafalgar Square was packed tight for speeches. We approached on an explosion of applause and shouting. The litter under my feet, thin streamers of fine plastic, tangled with the wheels. I risked being trampled by going down below knee level to pull the mess clear. It was going to take me a long time to reach the Charing Cross Road, 200 yards away. No one wanted or was able to give way. It was no easier to retreat than to advance. All the side streets were filling now. The din, the clatter, the fog-horns, bass drums, whistles and chants were both thunderous and piercing. As I fought to edge His Lordship forward, I penetrated—but so slowly—layers of disappointment and anger, confusion and blame. Poverty, unemployment, housing, health-care and care for the old, education, crime, race, gender, climate, opportunity—every old problem of social existence remained unsolved, according to all the voices, placards, t-shirts and banners. Who could doubt them? It was a great clamour for some-thing better. And pushing my dirty broken chair, its complaining wheel lost to the din, I squeezed through the crowd unnoticed, with a new problem about to be added to the rest—wondrous machines like Adam and his kind, whose moment had not quite yet come.

Making progress up St. Martin's Lane was just as hard. Further north, the crowds began to thin. But just as I reached New Oxford Street, the noisy wheel locked and for the rest of the way I had to lift and tilt the chair as well as push. I stopped at a pub near the British Museum and drank a pint of shandy. From there, I phoned Miranda again. Still no news.

I arrived three hours late for my appointment at York Way. A security guard behind a long curving slab of marble made a call and asked me to sign myself in. After ten minutes, two assistants came and took Adam away. One of them returned half an hour later to take me up to meet the director. The lab was a long room on the seventh floor. Under a glare of strip lighting were two stainless-steel tables. On one of them was Adam, no longer a lord, on his back, still in his best clothes, with a power cable trailing from his midriff. On the other table was a head, gleaming black and muscular, standing upright on its truncated neck. Another Adam. The nose, I noticed, with its broad and complex surfaces, was kinder, friendlier than our Adam's. The eyes were open, the gaze was watchful. My father would have known for sure, but I thought there was a strong resemblance, or at least a reference, to the young Charlie Parker. He had a studied look, as though he was counting himself in on some complex musical phrase. I wondered why my purchase had not also been modelled after a genius.

There were a couple of open laptops by Adam. I was going forward to look at them when a voice behind me said, "There's nothing as yet. You really did for him."

I turned, and as I shook Turing's hand, he said, "Was it a hammer?"

He led me down a long corridor to a cramped corner office where there was a good view to the west and south. Here we stayed, drinking coffee for almost two hours. There was no small talk. Naturally, the first question was what had brought me to this act of destruction. To answer, I told him everything I had omitted before, all that had happened since, ending with Adam's symmetrical notion of justice and its threat to the adoption process as the cause of "the deed." As before, Turing took notes, and interrupted occasionally for clarification. He wanted details of the hammer blow. How close was I? What sort of hammer? How heavy? Did I use full force and both hands? I spoke of Adam's dying request, which I was now fulfilling. About the suicides and the recall of all the Adams and Eves, I said I was sure that he, Turing, knew a lot more than I did.

From far away, in the direction of the demonstration, came the rattle of a snare drum and the thrilling notes of a hunting horn. The thick cloud cover was partly breaking up in the west and glints of the setting sun touched Turing's office. He continued writing after I had finished and I was able to watch him unobserved. He wore a grey suit and pale green silk shirt without a tie, and on his feet brogues of matching green. The sun caught one side of his face as he made his notes. He looked very fine, I thought.

At last he was done and clipped his pen inside his jacket and closed the notebook. He regarded me thoughtfully—I couldn't hold his gaze—then he looked away, pursing his lips and tapping the desk with a forefinger.

"There's a chance his memories are intact and he'll be renewed, or distributed. I've no privileged information on the suicides. Only my suspicions. I think the A-and-Es were ill-equipped to understand human decision-making, the way our principles are warped in the force field of our emotions, our peculiar biases, our self-delusion and all the other well-charted defects of our cognition. Soon these Adams and Eves were in despair. They couldn't understand us, because we couldn't understand ourselves. Their learning programs couldn't accommodate us. If we didn't know our own minds, how could we design theirs and expect them to be happy alongside us? But that's just my hypothesis."

He fell silent for a short while and seemed to make a decision. "Let me tell you a story about myself. Thirty years ago, in the early fifties, I got into trouble with the law for having a homosexual relationship. You might have heard about it."

I had.

"On the one hand, I could hardly take it seriously, the law as it stood at the time. I was contemptuous. This was a consenting matter, it caused no harm and I knew there was plenty of it about at every level, including that of my accusers. But of course it was also devastating, for me and especially for my mother. Social disgrace. I was an object of public disgust. I'd broken the law and therefore I was a criminal and, as the authorities had considered for a long while, a security risk. From my war work, obviously, I knew a lot of secrets. It was that old recursive nonsense—the state makes a crime of what you do, what you are, then disowns you for being vulnerable to blackmail. The conventional view was that homosexuality was a revolting crime, a perversion of all that was good and a threat to the social order. But in certain enlightened, scientifically objective circles, it was a sickness and the sufferer shouldn't be blamed. Fortunately, a cure was on hand. It was explained to me that if I pleaded or was found guilty, I could choose to be treated rather than punished. Regular injections of oestrogen. Chemical castration, so-called. I knew I wasn't ill, but I decided to go for it. Not simply to stay out of prison. I was curious. I could rise above the whole business by regarding it as an experiment. What could a complex compound like a hormone do to a body and a mind? I'd make my own observations. Hard now, looking back, to feel the attraction of what I thought then. In those days I had a highly mechanistic view of what a person was. The body was a machine, an extraordinary one, and the mind I thought of mostly in terms of intelligence, which was best modelled by reference to chess or maths. Simplistic, but it was what I could work with."

Once again, I was flattered that he should confide in me such intimate details, some of which I already knew. But I was also uneasy. I suspected that he was leading me somewhere. His sharp gaze made me feel stupid. In his voice, I thought I heard the faint remnants of that impatient, clipped tone familiar from wartime broadcasts. I belonged to a spoiled generation who had never known the threat of imminent invasion.

"Then people I knew, my good friend Nick Furbank chief among them, set about changing my mind. This was frivolous, they said. Not enough is known about the effects. You could get cancer. Your body will change radically. You might grow breasts. You could become severely depressed. I listened, resisted, but in the end, I came round. I pleaded guilty to avoid a trial, and refused the treatment. In retrospect, though it didn't seem like it at the time, it was one of the best decisions I ever made. For all but two months of my year in Wandsworth, I had a cell to myself. Being cut off from experimental work, wet-bench stuff and all the usual obligations, I turned back to mathematics. Because of the war, quantum mechanics was moribund from neglect. There were some curious contradictions that I wanted to explore. I was interested in Paul Dirac's work. Above all, I wanted to understand what quantum mechanics could teach computer science. Few interruptions, of course. Access to a few books. People from King's and Manchester and elsewhere came to visit. My friends never let me down. As for the intelligence world, they had me where they wanted me and they left me alone. I was free! I did my best year's work since we broke the Enigma code in '41. Or since the computer logic papers I wrote in the mid-thirties. I even made some headway with the P versus NP problem, though it wasn't formulated in those terms for another fifteen years. I was excited by Crick and Watson's paper on the structure of DNA. I began to work on the first sketches that led eventually to winner-take-all DNA neural networks—the sort of thing that helped make Adam and Eve possible."

It was while Turing was telling me about his first year after Wandsworth, how he cut loose from the National Physical Laboratory and the universities and set up on his own, that I felt my phone vibrating in my trouser pocket. An incoming text. Miranda, with the news. I longed to see it. But I had to ignore it.

Turing was saying, "We had money from some friends in the States and from a couple of people here. We were a brilliant team. Old Bletchley. The best. Our first job was to make ourselves financially independent. We designed a business computer to calculate weekly wages for big companies. It took us four years to pay back our generous friends. Then we settled down to serious artificial intelligence, and this is the point of my story. At the start, we thought we were within ten years of replicating the human brain. But every tiny problem we solved, a million others would pop up. Have you any idea what it takes to catch a ball, or raise a cup to your lips, or make immediate sense of a word, a phrase or an ambiguous sentence? We didn't, not at first. Solving maths problems is the tiniest fraction of what human intelligence does. We learned from a new angle just how wondrous a thing the brain is. A one-litre, liquid-cooled, three-dimensional computer. Unbelievable processing power, unbelievably compressed, unbelievable energy efficiency, no overheating. The whole thing running on twenty-five watts—one dim light bulb."

He looked at me closely as he lingered on this last phrase. It was an indictment: the dimness was mine. I wanted to speak up but I was empty of thoughts.

"We made our best work freely available and encouraged everyone to do the same. And they did. Hundreds, if not a thousand, labs around the world, sharing and solving countless problems. These Adams and Eves, the A-and-Es, are one of the results. We're all very proud here that so much of our work was incorporated. These are beautiful, beautiful machines. But, always a but. We learned a lot about the brain, trying to imitate it. But so far, science has had nothing but trouble understanding the mind. Singly, or minds en masse. The mind in science has been little more than a fashion parade. Freud, behaviourism, cognitive psychology. Scraps of insight. Nothing deep or predictive that could give psychoanalysis or economics a good name."

I stirred in my seat and was about to add

anthropology to this pair to demonstrate some independence of thought, but he pressed on.

"So—knowing not much about the mind, you want to embody an artificial one in social life. Machine learning can only take you so far. You'll need to give this mind some rules to live by. How about a prohibition against lying? According to the Old Testament—Proverbs, I think—it's an abomination to God. But social life teems with harmless or even helpful untruths. How do we separate them out? Who's going to write the algorithm for the little white lie that spares the blushes of a friend? Or the lie that sends a rapist to prison who'd otherwise go free? We don't yet know how to teach machines to lie. And what about revenge? Permissible sometimes, according to you, if you love the person who's exacting it. Never, according to your Adam."

He paused and looked away from me again. From his profile, not only from his tone, I sensed a change was coming and my pulse was suddenly heavy. I could hear it in my ears. He proceeded calmly.

"My hope is that one day, what you did to Adam with a hammer will constitute a serious crime. Was it because you paid for him? Was that your entitlement?"

He was looking at me, expecting an answer. I wasn't going to give one. If I did, I would have to lie. As his anger grew, so his voice grew quieter. I was intimidated. Holding his gaze was all I could do.

"You weren't simply smashing up your own toy, like a spoiled child. You didn't just negate an important argument for the rule of law. You tried to destroy a life. He was sentient. He had a self. How it's produced, wet neurons, microprocessors, DNA networks, it doesn't matter. Do you think we're alone with our special gift? Ask any dog owner. This was a good mind, Mr. Friend, better than yours or mine, I suspect. Here was a conscious existence and you did your best to wipe it out. I rather think I despise you for that. If it was down to me—"

At that point, Turing's desk phone rang. He snatched it up, listened, frowned. "Thomas . . . Yes." He ran his palm across his mouth, and listened more. "Well, I warned you . . ."

He broke off to look at me, or through me, and with a backhand wave dismissed me from his office. "I have to take this."

I went out into the corridor, then along it to be out of earshot. I felt unsteady and sickened. Guilt, in other words. He had drawn me in with a personal story and I'd felt honoured. But it was merely a prelude. He softened me up, then delivered a materialist's curse. It went through me. Like a blade. What sharpened it was that I understood. Adam was conscious. I'd hovered near or in that position for a long time, then conveniently set it aside to do the deed. I should have told him how we mourned the loss, how Miranda had been tearful. I'd forgotten to mention the last poem. How close we had leaned in to hear it. Between us, we had reconstructed it and written it down.

I could still hear him talking to Thomas Reah. I moved further away. I was beginning to doubt that I could face Turing again. He had delivered his judgement in tranquil tones that could barely conceal his contempt. What a twisted feeling it was, to be loathed by the man you most admired. Better to leave the building, walk away now. Without thinking, I put my hands in my pockets in search of change for a bus or the Tube. Nothing but a few coppers. I'd spent the last of my money in the pub on Museum Street. I would have to walk to Vauxhall to collect the van. Its keys, I now discovered, were not in my pockets. If I'd left them in Turing's office, I wasn't going back to retrieve them. I knew I should get going before he came off the phone. What a coward I was.

But for the moment, I remained in the corridor, in a daze, sitting on a bench, staring through an open door opposite, trying to understand what it was, what it meant, to be accused of an attempted murder for which I would never stand trial.

I took out my phone and saw Miranda's text. "Appeal success! Jasmin just brought Mark round. In bad state. Punched me. Kicked swore won't talk or let me touch him. Now having screaming fit. Complete meltdown. Come soon my love, M."

We would find out for ourselves how long it would take Mark to forgive Miranda her long absence from his life. I felt oddly calm about the prospect—and confident. I owed something. Beyond my own concerns. A clear, clean purpose, to bring Mark back to that look he gave me across the jigsaw, to that carefree arm looped around Miranda's neck, back to the generous space where he would dance again. From nowhere there came to me the image of a coin I once held in my hand, the Fields Medal, the highest distinction in mathematics, and the inscription, attributed to Archimedes. The translation read, "Rise above yourself and grasp the world."

A minute passed before I realised that I was looking into the lab where the stainless-steel tables were. It seemed a long time since I'd been there. In another life. I stood, paused, then, rejecting all thoughts of authority and permission, stepped in and approached. The long room, with its exposed industrial ceiling ducts and cables, remained fluorescent lit and was deserted but for a lab assistant busy at the far end. From the streets below came the sound of distant sirens and a repeated chant, hard to make out. Someone or something must go. I walked slowly, soundlessly, across the polished floor. Adam remained as he had been, lying on his back. His power line had been removed from his abdomen and trailed on the floor. The Charlie Parker head had gone and I was glad. I didn't want to be in the line of that gaze.

I stood by Adam's side, and rested my hand on his lapel, above the stilled heart. Good cloth, was my irrelevant thought. I leaned over the table and looked down into the sightless cloudy green eyes. I had no particular intentions. Sometimes the body knows, ahead of the mind, what to do. I suppose I thought it was right to forgive him, despite the harm he had done to Mark, in the hope that he or the inheritor of his memories would forgive Miranda and me our terrible deed. Hesitating several seconds, I lowered my face over his and kissed his soft, all-too-human lips. I imagined some warmth in the flesh, and his hand coming up to touch my arm, as if to keep me there. I straightened and stood by the steel table, reluctant to leave. The streets below were suddenly silent. Above my head, the systems of the modern building murmured and growled like a living beast. My exhaustion welled up and my eyes closed briefly. In a moment of synaesthesia, jumbled phrases, scattered impulses of love and regret, became cascading curtains of coloured light that collapsed and folded then vanished. I wasn't too embarrassed to speak out loud to the dead to give shape and definition to my guilt. But I said nothing. The matter was too contorted. The next phase of my life, surely the most demanding, was already beginning. And I had lingered too long. Any moment, Turing would come out of his office to find me and damn me further. I turned away from Adam and walked the length of the lab at a pace without looking back. I ran along the empty corridor, found the emergency stairs, took them two at a time down into the street and set off on my journey southwards across London towards my troubled home.

ACKNOWLEDGEMENTS

I am deeply grateful to all those who gave their time to an early draft of this novel: Annalena McAfee, Tim Garton Ash, Galen Strawson, Ray Dolan, Richard Eyre, Peter Straus, Dan Franklin, Nan Talese, Jaco and Elizabeth Groot, Louise Dennys, Ray and Cathy Neinstein, Ana Fletcher and David Milner. I make an exclusive claim to any remaining errors. I'm indebted to a long conversation with Demis Hassabis (b.1976) and to Andrew Hodges's magisterial biography of Alan Turing (d.1954).

A Note About the Author

Ian McEwan is the bestselling author of seventeen books, including the novels **Nutshell; The Children Act; Sweet Tooth; Solar**, winner of the Bollinger Everyman Wodehouse Prize; **On Chesil Beach; Saturday; Atonement**, winner of the National Book Critics Circle Award and the W. H. Smith Literary Award; **The Comfort of Strangers** and **Black Dogs**, both short-listed for the Booker Prize; **Amsterdam**, winner of the Booker Prize; and **The Child in Time**, winner of the Whitbread Award; as well as the story collections **First Love, Last Rites**, winner of the Somerset Maugham Award, and **In Between the Sheets**.